ZANE PRESENTS

W9-BZR-571

UNCORRECTED PROOFS
NOT FOR SALE

THE COST OF LOVE AND SANITY

COMPLIMENTS OF
THE PUBLISHER

Dear Reader:

Out of all the topics that I get advice emails about, being reluctant about entering into another committed relationship due to lack of trust is one of the biggest. It is hard for a woman to take a chance on love, expose her vulnerability, and become emotionally attached once she has been through a lot of heartbreak and pain. Such is the case with Alex Carter, in Jaye Cheríe's *The Cost of Love and Sanity*. Alex is concentrating on her career path, is recently single again, and is prepared to give up on love altogether. Then one day, at a crowded gas station, she runs into Nathan Chestnut, a man who betrayed her a decade earlier. He still looks good, he is still charming, but she remembers what he did. He professes to have changed, to have matured, and wants another chance.

This leads to another common topic from my email: second chances. Sometimes it is possible for people to be apart for years, even decades, and evolve into the soul mates that each desires. But Alex still has serious insecurity issues that she must overcome, along with suspicion, and overall trying to find something to disqualify Nathan yet again. *The Cost of Love and Sanity* is an interesting look at a dilemma that millions of women with tainted pasts face globally on any given day. Is love worth taking a chance on, or is it better to run from it? Will the next man be another example of disrespect, cheating, and being untrustworthy or will he be *the* example of what true love looks like?

As always, thanks for supporting the authors of Strebor Books. We try our best to bring you the future in great literature today. We appreciate the love. You can find me on Facebook @AuthorZane and on Twitter @planetzane.

Blessings,

Zane

Publisher
Strebor Books
www.simonandschuster.com

Also by Jaye Cheríe
The Gold Digger's Club

ZANE PRESENTS

UNCORRECTED PROOFS
NOT FOR SALE

THE COST OF LOVE AND SANITY

a novel by Jaye Cheríe

SBI

STREBOR BOOKS

NEW YORK LONDON TORONTO SYDNEY

Do not quote for publication until verified with finished book. This advance uncorrected reader's proof is the property of Simon & Schuster. It is being loaned for promotional purposes and review by the recipient and may not be used for any other purpose or transferred to any third party. Simon & Schuster reserves the right to cancel the loan and recall possession of the proof at any time. Any duplication, sale or distribution to the public is a violation of law.

Strebor Books
P.O. Box 6505
Largo, MD 20792
http://www.streborbooks.com

This book is a work of fiction. Names, characters, places and incidents are products of the author's imagination or are used fictitiously. Any resemblance to actual events or locales or persons, living or dead, is entirely coincidental.

© 2013 by Jaye Cheríe

All rights reserved. No part of this book may be reproduced in any form or by any means whatsoever. For information address Strebor Books, P.O. Box 6505, Largo, MD 20792.

ISBN 978-1-59309-509-3
ISBN 978-1-4767-3339-5 (ebook)
LCCN 2013933674

First Strebor Books trade paperback edition January 2014

Cover design: www.mariondesigns.com
Cover photograph: © Keith Saunders/Marion Designs

10 9 8 7 6 5 4 3 2 1

Manufactured in the United States of America

For information regarding special discounts for bulk purchases, please contact Simon & Schuster Special Sales at 1-866-506-1949 or business@simonandschuster.com

The Simon & Schuster Speakers Bureau can bring authors to your live event. For more information or to book an event, contact the Simon & Schuster Speakers Bureau at 1-866-248-3049 or visit our website at www.simonspeakers.com.

To every woman who believes in true love—
May you never give up on love and may God reward you for it;

To the real "Nathan,"—
It always trusts, always hopes, always perseveres. Love never fails.
—1 Corinthians 13: 7-8

ACKNOWLEDGMENTS

First, I want to thank God for giving me another opportunity to express my creativity through the written word. It is truly a blessing for me and I hope my work is a blessing to others. I want to thank the people that read and purchased *The Golddigger's Club*.

To my family—thank you for your continued support. First Coast Christian Writers Group—thanks for the feedback. As always, it makes a difference.

Toastmasters International, especially Lillian R. Bradley Toastmasters Club—thanks for your support.

My Strebor family—thanks for your guidance. It's helping me become a better writer.

"**U**h um," the VP of Operations, Mr. Eugene Sims, stood behind his executive chair and cleared his throat. The room acknowledged him with silent cooperation. "Surely, you all are wondering why I've called this meeting. Everyone is in a hurry to get out of here and enjoy their New Year's. Nevertheless, we have a pressing issue to discuss before the first of next month." He frowned.

"As you all know, our numbers are down twenty-either percent this quarter after being down nineteen percent last quarter. We've lost contracts. We aren't getting as many good people placed with our present clients and this is affecting our business." He leaned on the chair. "Golden Burch has been looking for a sales professional for four months. We haven't sent him anyone in four months!" the VP raised his voice, allowing his aggravation to erupt like a volcano.

For a second, you could hear a rat pee on cotton. Alexis Carter, one of three junior recruitment managers, blinked four times in rapid succession. Until Mr. Sims' outburst she'd been fighting hard to stay awake. She should have made herself a cup of tea that morning or at least stopped somewhere and bought a tea. A tea and two sunrisers. She could smell the steaming hot, peppered sausage, melted cheese and buns burning up her fingers as she pushed one into her mouth. Her stomach growled in response to her food fantasy. She quickly placed her hand over her stomach and looked to her left and her right to see if anyone heard it. Nobody showed any signs they did.

Suddenly, Dan Reece, a coordinator, raised his hand, looking like a fifth-grader about to ask his teacher if he could go to the bathroom.

"What?" Mr. Sims zeroed in on Dan.

"We haven't sent over any sales candidates because none of them fit their qualifications," Dan said.

"And what did you do about that?"

Dan fell silent, searching his colleagues' faces for ideas about what to say next. When no one offered him a lifeline, he answered on his own, sitting up straight in his chair. "Well, I…I called everyone I could in our database."

"And?" the VP said, without blinking.

Dan swallowed. This meeting was going further downhill by the minute.

"And no one matched," Dan said.

The VP pointed toward the embarrassed employee. "This is my point. As bad as the economy is, with all the people out there looking for jobs, all we're doing is making excuses. We're not doing everything we can to find the candidates. That's not gonna cut it."

Alex sat back in her chair. She knew this talk would come. The year started with a bang and ended with a whimper. She'd hoped their tongue lashing wouldn't come today, especially since her stomach seemed intent on gearing up for a second growl.

"Last year, we launched the Referral Program. Whatever happened to that? I heard it a couple of times in the meetings but not one person has mentioned anything about it since." Mr. Sims walked toward the right side of the room. "What about other ideas? Has anyone even attempted to find other ways to solve this problem?"

In an effort to look productive in this train wreck of a meeting, Alex answered. "I've had my people making triple the calls, to unemployed candidates as well as employed ones. I figured maybe some people are ready for a career upgrade."

She saw Dan smirk out of the corner of her eye.

Mr. Sims nodded. "Well, Alex, we'll have to continue finding ways to recruit. It's the company's goal to find people jobs, right?"

"Right," the room said in unison.

"Good. I'm glad we agree on something. In the meantime, we're going to have to make some changes." Mr. Sims scanned the board room. "The company will have to let someone go in a few months."

Everyone looked around at each other, except Alex. She couldn't see herself on the chopping block and, most importantly, she wouldn't see herself on the chopping block. She'd exceeded her recruitment numbers over the past two years. She became one of their top recruitment managers her first month there. *This can't apply to me. I'll make sure of it.*

"We'll be observing you guys. We should be making a decision around March or April. Until then, come up with ways to help our clients. Immediately. I'll be watching you."

After a few minutes of uncomfortable silence and exchanged glances, Mr. Sims dismissed the executive staff from the board-room. Alex sped away from the low chatters and panicked expressions and headed toward the elevator. Courtney Davis and Romero Martinez filed behind her.

"Wow!" Romero said. "I guess we'd really better get on the ball, huh? We need to work harder at protecting the image of the company."

"Forget the image of the company! I need to keep my job," said Courtney. As Alex watched her talk, she thought about Courtney's uncle—the CEO Mark Davis. Somehow, Alex didn't think the spunky redhead had anything to worry about.

Courtney bounced off the elevator onto the third floor.

Romero shook his head and said what they were both thinking. "Like she's gonna get fired. I hope they don't get carried away with the rest of us. I have a kid in private school." Romero narrowed his eyes and wrinkled his forehead.

"This only means it's really time to buckle down," Alex said.

Romero's eyes stared off into the empty space. "Yeah. I suppose you're right."

The bell rang and the elevator doors opened to Alex's floor. She turned toward the door and raised her foot to step off.

"Hey!"

She turned back toward Romero.

"Thanks."

Alex forced a smile and nodded.

"Say. Did you get my email?" Romero asked.

Her brain flashed back to the email she had received from him yesterday. Romero had asked her to attend an art exhibit with him. Refusing to allow recognition of the email to cross her face, Alex feigned ignorance. "What email?"

"Oh, I sent you an email about the art exhibit downtown tomorrow. I wanted to know if you would like to go check it out with me?" Romero asked, smiling.

Alex took a deep breath. She hated to tell him no. He really was a nice guy—but not the guy for her. Besides, she'd been seeing Phillip for about six months now. Even though she and Phillip were far from heading toward the wedding chapel, she couldn't see making a run for Romero.

She snapped her fingers. "You know what? I already have plans with my friend."

"Oh, yes. Yes, of course," he said, lowering his head slightly.

"But thank you. Thank you for the invite."

"Sure. Maybe some other time," Romero said.

"Maybe." Alex stepped forward and the elevator door closed behind her.

She shook her head. *Not a chance.* Romero wanted more than she could possibly give him and she did not believe in dating nice guys because they were, well nice. Besides, any romance between them would spark unwanted office gossip. Employees already had enough food for thought with the coming layoff. She had to concentrate on how to keep upper management off her back and what she wanted to do for New Year's Eve.

CHAPTER 2

Alex steered East onto Camelot Drive determined to release all thoughts of the emergency meeting. The crisp air seeped through the small cracks between her car doors, while hot air swished through the air vents, blowing her dark brown, shoulder-length hair off her neck. Christmas lights still lined most of the houses in her subdivision. Each house Alex passed seemed to out-shine the one before it. Her house, on the other hand, fit into the small group without holiday decorations. As she pulled her black Lexus up to the two-story home, Alex couldn't help but notice the lack of holiday spirit there. She should have been embarrassed but she had an excuse; she'd been too busy at work to bother with decorations and she didn't feel like asking Phillip to do anything these days.

The man initially represented himself as the perfect gentleman—patient, polite and thoughtful. But, over the last couple of months, Phillip had become impatient and a little selfish. Suddenly, his time and objectives took precedence over anything she had to do. Yet, he liked to present reasons for his requests as if they made more sense. He would have probably told her she didn't need light deco-rations because she had no children around to appreciate them.

Phillip's car was already parked in her driveway. Alex switched off her ignition and looked at his car, then, at the front door. She longed to go inside, eat, take a shower and curl up in bed with the

TV remote instead of feigning interest in conversation with him. Maybe the night wouldn't drag out too long. Maybe she could stop him before he harped on the problems with public education or government. She opened her car door and pushed herself out. Walking past Phillip's silver Audi, she placed her hand on top of the car. The cool hood indicated he'd been there awhile.

Upon opening the door, she smelled steak, rice, tomatoes and okra. *I hate okra and he knows this.* She sighed and placed her brief-case on the table in her foyer. Alex rounded the corner to see Phillip bent forward into the cabinet.

"Hey. What's up?" Alex asked, forcing herself to sound chipper.

His face emerged, showing neatly framed facial hair. "Nothing," Phillip said. He stood straight. "Did you bring some salt with you?"

"No," Alex said, sitting down on a stool.

He frowned and closed the cabinet door. "I thought you said you would stop to get some on your way home."

"No, I didn't say that."

"Yes, you did."

"No, I didn't." Alex furrowed her brow.

"Is it that you didn't say it or is it that you don't remember saying it?"

"I didn't say it, Phillip. I didn't even know I needed any."

"It's your house! You don't ever check to see what you need in your house."

Alex's blood boiled to 103 degrees. She pressed her fingertips to her temples and took a deep breath. "I don't have a problem with missing salt. You do."

He shrugged and tossed his hands up in the air. "Fine. I hope you don't mind the tomatoes and okra being bland because there wasn't enough seasoning."

"Since you didn't go to the store to get it, I'm sure it's fine." Alex rolled her eyes. She hated it when Phillip overdramatized things. It was salt. Not gold.

Phillip turned off the stove and they fixed their plates. They moved in silence with the tension of their argument still lingering in the air. Alex and Phillip sat down at opposite sides of the dining room table, allowing the sound of the TV to serve as a soundtrack.

She glanced up at Phillip and saw him focused on his steak. Pressing on his knife and fork, he cut his steak into bite-sized pieces before eating it. She cleared her throat. "So, how was work today?"

Phillip continued to study his steak. "Fine. They're implementing new computer software."

"Oh. Is it gonna be easier or better?"

He smirked. "Not really. Half of our staff barely knows how to use computers as it is. I can see them hitting my department up a million times a day."

"Well, if it gets too strenuous, maybe you guys can ask for a raise." Alex chewed on a piece of steak.

He snorted. "They are not gonna give anybody any more money. The employees didn't even get cost of living raises this year." He regained eye contact with Alex. "But I'll bet the head honchos got their bonuses."

What else could she say? He had a negative comeback for everything as usual. Alex nodded and sipped her water.

"What about you?" Phillip mumbled between bites.

"What?"

"What about you?" He repeated in a booming voice. "How was your day?"

She sighed. "I guess it could have been better. They called an emergency meeting and told us they are planning to let someone go."

"Really?" Phillip asked, raising his eyebrows.

"Yeah."

"That sounds bad but you don't sound worried. You don't think they're gonna do it?"

She shook her head. "No. I'm not worried. I've always been a top employee at the company. So, I'm sure I'll keep my job."

Phillip picked up his napkin, wiped his mouth and placed it back on the table. He leaned forward in his chair. "You can't count on that. Maybe it's time you look for something else."

"Like what?"

"I don't know. Something with less hours. It can't be healthy to work so much."

Alex frowned. "You work just as much as I do."

"Yeah, but I'm a man."

"Excuse me. What does that have to do with anything?"

He rolled his eyes. "As a woman, you shouldn't have to work so hard. You should be able to let your man do all the work."

Alex couldn't believe her ears. *What an idiot?* "And what should a woman be doing?"

"Enjoying her life. Shopping. Cooking. Whatever makes her happy."

Alex dropped her fork on her plate. She didn't go to college, work her way up the corporate ladder to sit at home and cook for him. She was a grownup—one fully capable of taking care of her own responsibilities, despite whatever he thought she should be doing.

"Phillip, if you have a problem, why don't you say it?"

He crossed his arms. "I don't have a problem. I only like a woman that can chill out and let her man lead sometimes. You know, be a woman."

Alex anger rose even higher. She'd had enough of this. "So, what are you saying? I'm not a 'woman?'" she yelled.

"Yes, you are but…I mean you're the type of woman that's super defensive and overambitious. You spend all this time on your *little* career. You can't even remember to restock your kitchen." He pointed toward the cabinet.

Alex scowled. "I'm fine in my *little* career. I like my life. But since you're the one with the problem, maybe you should start looking elsewhere."

"We'll see how great your life is when you're old and alone without anyone to care if you're sick or alive. It's gonna get real lonely staring at the four walls."

Is he trying to scare me? Alex's heart rate increased, as her chest swelled. She pointed her finger at him. "I think you need to go."

Phillip huffed and stood up from the table. "That's just as well. We should stop wasting our time anyway, right? We obviously don't have much in common." He walked over to the counter to pick up his keys. "You don't have to worry about me anymore, Alex. Goodbye."

With those words, Phillip stalked around the corner and stormed out the door.

CHAPTER 3

"**C**an you believe this? Can you believe Phillip?" Alex frowned in disbelief at her best friend, Izzy Parker, while the winter air escaped her mouth.

Groups of people stood throughout Mark's Landing waiting for the fireworks to indicate the start of a new year. Some ate candy apples, hot dogs or funnel cakes. Others people watched. Alex chose to talk her sympathetic friend's ear off. She must have told Izzy the breakup details twenty times but she could not resist lamenting on it once again. The spinning in her head began, as Alex replayed her and Phillip's argument like a DVD. Each time, she heard his words, saw his movements and seethed in her own anger. Complaining to Izzy helped her deal.

"I know," Izzy said, scanning the crowd.

"I mean, how could he do that? And he had the nerve to try and scare me into thinking his way of thinking is right. Like if I don't ascribe to being Mary Poppins, I'm destined to be alone forever. Was he high?"

Izzy broke into laughter. "Okay. That *was* kinda weird."

"I tell ya. You date someone for months only to find out that they're crazy."

Izzy chuckled. "Well, look at it this way. You said he was a little chauvinistic. From his argument, that's obvious. This should be a relief."

"It would have been if he hadn't made me so angry." Alex tugged the knot she tied on her coat, bracing herself for the extra wind picking up.

"Aww. I'm sorry it had to happen this way." Izzy patted her on the shoulder.

Alex shrugged and frowned. "At least it's over."

"Exactly. And the best way to get over somebody is to find somebody else." Izzy nodded at the man a few feet in front of them and nudged her.

Alex glanced over at the medium-height man with kind eyes. He looked her way and nodded. She smiled in response but remained unmoved. She couldn't imagine anything worse than sitting through a dinner with someone she didn't know and didn't care to know.

Alex shook her head. "I don't think so."

"Oh, c'mon," Izzy said.

Alex rolled her eyes.

A man's booming voice burst through the nearby speakers. "All right, everybody. It's time to count down!"

People bustled around, hunting for the best spot to see the fireworks.

" Five…4…3…2…1. Happy New Year!"

Alex watched the multi-colored fireworks light up the sky. The noise from party favors and cheers should have deafened her but she barely noticed. Images of her life flashed in between the blue, green and red bursts in the night. She closed her eyes and tried to think positive thoughts about the year ahead. Instead, she heard Phillip's prediction of loneliness. She couldn't help feeling a little disheartened.

She hated the way she and Phillip ended but, at the same time, their personalities clashed too hard. On top of that, he didn't respect her accomplishments. That meant he didn't respect her. And that would always be a problem.

Now she had another problem. She was 35, single with no children. She didn't even have a man anymore. It hurt to be back at square one all over again. She still believed in real love. Where should she find it? It felt like with everything she'd accomplished professionally, she was still failing in life.

Alex finally opened her eyes and looked up at the lights in the sky. The anxiety of another uncertain year almost suffocated her but she stuffed it back down before it could fully take hold. She took a deep breath and exhaled, just as Izzy grabbed and shook her.

"Whooo! Can you believe it? Last year went so fast but we made it. Yay!" Her friend bubbled over with her usual infectious brand of energy. "I can't wait to get started," Izzy said, smiling so wide Alex thought she could see all her teeth.

Despite her somber mood, Alex laughed. She admired Izzy's eternal optimism. No matter what life or relationships threw at her, she always looked forward to the next day.

After the fireworks ended, Alex and Izzy headed back to her car. Alex tightened her black trench coat around her fitted blouse and skirt. As soon as the two women jumped in, Izzy asked party questions.

"Where are we going next?" Her medium brown curls bounced with excitement.

"I don't know, girl. You know, I don't do the party scene too much, unless it's a company event. Have any ideas?" Alex asked.

"I hear Club Aqua is supposed to be lit up."

"Aww. I'm not in the mood to dodge some guy with bad skin and stanky breath. Any other ideas?" she asked, with a pleading look in her eyes.

"Not really. I mean, a club is about the only route right now. What do you have against clubs?"

"They're boring." Alex shot her friend a frustrated look.

"No. What's boring is going home, changing into your pajamas and climbing into bed with your laptop and work scattered all over your comforter."

Alex raised her eyebrow. "I don't know what you're talking about," she lied.

"Or maybe you'll mope around the house, feeling lousy about the way things ended with Phillip."

A wave of shame threatened to overtake Alex. Fifteen minutes into the New Year, and she already had plans to slide back into her old routine. She needed to move forward, not backward.

Suddenly remembering that her best friend sat right next to her, Alex snapped out of her thoughts with the shake of her head. "I'm tired of the same ole, same ole."

"How do you know a club is the same ole, same ole? Doing what you've been doing is the same ole, same ole," Izzy said.

Alex's brow furrowed. "I don't sit in bed and work all the time. Look, if I want to do something different, I can." She straightened her posture. "And I will."

Izzy smiled. "I know you will, Alex."

She threw Izzy a weak smile back. "Thanks." She sighed. "Okay, I guess you win. We'll go to Club Aqua."

"Yay!" Izzy shot her hands up. "I promise you won't be sorry."

"We'll see." Alex waited to pull into the sea of cars, hoping she would at least be able to avoid the stanky breath guy.

CHAPTER 4

Club Aqua had all the components of a New Year's Eve party. Drinks. Party favors. Lights. A ton of people. There were so many people that it was difficult to walk from one end of the room to another. On top of that, Alex could barely see anything in the smoke-filled space. Slight pathways through the dance floor made it a little easier to maneuver. She concentrated on finding those pathways so she could find a place to sit down. It looked like the only place to sit was up on the second floor. Alex longed to make her way to a comfortable chair up there. Izzy, on the other hand, was ready to get on the dance floor. The only thing that kept her from joining the other dancers was the drink in her hand.

"Isn't this great?" Izzy said.

Alex shook her head. "Not really."

Izzy tooted her lips up. "You need a drink." She proceeded to suck on the straw protruding from her glass.

Alex leaned closer to her ear. "I need a seat."

"You can't meet anyone sitting down," Izzy said.

"I don't care."

As they continued to wade through the bodies on the floor, Alex turned to her right. She saw a girl dancing with two guys. One in the front of her, the other in the back of her. While they danced, the guy in the front attempted to move his hand up the woman's shirt. He had almost accomplished his goal before the girl finally moved his hand. Alex rolled her eyes in disgust. *Why did I let Izzy talk me into coming here?*

Alex and Izzy made it to the stairs to go up to the second floor. The stairs were the clearest thing in the building. They quickly made their way up the stairs and found a high table with a couple of chairs. Alex plopped down in a seat. Izzy sat across from her still engrossed in her drink.

A scantily clad waitress with long brown hair and exposed cleavage approached their table.

"Can I get you anything to drink?"

Alex turned to her to respond but Izzy spoke first. "She'll have a cosmopolitan and I'll have an Apple Martini," Izzy said.

The waitress wrote down the order. Alex interrupted her. "Do you have any Daiquiris?" Alex asked.

"Sure," the waitress said.

"Which kind?" Alex asked.

"Whatever you want. Banana. Mango. Lime. Strawberry."

"I'll have a Mango Daiquiri," Alex said.

The waitress nodded and wrote the order down. "All right. I'll be back in a sec."

After she left, Izzy leaned toward her. "You had to go the safe route, didn't you?"

"You want me to get tore down. That's all."

Izzy chuckled.

Right then, the DJ started playing a familiar, popular tune. The people on the dance floor and on the second floor jumped up, Izzy included. "Oooh. I have to go downstairs. I'll be right back. Get my drink for me," she called over her shoulder.

Alex looked over the rail at the frenzied crowd. It was amazing what one song could do. She glimpsed movement out of the left corner of her eye. She turned her head and saw a couple wedged in the small space. At first glance, they seemed to be possibly moving to the music but, upon further gaze, it was apparent that the music had nothing to do with their movements; they were having sex in the club.

She rolled her eyes. *Ridiculous.* Her waitress returned with a smile and the drinks.

"Here you go. Mango Daiquiri for you and Apple Martini for your friend. Is there anything else I can get for you?" the waitress asked.

"No. Thank you."

Alex sipped on her Daiquiri, savoring the fruity taste. She'd forgotten about the couple in the corner and started to relax enough to take in the scenery. If she were in to the club scene, perhaps this would be a decent club. They sure put a lot of energy into the New Year's theme. Even the glittered ball on the ceiling said 2012 on it. Alex peered through the crowd on the dance floor, searching for Izzy. She thought she might be able to signal that her drink was there. No such luck. The mass of people on the dance floor had buried Izzy. What did Alex expect? Izzy was only about five-foot-two.

"Excuse me."

Alex turned in the direction of the voice to see a husky man in a business suit. He smiled at her, revealing one silver tooth on the right side of his mouth.

"I couldn't help but notice you sitting here alone but with two drinks. Are you here with someone?" he asked.

"Yes." Alex actually hoped she didn't have to clarify who she was there with. She hadn't come to the club to meet anyone. She was passing time; that's all.

"A boyfriend?"

"A friend," Alex said.

"Well, he can't be too good of a 'friend' if he left a woman as exquisite as you alone at a table. If I were with you, I wouldn't leave your side," he said.

Alex nodded. She was trying to be polite but she really had no interest in talking to him.

The man placed his hand on his chest. "I apologize. I failed to introduce myself. My name is Lenard. And your name is...?"

"Alexis."

"That's a beautiful name." He smiled.

This is so corny. "Thank you."

He started to sit down in Izzy's chair but Alex stretched out her hand.

"Please don't sit there. My friend will be back any minute," Alex said.

He eased back up from the chair. "Oh, of course. I don't want to take up your time or get in the way. Here." Lenard reached into his breast pocket and pulled out a business card. "Let me leave my card with you. It has my office and my cell number on it." He handed it to her.

She took it, fully intending to throw it in the nearest trash as soon as possible. "Okay."

"It was good to meet you." He leaned over to whisper in her ear. "Call me."

At that moment, Alex frowned up. Lenard's breath smelled like a dirty toilet. *I told Izzy this would happen.* She quickly looked the other way, trying to find relief for her nose. Anything would have smelled better than the air coming from his mouth. She blocked her nose with the back of her hand.

"Same here. Bye," she said.

Lenard walked away. Alex breathed a sigh a relief. She couldn't have pretended that she wasn't affected by his breath much longer. She wiped her nose with her hand, trying to rid herself of the smell. It wasn't working.

Izzy returned to the table in the midst of Alex clawing at her nose. "What's wrong with you?" Izzy asked.

"Your friend needs to wash his mouth out with bleach," Alex said, still rubbing her nose.

"Who?"

"This man who approached me."

"What? Did he talk dirty to you or something?"

"No. His breath smelled like boo boo!" Alex raised her voice over the music.

Izzy cracked up laughing and Alex followed suit.

"Whoo! That's awful to hear," Izzy said.

"It's even worse to smell. I didn't know whether to offer him a mint or some toilet paper," Alex said.

Izzy doubled over with laughter. In the distance, Alex heard the DJ playing the same song he had played earlier—the one that got everyone hype, including Izzy.

Alex frowned again. "Um. I'm ready to go. You're not ready to leave yet?"

Izzy chugged her drink. "Not quite. Why don't you get up and dance or talk to somebody cute?"

"I'm afraid Mr. Stanky Breath has ruined that for me."

"Girl, everybody in here doesn't have breath like that."

It didn't matter to Alex. She'd seen and experienced enough. She'd never been a club person and this experience hadn't converted her. The club was for people who only wanted to have a "good" time or a good laugh. Nothing else. You didn't go there to find a mate. You went there to party it up. Alex was in a stage of her life where she had more serious thoughts than what type of alcoholic beverage she wanted. She had no patience for games. She enjoyed hanging out with her friend but Alex had to find a way to get out of there.

"I hope not but I could really get out of here soon. When *will* you be ready to go?"

Izzy sighed. "I don't know. Why don't you try to relax and meet someone new?" she whined.

"There's no one to meet here."

"Look at all these men around here. Surely, there's someone worth talking to." Izzy took a sip of her Apple Martini. "It's New Year's. I didn't say you had to marry him. Talk to him."

Perhaps this little trip to the club was premature. It had barely been 48 hours since she broke up with Phillip. She wasn't ready to get out there and actively look for someone else, particularly in this environment. *This is what I get for trying to be a trooper.*

"Izzy, I appreciate what you're saying and I know you're trying to help but this isn't for me right now."

Izzy looked at her sympathetically. "You're right. This place is more for me than you. I'll tell you what. Let's have another drink and then, we'll leave. We can go get something to eat."

Alex smiled. "Okay."

About thirty minutes later, the two women left the club and went to a breakfast spot. Alex didn't walk into her house until 3:46 a.m. Even though the club was long behind her, she continued to wipe her nose, trying to rid herself of the stench from the stanky breath guy.

She trudged up the stairs and headed for the shower. As she ran the lavender-scented shower gel and water over her medium brown skin, the toilet breath odor disappeared. The events of the last few days, however, rushed to her mind as quickly as the water beat down on her body. The more she thought, the more Phillip leaving seemed best for her. He was a jerk. Therefore, she had no chance at happiness with him.

If she could stop herself from feeling lousy about their argument, she would be okay. She had to deal with the fact that she didn't have anybody now and she didn't know when she would find somebody else. Desperation crept up on her while she thought about her current prospect of having a family. If she kept losing relationships, she would have to have a child on her own. She sighed. She could do that but she really wanted a full family, complete with a husband.

Noticing that her hot water had turned ice cold, Alex switched the shower off and stepped onto her plush white rug. She changed into her T-shirt and pajama pants and walked into her room. She turned her comforter back, bent her knees to the floor and clasped her hands together.

"God, please keep me, my family and friends safe from harm. I also ask that you keep me focused and uplifted. I pray that you empower me to make the most of my life this year so that I might be a blessing to others. But God, there is one more pressing thing on my heart that I must address. A favor to ask." Alex took a deep breath and released it slowly.

"I know that you have a man out there—somewhere out there—for me. I have no doubt about that but if Phillip isn't it, could you show me who is? I mean, can I at least get a hint? I hope I'm not asking for too much. It's just that this searching thing is getting old. Kinda like me."

Tears welled in her eyes but she refused to let them fall. She felt silly asking for such a thing but the Bible said, "Ask and ye shall receive." She opened her eyes aware and somewhat ashamed of her own request. She unclasped her hands and stood up. Dashing to the bedroom door, she flipped the lights.

Once Alex crawled under the covers, she took momentary comfort in the cool, clean fabric. She lay on her back and stared up at the ceiling as if she expected the answer to her probing question to magically appear between the creases. It didn't. If anything, more questions followed with each passing minute. Squeezing her eyes closed, she turned on her right side. There was no use losing sleep over this.

CHAPTER 5

Alex's night fell short of restfulness but she managed to get up in time to watch the football game. Or at least she tried to watch the game. By the time third quarter hit, she'd stretched across her chocolate brown leather couch, nodding in and out. She finally gave in, rolling into a ball and closing her eyes. They remained closed until the teams were walking off the field. The final score appeared at the bottom of the screen. 24-14. Sorry she missed the last two quarters, Alex smiled when she saw that her team won.

She glanced up at the clock. Alex needed to go to the store, get some gas for her car and then come home to cook dinner. She really wanted to stumble into her room and fall out over her bed but that would not be productive.

So, Alex propped herself up off the couch and staggered to her bathroom. As she washed her face, brushed her teeth and fixed her hair, she psyched herself up for the errands. Once she finished, Alex slid on her shoes and jogged back downstairs—picking up the pace before she could change her mind about stepping outside.

She pulled into the gas station three blocks away. *Geesh, could they have made this parking lot any smaller?* The station had always been small but it seemed smaller now that the cramped space crawled with cars. Alex eased into the station, hunting for an open pump. To her surprise, she didn't have to search far; the second one stood vacant. She backed into the pump and hopped out of the car to slide her debit card in the machine. As she pumped her gas and music played in the background, her mind drifted to her prayer and her plans for the new year.

She didn't know if she would ever get an answer to her prayer but she had come to one important conclusion: a new year required a new direction. Her life needed change. She had to go after what she really wanted, instead of settling for the readily available. From now on, she would concentrate on moving her life forward. No looking back.

The gas pump clicked. Startled from the noise, Alex pulled the tube from her car and placed it back in the hook. She screwed the cap back into her gas gauge, yawning. She shook the sleep away and jumped back into her car. While she vigorously rubbed her hands together with hand sanitizer, she could see someone in her rear view mirror tapping their fingers on the steering wheel, waiting for her to pull away from the pump. She hurriedly cranked up the car.

Alex crept out of her spot and soon regretted it. A diesel truck had blocked the entrance of the station. Cars had piled into the pumps. She strained her neck to see the far end and noticed one lone pump vacant, providing barely enough space for her to exit. Alex pushed her foot on the gas pedal and wormed her way toward the carless space between pumps. But after she drove a mere few feet, a gray Acura pulled through her only escape route.

"Argh! I can't believe this," Alex screamed.

She scanned the other pumps and saw that cars were still beside each one. She turned behind her and saw that the truck blocking the entrance seemed to have no plans of moving.

Alex faced forward again and sighed. Her eyes wandered over to the Acura and, for the first time, she saw the driver blocking her exit. It was Nathan Chestnut, the man she had dated ten years ago. She winced and ducked her head down. *Aww, man. Not today.* She anticipated awkwardness between them. A lot of time had passed since she had last seen him and their breakup had left some issues unresolved. How would they treat each other now? She didn't know and she feared finding out. Yet, part of her wanted another glimpse of him. She peeked over the edge of the window and focused on his neat appearance. He hadn't changed much. He still possessed the same slender frame she remembered—almost like time had stood still for him. Not wanting to stare too long, she quickly darted her eyes downward, hoping he hadn't spotted her.

She had to do something; Alex couldn't keep her head down forever. Maybe she could find a way to get out of the station parking lot before he noticed. She turned to her right to check the entrance. The diesel truck still showed no signs of moving and the driver that had taken her spot had walked toward the store.

She decided to back up a little and try to wait for the driver to return to his car or for someone else to move. Alex turned to the left to see how much space she had. In that moment, she wished she'd kept her head down.

"Alex! Alex!"

Hearing Nathan call her from across the parking lot, she cringed. *Okay. I'm going to count to three and slowly face him. One...Two... Three.* When Alex did face him, Nathan closed his car door and took long strides around his hood. She watched his lengthy arms swing back and forward, while he glided in her direction. He had the same springy step. *I wonder if everything else is the way I remembered. The good and the bad.* Watching him walk toward her filled her with anxiety and want. Suddenly, Alex wanted to hear what Nathan had to say, even though her nerves were about to jump out of her skin. A part of her felt vindicated that he saw her and chose to greet her with such kindness. The other part of her still didn't know how to handle their interaction. She took in a large gulp of air and prepared for the inevitable.

"Hello, Nathan." Alex straightened her posture and replaced her worried frown with a fixed smile.

"Hey. I haven't seen you in awhile. How's it going?" Smiling, Nathan reached for her and ran his hand over her upper arm.

Her arm numbed at his touch. The sensation almost sidelined her response. "It's going. How's everything with you?"

"Oh, it's...well, going." Nathan laughed. "So, what have you been up to?"

Flashes of the last few days hit her like a frying pan over her head but she kept her composure. "You know. Life."

He nodded, with his eyes piercing into hers. If she didn't know any better, she'd think his eyes were searching for a more detailed answer. "I hear ya. What do you do now?" Nathan asked.

She looked away briefly. "I'm a recruitment manager at Priority One Recruitment Agency."

His eyebrows shot up to his hairline. "Wow. That sounds major."

Alex wanted him to think so but felt the need to play it down, for modesty sake. "I guess."

"Yeah, it sounds cool to me."

"I like it. What do you do?"

"I'm a customer relations coordinator for a dealership."

"Okay. Do you like it?"

He shrugged. "It's all right. I'm pretty good at it."

Alex waved her hand and rolled her eyes. "I'm not surprised."

He cocked his head to the side. "Why?"

"Because you always had a way with people, especially women." Heat rushed to her face. She wished she hadn't thrown in that last jab. She didn't want him to think she was still bitter toward him. Well, what could she say? Old habits die hard.

Although Alex's comment obviously referenced their breakup, Nathan maintained his relaxed, friendly demeanor, seeming not to notice. "I try to treat people how I want to be treated." He smiled.

"That's a good rule of thumb," Alex said, crossing her arms.

They lapsed into a brief, uncomfortable silence. Nathan looked down at his shoes. "So, um, are you married?"

Alex hesitated. When most people asked her this question, she avoided answering because she hated the questions that followed. She also hated the funny looks she received when she stated her single status. But nothing compared to the clever advice others had for her on snagging a man.

With Nathan, however, the question took on a whole other meaning. Anytime a man asked a woman if she was married, that usually meant he wanted to measure his chances. *Is that the case with Nathan?* Her heartbeat quickened to the rhythm of her nervous energy. "No," she said.

After hearing her answer, he looked back up at her. "Neither am I. Do you have any kids?"

Another sore question. "No. What about you?"

"I have a son. He's eight years old," Nathan said.

She nodded. "Good for you." She took her turn looking at the ground.

The truck blocking her way a few minutes earlier cranked up and pulled out of the parking lot. Alex's eyes shot over in unmistakable relief. Nathan's eyes followed hers. When Alex turned back to Nathan, she saw the unspoken question on his face and felt the need to explain out of politeness.

"I'd been trying to get out of this parking lot for the past five minutes," Alex said, with an apologetic expression.

"Oh. I don't want to keep you, if you have to go."

The fear she'd faced in talking to him had given way to calm and, surprisingly, she didn't want their exchange to end. Feelings of panic and disappointment threatened to escape her voice. She cleared her throat to cover them up. "It's fine," Alex said.

"Well, then can I have your number so I can call you sometime?" Nathan asked.

Alex's brain slammed on the brakes. She scanned Nathan's neatly pressed black slacks, Clorox white shirt and dark green tie and she thought about the man she had known ten years ago. Kind, sensitive and lighthearted. Yet, she had a hard time reading him back then. He had some enigmatic qualities and, in her twenties, she still didn't understand men all that well. Because she couldn't read him, Alex didn't always take him seriously. But now his appearance and his energy contradicted the unpredictable Nathan she'd grown to expect. A slight air of maturity and sincerity in his words set her at ease about talking to him again. After briefly closing her eyes, she stifled the voice in her head that tried to get her to run for the station's exit. Instead, she chose to make herself cooperate.

"Sure," Alex said softly.

Nathan pulled out his phone and punched in the number she gave him. He looked back at her and smiled. "I'll call you."

She nodded.

He turned to leave and after a few steps toward his car, he turned back around. "Don't be pretending like you don't know me when I call either," he said, winking at her.

Alex laughed in spite of herself. She shook her head, shifted her gear into drive and rolled out of the parking lot the same way she came.

CHAPTER 6

Alex sprung up in her queen-sized bed and looked at her alarm clock. When she realized she hadn't ironed any clothes for work, she hopped out of bed. The edge of her gold, embroidered comforter dragged on the floor behind her.

After setting up the iron and board, she reached for her remote and flicked on the TV. A perky news anchor appeared on the screen. Alex half-listened as she picked up her clothes and started to iron.

"And in Hollywood, actress Roxie Miller is going public with her new baby. The *Days of Forever* star will talk to Quincy Marx about her controversial decision to have a child via artificial insemination."

Pictures of the actress flashed across the screen. Roxie paraded down the red carpet with long, flowing hair, flawless skin and impeccable makeup. *How could a woman like her need to pay a man to impregnate her? Men fall all over her.* Conscious of the time, Alex hurried her ironing.

She trotted downstairs forty-five minutes later in her black and gold pencil skirt, matching jacket and high heel black boots. Alex reached into the kitchen cabinet and pulled out her favorite mug— a tall, green cup with a turning lid. Popping off the lid, she ran water into the mug and slid it into the microwave. She grabbed a cereal bar nearby and took a couple of bites, before picking up her iPhone. There were no urgent emails, only spam. And most importantly, there were no missed calls or voicemails. Alex closed her eyes and steeled herself to put the phone back into her holster.

She refused to focus on Nathan's impending call. If he called, great. If he didn't, fine. Either way, she shouldn't be worried about it. She finished making her tea and headed to work.

Walking through the corporate halls, Alex had replaced thoughts of Nathan with radio morning show jokes. She even caught herself smiling, as she stopped in front of the elevator. Courtney walked up beside her.

"Hi, Alex."

Her smile slightly faded. "Good morning, Courtney."

Alex stood silently praying that she could reach her floor before Courtney honed in on her with questions or requests for advice. She had no patience for either.

"Yes, it is a great morning, after such a superb weekend." Courtney giggled.

Here we go. Alex nodded. The elevator opened and she stepped on, pressing floor number five. She knew better than to expect Courtney to stay behind and Courtney did not let her down. The chatty woman fell right behind Alex, foot-to-foot, onto the elevator.

"Chris and I spent the whole weekend together." Courtney pushed a button and continued without missing a beat. She looked up at the elevator ceiling, dreamy eyed. "We drank champagne, talked and watched the sun set together. Then, we went out for a night on the town for New Year's Eve."

Alex couldn't help rolling her eyes. "Good for you."

"I mean, it's amazing how perfect we are for each other. You know what I mean?" Courtney asked, leaning toward Alex.

"Um hmm." Alex eyed the numbers. Unfortunately, the elevator had only moved to the second floor, where it opened. No one stepped on. *Great. No relief.*

Courtney turned to Alex and smiled. "How was your weekend? How did you spend New Year's?"

Her brain instantly summoned memories of her breakup with Phillip and running into Nathan. Her chest tightened. Unattached again, she still didn't know when she'd find someone else. She didn't want to explore these issues at work either, especially with Courtney. Alex blinked and shifted her purse on her shoulder.

"Mostly with my friend. We saw the fireworks and headed home." *That's right, Alex. Keep it simple.*

She was proud of herself. Maybe if she held off on giving too many specific details Courtney would get the hint that Alex didn't want to talk.

"Really? You didn't do anything else?"

"Um. No, not really." Alex pushed down the frustration on the verge of surfacing.

Courtney shook her head. "That's sad. It was the New Year. You were supposed to bring it in doing something extra fun. Like hanging out with your boyfriend. You could hang out with a friend anytime." She nudged Alex in the side.

Alex bit her lip. Moments like these, she really had to resist the urge to tell Courtney off. She didn't know anything about Alex's life. Yet, Courtney assumed she knew the best thing for her because of their imaginary "friendship." It was irritating.

"You have to spend more time with your man. How else are you gonna get him to marry you?" On that note, the elevator opened on the fourth floor and Courtney stepped off, completely oblivious to Alex's eyeballs burning fire into the back of her head.

How dare she tell me what I need to do? She needs to mind her business. A glare had replaced Alex's jovial expression. When she finally reached the fifth floor, she barged out of the elevator and stomped down the hall to her office, passing all familiar faces in her wake. She opened her office door and shut it behind her before anyone could come in and ask questions—professional or otherwise.

Alex dropped her briefcase on the chair in front of her cherry wooden desk. After placing her mug on the desk, she flopped down in her black, leather executive chair. She rubbed her temples as her head throbbed. *Ugh. I hope these aren't coming back.* Alex reached into her drawer and pulled out her prescription pills for headaches. She hadn't needed them in about a week. As she popped a pill and washed it down with her tea, she hoped this wouldn't become a habit. While the liquid ran down her throat, Courtney's words bounced around the walls of her brain. The more she tried not to think about them, the more she did.

She spun around in her chair. The morning sunlight and clear sky outside her window calmed her a little. She tried to remind herself that she didn't want to find just anyone. She wanted the real deal. Someone she could build a life with. But if this didn't happen for her soon, she would have to take matters into her own hands, like the actress, Roxie. *Could I do that?* In the midst of her brief minute of relief, someone knocked.

Alex swiveled around to face her office door. "Come in!"

The door opened and Mr. Sims walked in. "Morning, Alex."

She sat up straight. "Good morning, Mr. Sims."

He stood in front of her desk. "Did you ever receive our report?"

"Yes, I did."

"Good. What do you think of the numbers?" he said, moving her briefcase and sitting in the chair on the opposite side of her desk.

She sighed. "It could be better."

He nodded. "How do you propose we make it better?"

She thought fast. Amidst her relationship woes, she had forgotten that upper management expected feedback and ideas on improving their numbers—a rarity for her since she always remained on task. "Well, we could post ads on job search websites."

Mr. Sims shook his head.

"I was also thinking we could host a job fair with employers and potential candidates."

He frowned. "I don't know about that. We can't afford to waste our clients' time."

"It won't be a waste of time if we conduct the proper screening beforehand. The event would be invite only and the only candidates invited will be the ones that have required qualifications. We may even be able to get sponsors for the event, which will bring in money and—"

"—give us more clients," Mr. Sims finished her sentence.

Alex nodded with a satisfied smile.

"That might be worth considering. Prepare a proposal about the job fair and present it at our next meeting." He stood.

"Sure thing. I'd be glad to."

"Good. I hope this works out for you."

"I'm always happy to do whatever I can to help the company maintain its vision, Mr. Sims."

"That's what we're counting on, Alex. The numbers have been down for far too long. It's about time to trim the fat and more than likely, it will be a manager that gets the axe. If your idea doesn't come through for us…" He shrugged. "I don't know. It could be you."

He turned to leave. "See you at the meeting."

As her door closed, Alex sat with her mouth open. Suddenly, the little idea she had come up with carried a lot more weight than she'd expected. She reached for her mug and took a swig of the tea. She frowned. The tea had turned lukewarm between her elevator ride with Courtney and Mr. Sims' stark warning. She had to pull herself together and create a proposal. Alex stood up and grabbed her mug. After counting to ten, she took a deep breath and opened her door.

CHAPTER 7

The computer clock read 5:08 p.m. Alex blew out a mouthful of air. She'd barely finished half of the proposal for Mr. Sims. Tired and angry with herself, she began to shut off her computer. It shouldn't be so hard to finish a proposal for an idea she created. She had no excuse but she did have a reason.

Alex spent half the time pushing the events of the past weekend out of her mind. If she wasn't lamenting on her romantic future, she was scrutinizing her cell phone to see rather it worked or not. She wondered if Nathan had forgotten to call her but reasoned he wouldn't forget if he really wanted to talk to her. The back and forth had put her a little on edge. If she were a smoker, she would have run through a pack that day.

Picking up her belongings, Alex headed for the first floor, happy for an end to a frustrating work day. When she passed the break room, Dan walked out. He stopped short after he saw her.

"Hello, there."

"Hello, Dan. How have you been?" Times like these, Alex wished she could have cut him dead as opposed to maintaining her professional disposition. Talking to him felt like such a waste of time.

"I'm great!" Dan said. "Have you started working on improving the numbers yet?"

"Yes, I have."

"I already have a couple of ideas underway myself. It's gonna go so well that they're gonna give me a promotion." He smirked and stuffed his hands in his khaki pockets.

"Good for you. Well, I need to get going now. Nice talking to you." *Not.*

Alex trotted out of the building to her car and dashed down the street. She turned up her radio and rolled the window down, allowing the sounds of the wind and the music to drown out the concerns of her day. She looked forward to meeting up with Izzy. They hadn't talked since New Year's Eve and Alex sure could use her friend's stubborn optimism. After passing the churches and hair salons aligning Washington Street, Alex pulled into Terrace Springs, a gated apartment complex. When she punched in a code, the gates opened for her. Upon driving past the familiar brick buildings, she pulled up to the eighth one, walked through the glass door and up the carpeted stairs.

The sound of screaming little girls emanated from Izzy's apartment door. Alex rang the doorbell and covered her ears. After a few shuffled steps, Izzy opened the door in a brown colored, peasant skirt and a turquoise and brown blouse that exposed her shoulders. A brown scarf tamed her wild, curly hair.

"Hey!" Wide-eyed, Izzy reached out to hug Alex.

"Hey! What cha up to?"

"Trying to keep up with these girls."

With her arm still around Alex, Izzy led her into the apartment. Alex scanned the living room. The coffee table had been moved to the side to accommodate coloring books, watercolors and crayons. A scooter leaned against the window and doll clothes were scattered around it on the floor.

"Are you sure they're not trying to keep up with you?" Alex asked.

Izzy chuckled. "No, girl. I think they got me beat."

The girls shot out of the kitchen like bullets from a gun—one chasing the other.

"Hey! Stop all that running."

They screeched to a halt as they saw their mother had company. "Hi, Auntie Alex," they said in unison. They went up to give her a hug.

"Hey, girls. What ya'll doing today? Being bad."

"She is," Izzy's oldest daughter, Maya, said.

"Na uh," her sister, Kelis said, pushing Maya.

"Okay. That's enough of that," Izzy said to the girls.

"I have an idea. Why don't we go to the park for awhile and stretch out?" Alex asked.

"Yay!" Maya and Kelis cheered and danced around the living room.

"Okay, okay. You guys go get your jackets," Izzy said to the girls who dashed back around the corner.

The four of them packed into Alex's car for a noisy ride to Helmsman Park. When they arrived and stepped out of the car, the soft breeze caused a slight chill in the air. Maya and Kelis raced for the jungle gym, while the two women sat on the swings to talk.

"You know, Kelis has a little boyfriend at school." Izzy chuckled.

Alex's eyes widened. "What? Who?"

Izzy smiled and nodded toward her daughter. "Kelis? What's your boyfriend's name?"

The little girl stood at the top of the jungle gym and put her hands on her hips. "Warren."

Izzy laughed. Alex shook her head. "Where did the time go? It seemed like yesterday I was changing her diapers. Now, she has a boyfriend."

"I know, right."

"It's scary."

"Why? It's a part of life. They all grow up." Izzy turned to her friend. "Don't tell me this is why you haven't had kids."

"No. I want kids. Just haven't had them yet."

"Really?" Izzy wrapped both her hands around the chain on the swing. "Well, what are you waiting on?"

Alex frowned. "A man."

"Is that all?"

"Well, that's usually how the reproductive process works."

Izzy tooted her lips up at Alex. "Yeah, you had one of those."

"And he was a jerk. I need someone permanent in my life to help me raise my children. I want the right man for me."

Izzy tossed her head back and laughed. "Girl, if I had waited for the right man, I wouldn't have those two beautiful little creatures over there. And though they are a handful and I have very little help from their fathers, I would never regret them."

Alex sighed. "As you shouldn't." She glanced over at the two girls fighting over who would go down the slide first. "But I want to marry. I want the whole thing. I want the kids and a husband who I adore and who adores me. Is that so wrong?"

"No, it's not. Listen, when I met Carlos, I thought he was it. We were going to get married, have kids and live in a house with a white picket fence. I even had the date picked out."

"You were really in to him."

Izzy nodded. "Yes, but two years in, I realized he wasn't ever going to marry me. He still wanted to hang out with his friends, run around. I had to move on so I could find someone else."

"That's great. No matter what, you stayed optimistic."

"Only because I knew that even though I didn't get what I wanted then, things would still work out."

"So, does this mean that you're going to settle now?" Alex asked.

Izzy shrugged. "I don't know. Maybe. Depends on what I want at the time."

Alex shook her head. "That doesn't sit well with me."

"But what if you don't get your husband wrapped up in a neat little bow? What if you find a guy who is nice and a good father but you don't have that 'adoring' feeling for him? Can you live with that?"

Alex pressed her lips together. It's a thought that she'd considered too many times and she'd always come to the same conclusion. No. She couldn't imagine life with someone who was an "okay" choice at the time. The day in and day out of interacting with someone that she had nothing in common with or didn't really love made her want to give up on the relationship before it even started. On the other hand, she often wondered if she was being unrealistic. Maybe she didn't really need to adore someone. Maybe she could be with someone who respected her, treated her right and that's it. In that case, she might have to settle, so she could have the home she hoped for.

She frowned at the thought of living that type of lie. Izzy caught her frowning.

"Who am I kidding? You always get what you want." Izzy bumped Alex.

"Yeah, right."

"No. Let's think this through. Do you have any irons in the fire now?"

Suddenly, Alex remembered Nathan. Butterflies danced around her stomach before she could utter his name. She planned to tell Izzy but now she hesitated. She didn't want to make him sound like he was a prospect; he hadn't even called her yet. Knowing Izzy's overactive imagination, she would have them married next month but Alex bit her lip and told her anyway.

"Not really." She took a deep breath. "I did run into Nathan yesterday, though."

"Nathan?"

"You remember him. The guy I dated a decade ago?"

Izzy's eyes shot open like she'd swallowed a hot chili pepper. "Oh! Him! Yeah, I remember. He was nice. What did you guys talk about?"

"Where we work, so on and so forth."

"Is he married?"

"No."

"Did you tell him you weren't either?"

Alex sensed where this was going. "Yes."

Izzy nodded. "Did he give you his number?"

"No." Alex shot back.

"Did you give him yours?" Izzy leaned over.

"What's the point of these questions?!"

Izzy laughed so loud her daughters momentarily turned in her direction. "I knew it!"

"You knew what?"

"The second you said you ran into him. I knew he was gonna ask for your number and you would give it to him."

"How did you know that?"

Izzy smiled wide. "It was a hunch."

Alex rolled her eyes. "Well, don't get too excited. He hasn't called yet."

"So, you *are* waiting for his call?" Izzy raised her eyebrow.

Alex threw up her hands. "Forget it!"

"Oh, c'mon. I'm kidding. It's okay to want him to call you. What happened was ten years ago. Both of you have grown and the fact neither of you are married may be a sign."

"A sign of what?"

"A sign from God that this may be a relationship worth revisiting."

Ugh. Here we go. "Izzy, it is not a sign."

"How do you know? For all you know Nathan could see you as the one that got away. He did ask for your number."

"Yes, he did but—"

"See? He wants to rekindle the relationship. Alex, this could change everything." Izzy's breathing quickened.

"This changes nothing. All I did was give him my number."

"And he took it. He wants something else and so do you. The man has a plan."

"Let's drop it." Alex didn't know why she tried explaining this to Izzy. She'd have better luck talking to the ocean. No matter what Alex said Izzy continued to flow her own way and romanticize this whole scenario—the opposite of what she wanted. Although she would like for Nathan to call her, she also needed to keep her head on straight. No use making mountains out of ant beds.

Surely, Nathan had changed. Besides growing older, he had new responsibilities but she had no way of knowing if a relationship between them would develop now. He hadn't called her yet. So, she couldn't see any solid proof that he wanted to rebuild their relationship. She preferred to focus on that reality.

Alex faced Maya and Kelis as they ran up to her and Izzy.

"Mama, can we go get some ice cream?" Maya asked.

"Sure, Hon. Let's go." Izzy stood up and the two sisters began debating the kind of ice cream they would choose. Izzy turned back to Alex.

"You know what your problem is?" Izzy asked.

Alex raised her eyebrow.

"You're afraid to believe. You have to believe your life is going to change. You have to believe this is going to be different. Even though I've had my share of man problems, I enter each new relationship with a clean slate, determined to believe the best will come from it. You have to do the same thing, Alex. If you don't think anything good will come out of it," Izzy shrugged, "nothing will." She faced her daughters. "C'mon, girls. Race you to the car."

While Izzy ran lightly behind her daughters toward the car, Alex sat on the swing, pondering her words. Could it really be that simple? Had she asked for something she didn't even believe she could have?

CHAPTER 8

That night, Alex's briefcase lay untouched against the gold wingback chair in her room. An unfinished proposal called out to her but she continued to lie motionless on her bed, staring at the TV. There weren't even any papers or a laptop skewed across the covers. *Hey, maybe I am breaking habits this year. Now all I have to do is find a man.*

Alex switched channels and landed on *Quincy Marx Tonight*. She adjusted her pillow, as the interviewer introduced his guest for the evening. Quincy turned toward actress Roxie Miller after the intro.

Roxie appeared calm and serene. Cheerful, even. She wore a cream blouse with a scarf draped around her neck and blue jeans. Quincy jumped right into the interview, asking her specifics about her baby.

"Let's talk about your wonderful new baby. What's her name?"

"Marie," Roxie said, smiling.

"That's beautiful. How did you come up with it?"

"It was my grandmother's name."

"Your grandmother's name? All in the family, huh?"

"Yes." She nodded.

"How long have you wanted a child?"

Roxie crossed her legs. "For a while. Several years. My life didn't always allow for it."

"How is that?"

"Booming career. A couple of years ago, I filmed two movies in one year. I was also making some guest appearances on *Summer's Lane*. I barely had time to breath, let alone have a child. And then there was the issue of having no man." She chuckled.

"So, why now?"

"It's a better time all the way around."

"But your career is still good and you've said there is no man."

"Right but I've learned how to make some adjustments to my schedule and I'm ready now."

"Who is the father of your baby?" Quincy asked, leaning forward. Alex leaned forward with him.

"I don't want to say his name." Roxie shifted in her seat.

"Is it your co-star, Greg Long?"

"I will not talk about the father of my child."

"Okay. Why go this route?"

"Which route?" Roxie cocked her head to the side.

"The route that would mean having and raising a child on your own?"

"Oh, well. Simply, I wanted a child now."

"But you know people are criticizing you for it."

"I can't live for the 'people.' I can only do what feels right for me." Roxie leaned forward. "Look. I could wait five more years to meet the right man or I can do what I want right now. I chose not to leave my life up to fate."

Roxie's words pierced Alex to the core. Roxie had received flack for her decision to have a child alone but the more she talked about it, the more Alex understood her position. Sometimes you have to make things happen for yourself.

"Is there anything that you would like to tell someone who may consider becoming a single mother?" Quincy asked Roxie.

"That no matter how scared you are, if you really want this, you can make it happen. I did it and I'm very happy with my decision."

Alex muted the show and stared at the screen. Although Roxie had disappeared, her confident and poised demeanor lingered behind. Alex and Roxie had two different vocations but they were fundamentally in the same situation. They both wanted a family. Roxie simply chose to take her dreams into her own hands. What was wrong with that? Nothing, in Alex's opinion.

Roxie didn't really need a man in her life to have a child. She had more than enough to support the child financially. So did Alex. With forty right around the corner, she couldn't wait forever. Not if she really wanted a child.

Besides, why should she wait? Love? Roxie didn't. The more she thought about it, this sounded like a viable option for Alex. She took comfort in the idea that even if her relationships bombed, all was not lost.

Alex leaned her head against the headboard and closed her eyes. In spite of her alternative, sadness fell over her like a dark cloud. Before she could succumb to it, her phone rang. She looked at the phone as if it were an alarm. It rang again. She didn't want to answer it but when it rung a third time, she decided to pick it up.

"Hello."

"Hey, Alex. It's Nathan."

Alex sat up in her bed. *I can't believe he finally called. I thought he'd never call.* Butterflies gathered in her stomach, while she glanced at her clock. Eleven thirty-two. "Hi. I wasn't expecting anyone to call this late."

"Sorry. Is it a bad time?" Nathan asked.

"No, I was just watching TV."

"Really? What were you watching?"

Alex cleared her throat. "A news show." She should not be talking babies right now. He did not need to know how desperate she had become. "So, uh, what's up?"

"I wanted to touch base with you. I meant to call you a couple of days ago but I had a lot of things come up. I've been absolutely swamped," Nathan said, sounding apologetic.

She smirked. Nathan's apology irked Alex a little. For all he knew, she'd been busy as well. Yes, thoughts of his impending call had lurked through her mind but she couldn't let him assume his call mattered to her. She preferred to pretend she hadn't even thought about it. "Me, too! I've been up to my hair follicles in work."

"I guess it's that time of year, huh?"

"Yep," Alex said.

"Well, I wanted to ask you if it would be all right...I mean. Would you like to go to dinner with me sometime?"

A faint sense of resentment made her stall in accepting the dinner invitation. She couldn't help wondering why he had taken so long to call her. Was he playing a game or did he really have something important to do? She toyed with the idea of turning down his invitation. But then she thought about her current patterns and habits and how badly she wanted to change them. She could turn him down but what would that prove? That she had a stubborn personality? She already knew that. Would she prove her feelings were still raw over the way things ended the last time? Thinking about it made her heart sink.

After Alex didn't respond right away, Nathan filled the empty sound with obvious self-doubt. "It's okay if you don't want to—"

"Uh, no. I mean. Yes, I would like to go to dinner with you," Alex interrupted him.

"Okay. Great! Um, how does seven-thirty this Friday sound?"

"Sounds good."

•••

Alex stared at her computer screen, studying the words in her proposal. Thankfully, her concentration had increased and she was about three-quarters done. She hated to think that this had anything to do with Nathan's call the night before. Yet, she couldn't deny that she was finally focused without wondering when he'd call her. While in the middle of thinking of the next line in her proposal, her phone rang. She sighed and picked it up.

"Alex? I need you to come down to my office," Mr. Sims said, absent a greeting.

"Sure," she said, puzzled.

Once she hung up, Alex grabbed her notepad and pen out of instinct. Whenever she had to go talk to her boss, she always wanted to have a pen and paper, certain that he would say something she needed to remember. From the way he sounded over the phone, he had important things to discuss.

Within five minutes, Alex was knocking on his door.

"Come in," Mr. Sims said.

Alex walked into the plush office and shut the door behind her. It looked like something out of a magazine. The dark brown wooden furniture matched the rest of the wood décor. A chess game was set on a small round table next to an unlit fireplace. Three historical paintings on the wall were lit from above. He motioned to her to come forth. She walked carefully over the thick, beige carpet. When she reached his cherry brown executive desk, she stood in front of it while he finished a call.

He hung up and pointed toward the seat in front of his desk. "Have a seat."

Alex sat down and leaned forward, awaiting his words.

"How's everything going?"

"Pretty well, sir."

"Great. How's the proposal coming along?"

"Very good. I am putting the finishing touches on it now."

"Now?"

Why didn't I just say it was complete? "Yes, Sir. Finishing touches."

He nodded. "Is there anything that you need?"

"No, Sir. Everything is under control. Once I present the proposal, we can hash out the details and I will get started."

"Okay. As I'm sure you recall that we've been having a tough time over the past year with recruiting. As a result, we've had to pull back on a lot of our resources." He sighed. "Your event is not only going to require a lot from our clients but it's going to require a lot from us as well. With that said, if we do it, it must be a success."

"Oh, it will be. Absolutely. Without a doubt."

"Let's hope so because if it is not," he paused, "let's just say it won't look good for you."

Alex swallowed the lump in her throat. She understood what this meant. If this job fair did not succeed, she could kiss her job goodbye. A small surge of panic crept up her spine but she headed it off before it could go all the way up.

"I understand, Sir. You nor the clients will be disappointed."

He smiled for the first time since she arrived in his office. "Good. I look forward to that. Well, that's all I had. Let me know if you need anything."

"Sure."

Alex stood up and walked out the door. She couldn't get back to her own office fast enough. She walked with her head down deep in thought about Mr. Sims' little "pep talk." Alex didn't expect to feel this type of pressure. He was obviously sending her a warning that she'd better heed. Alex had to make this job fair work and she would start with this proposal. It would be done before she left the building. No exceptions. *I will make this the best event this company has ever had.*

CHAPTER 9

A t seven on the dot Friday night, Alex stood in front of her mirror half-dressed. It took some time to decide what to wear. The cleaners still had her preferred outfit, which meant she had to find something else quickly. She thumbed through the clothes in her closet. She pulled out a pink and black dress she'd worn about five months ago but it looked too summery to her. Her eyes rested on a long skirt with two five-inch slits up each side. She frowned. The matching shoes were unsuitable for winter weather. Alex chose a long sleeve, beige sweater dress and matching boots. After she laid it out on her bed, she returned to her mirror to figure out what to do with her hair.

As she pulled her hair backward and turned it sideways to view it from different angles, her nerves set in. She'd managed to avoid them all day but, in her quiet moment of getting ready, they were threatening to overtake her. She had so many thoughts and feelings that were unresolved. She wanted to ask Nathan many questions. Like did he ever love her? Did he regret cheating on her? Had he changed? Yet, she didn't know how to ask these questions casually. Alex plugged her flat iron into the wall and slid into her sweater dress.

After parting her hair a few times and smoothing out the rough edges, Alex unplugged her iron and brushed her hair over her shoulders. She gave herself a nod of approval in the mirror and walked downstairs. She passed the clock on her stove. It read seven forty-eight. Alex sighed. *I wonder where he is.* With no call, text or email, she didn't know what to think of his tardiness but decided not to draw a conclusion about it yet. She paced the floor a few times. Alex finally picked up her phone, walked over to her living room and flipped on the TV. She placed the phone on the coffee table and switched the channels. She landed on Lifetime. She didn't usually watch that movie channel but she figured she'd watch the current movie while she waited.

Three commercial breaks passed. Alex picked up the remote and hit Select. The clock read eight thirty-five. She stared at it hoping it would magically subtract an hour and five minutes. It didn't work. She didn't have an explanation for Nathan's absence but one thing she did know for sure; her anger felt like lava heat ready to ooze out of her and melt everything within her reach. She let the screen return to the movie and crossed her arms. Her cell phone rang.

She picked it up off the coffee table.

"Hello?"

"Hey, Alex," Nathan said, as his voice came through the line. "I'm so sorry. My friend's car broke down. He called me to help him at four and I thought sure I had enough time to get to you but..." His voice trailed off. "I just got home and I'm covered in grease."

Alex closed her eyes and sighed.

"I'm sorry. We can reschedule this for another time. How about tomorrow?"

Alex's chest felt heavy, almost too heavy to suck in enough air to speak. *How could he do this? Does he expect me to be available at his whim? What kind of game is he playing?* This must have been a mistake. She didn't even know why she gave him her number. "I have a lot to do tomorrow," she uttered.

"Oh. Well, what about next Wednesday or Thursday?"

"I'm not sure about then either. Look, thanks for giving me a call. I hope your friend's car is working again," Alex said, devoid of any emotion.

"I think it'll be fine. I'm gonna call you later so we can set something up, okay? I'd really like to see you again," Nathan said.

Alex took a deep breath. "Sure. Goodbye, Nathan."

She hung up without hearing his goodbye. As she kicked off her shoes and threw her legs onto the sofa to finish the Lifetime movie, she felt the heaviness again. Except this time it wasn't just her chest that felt heavy; it was the heart underneath it that weighed a ton.

•••

On the following warm and sunny Saturday afternoon, Alex sat in the office inside of her house. The room overlooked the subdivision's neat and clean landscape. She glanced out the window and caught a glimpse of the sunlight bouncing off the tree leaves—so inviting. She wished she could go outside and at least take a walk somewhere but she needed to work. Even though she'd finished her proposal, Mr. Sims' warning still rang in her head. She needed to stay ahead of the game. So, she decided to start planning for the fair.

However, in the middle of looking through venues, she found her mind wandering. Alex leaned back in her black, executive chair, unable to resist allowing her mind to replay Nathan standing her up. She couldn't believe she wasted time wanting him to call and then, when he finally called and set up a date, he missed it. A mixture of sadness and anger engulfed her heart all over again.

Alex usually figured things out quite quickly but relationships were kicking her butt. It was enough to make her forgo them in favor of taking matters into her own hands. But where would she start? She sat up in her chair and switched back to the Internet. Alex went to Google and searched for sperm donors. A sperm bank popped up first. She reluctantly clicked on it and the yellow and white website appeared before her eyes.

The phone number and hours of operation for the bank sat at the top left-hand corner of the site. Farther down, she saw one of the most thorough search boxes she'd ever seen. It was like a catalogue. She had the choice from a variety of hair colors, eye colors, heights, weights and ethnicities. Out of curiosity, she clicked on black hair, any eye color and around six feet tall. She clicked on search and leaned into the computer for the results.

Up came the basic demographics for donors, along with a code number. She clicked on the African-American donor who was six-one and 185 pounds. She immediately saw a list of information on his hair type, blood type and other profile information. They even provided a description of his personality. On the right side of the screen, she saw the price for the donor's sperm. *$565*. Alex leaned back in her chair, floored.

Instinct led her to pick up the phone to dial Izzy's number. She had to tell somebody about this. Izzy picked up on the second ring.

"Hello?"

"Girl, you will never believe what I am looking at."

"What?"

"I am looking at an online sperm bank."

"What? Why are you looking at that?"

Alex gasped. She remembered that she hadn't told Izzy about her thoughts of pursuing motherhood on her own. She placed her hand over her mouth, trying to think fast and figure out what to say.

"Oh. I happened to be on Google searching for something else and you know how other stuff pops up on the search engine? Well, it was there." Alex crossed her fingers, hoping that her friend bought her excuse.

"Oh! Whew! You scared me for a minute there." Izzy laughed.

"Yeah. Well, I had to click on it to see what it was about. It's like a catalogue," Alex said.

"Really?"

"Yeah. They got prices and all."

"OMG! I gotta see this. What's the website?"

"www.theasibank.com."

"Hold on." Izzy disappeared from the phone. A few minutes later, she came back.

"Wow! I am blown away. Who knew it was this deep?" Izzy asked.

"I didn't," Alex said.

"Well, thank God we don't have to do this. Paying for what should be free is not the way to go."

Izzy's comment felt like an arrow piercing Alex's skin. She winced a little.

"Yeah, but I guess it helps a lot of people," Alex said.

"Sure but it's also a business. Someone is making money off of what should be a part of nature. Selling our blood on the corner. It's an abomination."

"What?" Alex looked at the phone.

"Okay, maybe that's going a little overboard but it's definitely unnecessary," Izzy said.

Mixed emotions ran through Alex's body. On one hand, she was happy that she hadn't told her friend that she'd been thinking about doing this on her own. As free-spirited as Izzy had always been, she never expected her to be so judgmental about this but she guessed everybody had an opinion. On the other hand, she was disappointed that her best friend opposed another woman's choice. Sure, she didn't know that Alex had considered this choice but it still stung to know that in this decision—the most important one of her life—she may not be able to count on her friend.

She supposed she might have received a different reaction had she told Izzy that Nathan had stood her up. Sympathy, perhaps. But Alex wasn't in the mood to talk about that disappointment. She looked up at the ceiling as if expecting some reassurance from God.

"Well, I saw that and had to share. Let me get back to work," Alex said, seeking to end the call before she began to show her true feelings.

"Okay. I'll call you later," Izzy said.

"All right. Bye."

After Alex hung up the phone with Izzy, she went back to searching the bank website. She spent forty-three minutes looking at the donor descriptions. There was only one that stood out but he cost $700. *Why in the world does sperm cost so much?* These people really were trying to get rich off a delicate situation.

She clicked on the x at the top of the site's window. She didn't see anyone on the website that was worth $700, even if he was a Ph.D.

Alex turned back to the window she originally opened. She needed to get back to work and focus but the words on the page seemed to run together. Baby thoughts were still occupying her mind. She had searched the bank, hoping she would find answers to help clarify her direction. Instead, she had more concerns. She didn't know how Roxie was able to reach such a happy destination but the road Alex occupied seemed to twist and turn, leaving her as confused and lonely as before.

CHAPTER 10

The meteorologist on Channel 14 predicted a sixty percent chance of rain. So far, the sky only had a slight overcast. Alex almost cancelled eating dinner with her mother. Between the weather and her unexpected letdown from Nathan, she didn't feel up to it but she decided she still craved some good food and hoped the sky would stay clear. Maybe her mother wouldn't notice her distraction.

Alex turned onto Robin Avenue with her mother in the passenger seat. As she approached the red light, her mother held out her hand.

"Wait!"

"What, Mama? I was stopping. What do you think, I'm gonna run through the red light?" Alex asked.

"Well, I don't know. You kept going," her mother said.

"I wasn't going to run a red light, Mama." She couldn't wait to reach The Seashore Restaurant. She really hated driving her mother anywhere. She complained even without anything to complain about. She tried to insist that her mother drive but she climbed into Alex's passenger seat and refused to move.

Alex finally pulled into the restaurant parking lot. As soon as they walked in, she noticed a long line of people waiting for a table. They approached the chipper, young hostess.

"Hi. Welcome to The Seashore. Will there be two?" the hostess asked.

"Yes," Alex said.

"Okay. It's going to be about a fifteen-minute wait. Is that okay?"

"Not really," Alex's mother mumbled.

"Ma," Alex said. "That'll be fine," she said, turning back to the young girl.

The hostess nodded and handed Alex a beeper. Alex looked around the waiting area for a place for her and her mother to sit but all the seats were taken. She remembered seeing empty chairs outside. When she peeped through the window, she noticed that they were still available.

"C'mon, Ma. We can sit outside."

Alex opened the door for her mother and they walked over to the empty, wooden chairs. She sat down and crossed her legs. Her mother plopped her stocky frame down in front of her.

"Ooh. These chairs are too low," her mother said.

"Well, I didn't see anything higher, Ma. Unless you want to go back to the car or sit on those bricks over there." Alex pointed to the stack of bricks that were holding the greenery close to the building.

"Then, I won't be able to enjoy the dinner for itching." Her mother tooted her lips up. "I guess I might as well stay here."

If the Olympics made complaining an event, her mother would win a gold medal. Alex prayed that she didn't spend the whole lunch complaining. She didn't feel like hearing it today. She had too much on her mind. She frowned.

"What's going on in your life?" her mother asked, peering at her daughter. She leaned forward to hear what she had to say, seeming to sense something wrong.

Although Alex knew what her mother wanted to hear, she chose to give her what she wanted to give her: work talk.

"Well, my company is undergoing a lot of changes. Executives say we aren't doing as well as usual and someone will lose their job soon."

Her mother's eyebrows shot up. "Who?"

"They haven't said but we are all instructed to be on our Ps and Qs."

"You do not need to lose your job, especially with that big house you're living in. Who ever heard of a single woman living in a house that big?" Her mother shook her head.

"It's a two-story house. Not a mansion."

"Still. It's too big."

Just like her mother to see the negative. She couldn't be happy she had a successful daughter. She had to find a means to point out Alex's shortcomings. It never failed. "Anyway, I don't think I'm going anywhere," Alex said.

"I hope not." She scanned Alex. "Anything else going on? Met anyone new?"

"No, Ma."

"Why not?"

The beeper flashed and buzzed. Grateful for the distraction, Alex stood up and led her mother inside the restaurant.

The hostess sat them in a booth near the window, offering full view of the busy intersection and a Babies "R" Us store across the street. Alex immediately thought about the sperm bank she found on the Internet. She quickly turned away, hoping that the baby longing she felt in her heart didn't show in her eyes.

The women ordered and within twenty-five minutes the server brought their food to the table. Alex ordered a Wood-Grilled Shrimp Fest. Her mother had a full plate of pasta and a side of broccoli.

"Enjoy your meal, ladies," the server said.

Alex nodded. As she picked up her glass of water and took a sip, her eyes fell back on the Babies R' Us store and she began to ponder the bank again. *Was it really all that bad of an idea?* Maybe she needed more than one opinion.

"Ma?"

"What?"

"Have you watched the news lately?"

"A little bit but I don't listen to the radio shows anymore because I don't work. So now I only catch the evening news, except for last Wednesday. I had to wash my car. It's been so cold outside but I couldn't take looking at that car another day. It had dirt spots all over it. You know the kind that look like they've been on there for days, accumulated from when it spot-rains? That's how mine—"

"Ma," Alex said, sighing. "I asked because I wanted to know if you saw the story about the actress, Roxie Miller."

"I'm not sure. What about her?" her mother asked, digging into her plate of pasta.

"She recently had a baby."

"Oh. They were talking about her this morning. Who's the daddy? Some big Hollywood hot shot?"

"No. Actually, she had artificial insemination."

"What?"

"You know, where they insert the sperm manually."

"Ugh. I know what it is. Why in the world would she do that?"

"I guess because she wanted a baby."

"Then, why didn't she go out and get a man like everybody else?"

"She did get a man. Many men but none of them worked out. So, she did it on her own," Alex said, blowing on her shrimp.

"Nonsense. No woman has to do it on her own, unless she wants to. There's always a man around. You have to pay attention and stop making excuses."

Even though Alex knew that her mother was talking about Roxie, she couldn't help feeling like those words were for her. She seemed to always struggle with relationships and men. It had become a sore spot for her. She and her mother had discussed it several times. The conversation never ended well. Alex hesitated to even mention her break up with Phillip. From the way her mother talked, it wouldn't be any easier than previous conversations. She opted to wait a little longer to tell her. Maybe her mother had even forgotten about him. She'd only mentioned him a couple of times.

"Whatever, Ma." Alex's eyes wandered down to her mother's half-empty plate. "So, how's your diet going?"

Her mother almost choked on her pasta. Alex laughed.

"It's been going good until today."

Both chuckled. "That's okay. There's always tomorrow," Alex said.

Alex's phone buzzed from her purse. She pulled it out and saw Nathan's number. She frowned, muted the ring and threw it back into her purse.

"Who was that?" her mother asked.

"An unknown number."

"Oh." Sandra glanced through the window and spotted the place that made Alex think about Roxie. "Babies "R" Us. That reminds me. Gerard called me yesterday and said that he and your cousin Nikki are having a baby shower Saturday. We can go across the street and get the gift out of the way."

Alex rolled her eyes. *Another baby for Cousin Nikki.* "I don't know if I'm going to this one." This would be number four for Nikki. Alex bought her a gift last year. She didn't feel like doing it again.

Her mother stretched her eyes. "Oh, you're going. Or I'll tell the family where you live so they can randomly stop by your house to say hello."

Alex grimaced. Sometimes her mother could be so cruel. "Why would you do that?"

"Because you need to be more supportive of your family."

"Well, if you want to go to the store, you might want to hurry up cuz they may close soon and I have work to do."

She could feel the nightmare coming. The store alone gave her mother way too much space and time to torture her. She could see her pointing out all the things Alex should be buying for herself. She felt bad enough already. She didn't need help.

Her mother took her time with her meal, despite Alex's warning. She not only got a couple of refills on her drink, she ordered dessert: chocolate cheesecake with a side of vanilla ice cream. She took a bite and rolled her eyes in taste bud heaven. Alex rolled her eyes in annoyance.

"Umm. This is good. You want some?" Her mother pointed her fork at the cake and ice cream.

"No, thank you, Mama."

"Are you sure? This is really good."

"Yes, Mama."

"Why not? Are you watching your weight again? What for?"

"Ma."

"I mean, that would be fine if you were watching it to catch a man but since there doesn't seem to be one in sight, what's the point?"

"Ma?"

"It's not like you're gonna make me a grandmother this century."

Alex saw red. She'd had enough. She grabbed her Dooney & Bourke purse straps. "Ma, I'm gonna go ahead and go to the store. You can come over once you're finished with your cake and ice cream. Okay?"

"All right, all right. I'm almost done." With that, her mother wolfed down the remains on her plate and took one last sip of her drink. "Okay. I'm ready to go."

Alex waved for the waitress. After she paid and left a twelve-dollar tip, the women exited the restaurant and rode across the street to Babies "R" Us.

Every time Alex passed the store, it seemed to be a wasteland but the day that she had to go in there, the parking lot burst with cars. While she took her time going in, her mother practically jumped out of the car while it still moved.

"C'mon, girl," her mother said.

Alex walked slowly behind her toward the store and paused briefly when she reached the automatic doors. She took a deep breath and stepped forward.

In midstride, her mother turned backward to look at Alex. "C'mon!" she said with much more force in her voice.

Someone needs to tell this lady I'm not two years old anymore.

Alex picked up speed, figuring it better to speed up and get this whole thing over with. She followed her mother, who led her down the aisle with the bottles and the bags. Her eyes rested on a black stretchy stomach band. She picked it up and read the instructions. The mother-to-be simply wrapped it around her stomach to help bring her tummy back in after childbirth. And it was fairly inexpensive. Alex shrugged. Maybe she could buy this for her cousin. Goodness knows she could use it.

She walked over to her mother, who stood studying the diaper bags. "I'm going to get her this."

Her mother eyed the product and without missing a beat said, "And what else?"

Alex's head fell to one side. "What do you mean, 'and what else?'"

"I mean, what else are you buying her? You're not going to stop with that, are you?"

Alex looked away. Why did her mother have to make this so complicated? "What else am I supposed to be getting her?"

"Toys, clothes, bottles." She dropped the diaper bag to her side.

"You've never had one of these before but there's enough stuff around here to give you an idea of what one needs when they have a child."

"Mama, you act like she's never had a baby before. She has some of this stuff already."

Her mother sighed. "Alex, this is your cousin. She's family. We're supposed to do for family. Now, I wanted you to come along because you have good taste. Please don't act like you don't want to help. Okay?" She turned back around to examine the diaper bag again.

Alex turned in the opposite direction. She hoped her mother didn't expect her to buy up the store for her cousin because that would not happen. Alex walked down the clothes aisle. She spotted dressy and casual shoes, as well as little jumpsuits. She wrinkled her forehead. Alex didn't know what to pick. She also hated that she had to be there doing this for someone else. She looked up and saw a big poster of a baby with black curly hair. The little girl in the photo appeared to be shot right before a smile. Her facial expression was gentle and playful. For a minute, Alex stood there, staring at the little girl as if she were someone she recognized in a missing persons flyer.

All her thoughts about her cousin disappeared. She could only think about her own dreams—dreams she'd held for a long time but pushed aside, figuring she would get to them later. In looking at the little girl on the poster, she now realized that later had turned into now. She really needed to get started on making her dreams a reality.

CHAPTER 11

Alex sat at her desk, scrutinizing her proposal with a shrewd eye. There was no room for errors. Luckily for her, there weren't any. Now she had to deliver it well. She'd practiced her points the night before and prepared herself for any objections to the idea. Management would definitely see the benefit of the job fair. She glanced at her clock and saw that she had ten minutes before the meeting started. *I'd better get down there.* Alex gathered her presentation and a pen.

When she walked into the conference room, a couple of people were standing around conversing. Alex nodded a greeting to the executives she passed and sat at the table. Dan strode in and greeted others loud enough for most people to hear. He saw Alex and stopped short of heading to his seat.

"Hello, Alex."

Alex glanced up at him. "Hello, Dan."

"I hear you're doing your presentation today. Are you ready?" He shot her a sly smile.

"Always." *Games.* She hated playing these competitive games and Dan seemed to always want to play them. Despite his underhanded provocation, she maintained a neutral expression on her face.

"I look forward to hearing it. Mine is going to blow Mr. Sims away. Good luck."

Dan walked to his seat in time for Mr. Sims to take his place at the front of the room. The VP's commanding presence caused a hush to fall over the room.

"Good morning, everyone."

They returned his greeting.

"We have a bit of sad news. One of our board of directors, Tom Gidder, is retiring and leaving the board. He's been here for fifteen years and seen the company through many changes."

The staff offered sympathetic expressions to the occasion.

Mr. Sims nodded. "His influence will be missed." He walked toward the left-hand side of the room. "On another note, I've continued to monitor our numbers over the past couple of weeks."

Alex scanned the room to see everyone else looking around, too. They all seemed to brace themselves for the tongue-lashing headed their way.

"Many of you have made an effort to improve the placements. I appreciate all of the extra hours and extra calls made to help us reach our goal," Mr. Sims paused, "But I'm afraid we are still falling short. Our placement numbers are 17 percent lower than they need to be and this is because we have some catching up to do from last year. "Now I know our company can do much better and today Alex and Dan are going to share their ideas as to how we can turn this situation around. Every meeting, I'll select a couple of you to present your ideas. So, get prepared. But right now, we're going to start with Alex."

Alex stood up and practically flew toward the front of the conference room. She was eager to get this over with. It felt like she'd been holding on to that proposal forever.

"Good morning, everyone," Alex greeted the staff.

They murmured a lackadaisical, "Morning."

"As Mr. Sims has indicated, we have all been charged with making a positive change in our numbers. Well, I have come up with a way for us to gain a load of placements in one swoop." Alex paused for effect. "A job fair."

She browsed the staff and thought she saw some of her coworkers roll their eyes.

"I know what you're thinking: 'Those rarely work out for the job seeker or the employer.' And you know what? You're right. But I'm prepared to do it differently. Instead of printing a bunch of flyers and paying for ad space, I'm going to pull exclusively from the pool of applicants we already have, select the best of the best and match them with our most prized employers. The event will not be advertised in the paper. The fair will be strictly invitation only. This will allow me to screen the applicants thoroughly so that when they arrive to the job fair they are five steps closer to getting the job of their dreams."

After going over a few more points, Alex breathed a sigh of relief inside. She'd gotten through it and now the presentation was almost over. She believed she'd done a good job explaining her plan of action and its benefit to the company.

Courtney raised her hand. "How many candidates do you plan to invite?"

"At least four hundred," Alex answered.

Brian Stacks, a coordinator, whistled. "When are you going to find time to invite all these candidates and perform your regular responsibilities?"

"I'm going to have the call center line up a number of candidates for the individual companies," Alex answered.

"It sounds good, Alex, but that's a lot of people. How are the companies going to see them all?" Mr. Sims asked.

Alex faced him. "Well, they won't. They're going to be split into groups. Thirty-minute increments. The candidates' first stop will be in a separate room for background checks and those that make it through that will interview with the companies' HR departments."

Mr. Sims raised an eyebrow. "Well, it looks like you have it all figured out. Good job." He nodded and motioned permission for Alex to have a seat. He then turned toward the rest of the room. "I'm glad to hear you have a plan because we are planning to have a big going away party for Tom in March. That means we need to get this job fair done soon. We'll schedule it for February 23rd. That's about four weeks from now."

She nodded and wrote the date at the top of her presentation paper.

Looking back at her, Mr. Sims continued. "Go ahead and get started with the fair." He pointed to his left. "Dan will help you."

Excuse me? Dan? Why do I have to work with Dan? She peered over at Dan. His eyes were stretched open. She could tell he didn't like the news anymore than she did. She imagined him with that same expression throughout the whole planning stage of the fair. Her main job would entail putting out his fires. She tried to speak but her voice would not cooperate. Dan, however, did find a way to speak.

"Uh. Mr. Sims? I still haven't given my presentation yet. I had other ideas of how to improve the numbers."

"Hold on to them for a later date. We don't want to spread ourselves too thin," Mr. Sims said.

"Maybe he has a proposed project that will benefit mine," Alex said, finally finding her voice.

"Perhaps, but I really want us to focus on the fair. You and Dan will be working together. Any questions?"

Alex shook her head. No one else said a word. "Good. I'll expect a full briefing on the progress next week. Any other updates?"

The staff remained silent.

"All right. Until next week."

Alex stood up from the table and caught a glimpse of Dan. He was grabbing his papers and folder quickly, scowling the whole time. *I know, Buddy. I don't like it anymore than you do.*

She headed to the elevator to go back to her office, dreading the headaches to come. Romero caught her in the elevator.

"Good job today, Alex."

"Oh. Thanks." Alex shrugged.

He held up his hand. "You must be annoyed having to work with Dan. He isn't the easiest person to work with. He has quite a bit to learn but has a problem listening. Well, at least you guys won't have to work together long."

"Four weeks."

"I'm sure it'll fly by." Romero smiled.

Perhaps she could have said more to Romero but she was too busy thinking of how to get companies to commit to the job fair *and* how to recruit hundreds of qualified candidates to attend.

"It's going to go great." He looked her up and down before clearing his throat. Before he could say anything else, the elevator door opened on her floor. *Ha! Quicker escape this time.*

"I'm sure it will. See you later, Romero."

Alex marched into her office and flopped down in her chair. It was safe to say the meeting didn't go the way she thought it would. She should have been ecstatic about Mr. Sims enthusiasm for her job fair but, for the life of her, she couldn't understand why he would pair her with Dan. With all his talk and competitive behavior, he had yet to prove himself a leader in the company. That meant, in this project, he would have to follow her lead. Alex moaned and leaned her head back in her chair. She had no time to babysit, especially a grown man.

She had to figure out how she was going to handle Dan. She could ignore him but if she did that, he might take matters into his own hands and create all kinds of chaos, trying to be relevant. Bad idea to leave him to his own devices. She could try to talk to him about what she expected. Then again, she didn't see him responding well to that; he responded better to ego strokes. Alex didn't have enough patience with him to do that. *Why don't I assign him things to do?* That sounded like a good idea. This way she'd know what he was doing and he'd have an active hand in the fair. She'd also get to look like a team player who gets along with others, even difficult coworkers. A real win-win.

She smiled at her plan of action. Dan could start on sponsors while she worked on obtaining the employers. She'd talk to him about his tasks later. For now, she would give him a chance to cool down after getting run over in the meeting. Alex stretched then reached into her desk drawer for her cell phone. Unlocking it, she immediately searched for new emails. She found emails, as well as three missed calls. She tapped on the screen to show the numbers and saw Nathan's number.

Suddenly, all the memories of the date that never happened rushed back to her in a flash. She'd successfully pushed them out of her mind until then. She searched for ways to make it disappear again, along with the sadness and shame that came with it but they remained. She stared at Nathan's number. Her eyes were drawn to it as she toyed with the idea of returning his call. Her heart wanted her to do it but her pride would not allow it. He messed up *again*. She could not forget that and she didn't think she should try. Alex closed the call log, opening her emails to focus on them instead.

CHAPTER 12

Alex's phone sung a ditty for her while she was driving. She glanced at it quickly but refused to answer. As the sun rays beamed through her windshield, she pulled on her sunglasses and concentrated on the street signs. She didn't visit her cousin's house often so she always had to seek directions to get there. This time, however, she believed the Internet directions led her astray. She found herself rolling down a dead-end street. Maybe this would have been easier had she picked her mother up and they went over together but she didn't think she could handle dealing with her mother the whole way. She could not withstand her mother's incessant nagging.

To tell the truth, she really wanted to stay home. She had plenty of work to do. Catching up on work sounded much better than pretending to enjoy this family gathering. It wasn't that she wished her cousin ill or lacked happiness for her; she wasn't in the mood to be reminded of something she didn't have—a family of her own.

Alex reached the end of the street and circled around. She finally gave in and reached for her phone to call her mother for the tongue-lashing she knew awaited her. When she clicked on the screen, the missed call symbol popped up. She touched her screen and slid it down to see Nathan's number. He called her while she was driving.

She rolled her eyes. *I'm glad I didn't answer.* She didn't have time to talk to him, listen to him or try to decipher his sincerity. With that said, she did wonder what he had to say. What could he say after standing her up? Alex shook her head and dialed her mother's number.

"Ma, I'm at Winchester and it dead ends. Where should I go next?"

"How did you get down there?"

"It was on the directions."

"What directions?"

"The ones I printed out."

"I told you how to get here. You should have written down what I said instead of going to some computer. I told you to turn on Forsyth, not Winchester. I don't know why you don't listen to me."

Alex sighed and grabbed a pen from her arm rest. "Okay, Ma. So, go back through Kingston Road." She scribbled on the defunct directions.

"Go back four streets the way you came. That should lead you to Forsyth. Once you get to Forsyth, turn left."

"Okay, okay. Hold on. Let me write this." Alex wrote down the directions as fast as she could.

"Got it?" her mother asked.

"Yes."

"After you turn left onto Forsyth, you're gonna go through three lights. Turn left at the forth light. That will be Peach Street. Go down one block and it's the house on the right with all the cars and balloons."

This time, Alex had a better understanding of the directions.

"Thanks, Ma."

"Um hmm. Hurry up! We're ready to eat."

Alex followed her mother's directions to the letter. When she finally pulled up to the house, she squinted at the scene in front of her. Like her mother said, there were a lot of cars in the yard and pastel-colored balloons tied to the mailbox but there were also people standing outside. Alex pulled to the side of the curb, grabbed her bag and exited the car. As she got closer, she heard loud talking.

"Uh uh. She cannot come inside!"

Alex continued to hear the commotion and moved closer. She saw her cousin standing on the porch, looking down at their other cousin, shaking her head in disapproval.

"That's fine. Me and my gift can go elsewhere," the other woman yelled.

Alex spotted her mother off to the side of the action. She walked over to her. "What's this about?"

"Oh, child. Pinky came in the house sneezing and blowing her nose. When Nikki heard it, she came out of the back like a bat straight out of its cave. Yelling and screaming about whoever is doing all that sneezing has to get out of her house because she can't get sick while she's pregnant."

Alex looked over at the women who continued to go back and forward with each other.

"So, how did we get to this?" Alex motioned toward the two women.

"You know how Pinky is. She refused to leave and they got into this big argument. So, here we are."

Alex happened to look backward and noticed that a couple of the neighbors had stuck their heads out the door. Embarrassed, she turned toward the house.

"Ma, I'll be in the back. I don't wanna look like I'm a part of the spectacle."

Heading for the backyard, Alex maneuvered through the crowd

of people watching the racket. The sound of music began to drown out the yelling in the front yard. She rounded the corner and found her cousin's husband sitting down with a beer in his hand. He leaned his head back, letting the faint breeze envelope his face. Alex hesitated for a second and then, decided to move forward.

"Hey," she said.

Gerard snapped his head up and opened his eyes. "Hey, Girl! Where you been?" He stood up and reached over to give her a big hug. Alex smiled. Gerard's friendly demeanor always impressed her. So did his caring and loyal attitude toward Nikki. Their relationship gave her hope. If Nikki could have a husband who loved her and devoted his life to making her happy, surely she could, too.

"Oh, I've been around," Alex said, sheepishly.

"Have a seat." Gerard motioned to the chair next to him.

"Where do you want me to put this?" she asked, holding up the large bag she brought.

"Here. I'll take it." He reached over for it. "Whew! What is this? The baby's a little young for a car, isn't he?"

Alex laughed. "It's not a car."

She sat down and, for the first time, she got a good look at the decorations. Three white tents were set up outside. Yellow, blue and green pastel balloons aligned the poles and baby-inspired centerpieces were set in the center of the tables. The gifts sat on a table across from them in front of the blaring stereo.

She suddenly found herself envisioning her own baby shower. The only way she would hold it under white tents is if she had rented a country club with super green grass. Otherwise, she would probably hold it at a hotel like the Rico Marco in Amelia Island or the Carloto Hotel in Sawgrass. The tables and the chairs would be covered in lavender and cream. She'd have a three-tier cake with butter cream icing and a silver shaker at the top. She'd also make all the guests wear cream. Alex couldn't help smiling as she thought about her dream baby shower.

Before her dream could linger too long, Alex shook it away and turned her attention back to Gerard.

"So, are you excited about the new addition to your family?" she asked, tapping him on the knee.

"Oh, yeah. I mean, this is like old hat to us but we're always happy to have another one."

"Have you thought of any names?"

"I like Michael."

Alex nodded. "Nice. Stick with the traditional. I respect that."

"Um hmm but I had to fight for it." Gerard leaned over and put his beer on the ground.

"What do you mean?"

"Originally, Nikki wanted to try and be creative. I told her this was not the time to experiment. It's our child's name. Why give them one they'll be embarrassed about later?"

Alex nodded and smiled. "I agree. No child should have unusual names, like Tree. It's like naming your child Tuesday."

Gerard laughed.

"Tuesday, come back here. Uh, Wednesday, where are you going?" Alex mocked.

Gerard bent over in laughter and held his side, trying to regain his composure. "Oh my gosh. I know exactly what you mean."

Alex took a deep breath. "Seriously, I admire you guys. You're doing what you want to do. You're raising a family. I think it's great."

Gerard raised an eyebrow. "Aren't you doing what you want to do?"

Caught off guard, Alex hesitated. "Yes but..."

Gerard continued to stare at her. "What?"

She contemplated her next words. She'd always kept much of

the personal details of her life away from her family. Alex didn't want to be gossiped about or given unsolicited advice and she knew that's all they would do but she thought maybe it was time to confide in Gerard. He'd always been encouraging toward her.

"I would like to have a family, too, someday," Alex said.

His eyebrows shot to his scalp. "Really?"

"Yes. Surprised?"

"A little. You never expressed this before."

She shrugged. "I don't like putting my whole life out there for public commentary."

"Okay. Do you have anybody in mind now?"

Nathan popped into her mind. Alex looked downward.

"Uh oh. Is everything okay?" Gerard asked.

She hesitated. "Can you keep it to yourself?"

He nodded. "Whatever you say won't go any further than me."

She sighed. "I broke up with someone recently and I find myself a little concerned about my chances of having a child."

"Well, Alex. You still have time."

"I won't always have time. I need to get this together now."

"Don't rush. When it's supposed to happen for you, it will happen for you."

"That sounds good but what if it's not going to happen. What if I have to make it happen?"

His eyes widened. "How are you going to do that? Adopt or something?"

She shrugged. Alex had shared some of her fears and concerns but she felt the need to stop short of telling him her thoughts about artificial insemination and other fertility options. That would probably be too much for him to handle. "I'm stressed over breaking up with Phillip and running into my ex."

"Your ex? Who?"

"His name is Nathan."

"Nathan. Where did you run into Nathan?" Gerard asked, picking up his beer and taking a quick sip.

"The gas station but we initially met several years ago through friends. We dated for about a year."

"Um. So, why did you break up?"

Alex inhaled, wondering if she should tell the truth. She would be so aggravated if all this spread around the family. She imagined herself having to field questions that weren't her family's business anyway. But then she remembered that Gerard had always been a stand-up guy. He'd agreed to keep her admissions to himself and she believed he would do that. "He cheated on me."

"With who? Your friend?"

She shook her head. "No. With some girl at a friend's party."

Gerard leaned back in his chair. "Do you think you can trust him now?"

"I don't know."

"But you have doubts, right?" His eyes bore into hers.

"Yes. I mean, I don't know if he's changed or not. I only ran into him recently." She frowned at him.

"Well, be careful. Follow your gut on this guy."

So far, Nathan had proven unreliable. Maybe she should let any thoughts of reconnecting with him go. Yet, Alex thought about her missed call from him. She again wondered what he wanted from her.

"Sure," Alex said.

As if sensing that she needed to be saved, the "party" migrated toward the back yard. Several of the guests, including Alex's mother, joined her and Gerard, picking right up where they left off.

"Chile, you should have seen that foolishness," her mother said, stopping in front of Alex. "Those two would still be going on and on had the neighbor not threatened to call the police."

"Well, I'm glad it's over," Alex said, distracted.

Alex's aunt, Martha, walked through the sliding door carrying a tin pan. A few others followed her carrying similar pans.

"Okay, everybody!" Aunt Martha chirped.

By the time the pans reached the picnic table, the smell of fried chicken, potato salad, greens and sweet potato pie took her nose hostage. She almost forgot about Gerard's skepticism but not quite.

Alex excused herself to the bathroom. Once she locked the door behind her, she washed her hands and tried to clear her mind so that she could rejoin her family in good spirits. She stared at herself in the mirror and shook her head. She willed herself to stop thinking about Phillip, Nathan or anything else that had to do with her failing romantic life. After a few deep breaths, she stepped back outside, where she tried to focus on the delicious food her aunt had cooked.

CHAPTER 13

The cell phone vibrated. Alex reached into her desk drawer to look at it and saw Nathan's number again. She quickly silenced it and slid the phone back into the desk. Alex sat in her executive chair, bouncing her knees under the desk. While Mr. Edward Allen, talent manager at PharmScope, read over her proposal, she thought about every word she'd written. She wondered if all her words were spelled correctly and even if she'd practiced proper grammar. So far, she'd secured two possible companies for the job fair. She desperately needed a confirmed participant. She never thought it would be this hard.

As Mr. Allen flipped through the pages, he fluctuated between expressions. At one point, he would furrow his eyebrows. At another point, he would nod. Watching him do this over and over nearly drove Alex wild.

"Do you have any questions, Mr. Allen?"

He sighed. "Yes. What do you expect the return on this to be?"

"As I stated in the proposal, we should be able to find at least twenty-five great candidates for your company. Even more than that."

Mr. Allen sat back in his chair. "It's a nice idea but we can't afford to send our staff out to an event that may not prove successful. We need them back at the office."

"I understand your point of view, Mr. Allen, and my point is that attending this job fair may cut your staff's work in half, freeing them up to concentrate on other tasks, develop other programs."

Mr. Allen cocked his head to the side. "That sounds good but how can you assure me that I will get the most out of this?"

Before Alex could respond her cell phone vibrated. *I thought I silenced that thing. She frowned and swiftly reached into her desk drawer to silence* it without missing a beat. "I'll tell you what. We will get you at least fifty prospective candidates at this job fair. If by some strange event we are not able to deliver on that, I will personally screen and host another site event just for you. With no additional cost."

Mr. Allen pushed his two pointer fingers together and pressed them to his lips. "I like the idea."

"You'll like the results even better," Alex said, leaning forward.

He nodded. "Okay. Here's what I'll do. Let me have a little pow-wow with the rest of the staff and I'll get back to you by noon Thursday. Does that sound fair?"

Alex smiled big but inside she wanted to scream. On one hand, she knew he would end up participating in the job fair but, on the other hand, she would rather have had him sign on now, especially since she had a meeting with the VPs Thursday morning. Yet, Alex knew if she pressed the issue she risked losing his cooperation altogether. So, she let up.

"Sure. Absolutely. Noon Thursday it is." She leaned forward to shake his hand. When he walked out of her office, Alex slid down in her chair. *Great. I wanted this one so badly.* She racked her brain for a solution to this problem. She desperately needed employers to sign on as soon as possible. Lost in thought, she jumped when her extension ring.

Flustered, she grappled with the receiver.

"Yes."

"Ms. Carter? You have a delivery downstairs," the receptionist, Betty, said.

Alex jerked her head back. "Oh, okay."

She walked out of her office and headed for the elevator. When she saw Courtney, she rolled around to the other elevator. She stepped into the vacant elevator with her mind wondering. What kind of delivery did she have? She hadn't ordered anything.

When the elevator opened up on the first floor, Alex walked toward the front desk. The closer she came to the receptionist's desk, she could see a massive object setting on it. Sticking out of an elegant Couture vase, Alex saw two dozen long-stemmed red and pink roses mixed with smaller white and light pink spray roses and fresh green bupleurum.

Alex crept up to the desk, looking around. "Uh, hey, Betty. You said you have a delivery for me?"

"Right here." Betty motioned toward the large display of flowers.

Alex rounded the flowers and saw the card with her name on it. She started to open it but happened to glance up and see Betty sitting with her hands folded, waiting for Alex to open the card. Suddenly feeling uncomfortable, she tucked the card back into the bouquet and grabbed the vase.

"Thank you, Betty," Alex said, moving away from the desk.

"Sure thing." Betty watched her round the corner.

Alex's palms were getting sweaty. She darted her eyes back and forth, looking to see if anyone noticed the large display of flowers eclipsing her. So far, people in the building seemed to be minding their own business. She relaxed a little and relaxed even more when she pushed the elevator button and it opened right away. *It looks like I'll get this upstairs without any fuss.*

She stepped on and pressed the fifth floor. Right before the door closed, Romero put his hand in the way and strode on in. He smiled when he saw Alex but his smile dimmed a little when he saw the flowers.

"Hey. What you got there?" he asked.

Alex shrugged. "Flowers."

He nodded. "They're beautiful. From someone special, eh?"

"Well, I don't know about that. Someone decided to surprise me." She nodded. "I'm surprised."

They both laughed a nervous laugh. *C'mon, floor five.*

"So, have you been seeing this friend for awhile?"

"Uh, no."

The elevator door finally opened up on her floor. Grateful for an escape from this uncomfortable conversation, she hopped at the opportunity to leave it behind. She always hoped that Romero got the hint—that they would never be a couple but, moments like these, she wasn't sure. She really didn't like to hurt anybody's feelings. She also couldn't lie. Handling her interactions with Romero poorly could lead to real problems for her at work, something she wouldn't tolerate.

"Have a good day, Romero." Alex stepped off the elevator.

"You too, Alex."

Alex rushed to her office before anyone else asked her about the flowers. She bolted through the door and bumped it closed behind her. After leaning against the door for a few seconds to catch her breath, she carefully escorted the vase over to her desk. She sat it down and parked herself in the chair to read the card.

I hope you accept these flowers as an apology. I kick myself for not catching up with you and I would like for us to try again. I accept responsibility for my part in destroying our first attempt. Please let me make up for it with a date (yeah, I said it). Promise you won't be sorry.

Sincerely, Nathan

Alex leaned back in her chair, as the card dropped to her lap.

Nathan had never sent her flowers before and he'd certainly never written anything like this to her. Before she could think about the card any deeper, someone knocked on her door. Alex rushed the card in her desk drawer.

"Come in!"

"Hey. Hey! You got flowers." Stanley walked in the room.

"Yeah. Just a friendly gesture." Alex waved it off.

"Some gesture. Listen. We need some help with the new outline. You gotta minute."

"Sure. I'll be right over."

As Stanley walked out the door, Alex made sure she'd tucked the card away in her drawer under several pieces of paper. As if sensing the card's presence, her phone vibrated. She looked over and saw Nathan's number—again. Something in her grew excited, despite her attempts to be level-headed. After a moment of standing still, the phone finally stopped and rung once signaling a message. Satisfied with her composure and self-control, she smoothed her skirt and walked out of her office.

CHAPTER 14

"Oh! So, he bought you flowers, huh?" Izzy teased.

Alex shook her head.

Izzy had a couple of hours to kill between hair clients and Alex left the office an hour and a half early. The two met up and walked through the mall that afternoon. Alex munched on a chocolate chip cookie, while Izzy licked her Rocky Road ice cream off the waffle cone.

"Yeah. It's no big deal."

"Alex? Please. Men don't spend money on a woman because it's no big deal. Okay? I mean, rich men might but the average Joe will not spend extra money on a woman unless he's really into her. I don't care how nice he is."

"All right. So, you have a point. That still doesn't mean anything."

Izzy quickly licked the ice cream oozing down her cone. "You know what your problem is?"

"No, but I'm sure you're gonna tell me."

"Your problem is that you're too negative. You're not willing to believe in anything. Every time Nathan does something nice for you, you figure out a reason to dismiss it."

"Can you blame me? I gave him my number. He took a week to call. We make a date. He doesn't show up. Every nice gesture is not cause to call a wedding planner. I'd rather be realistic about what's happening. He's already proven to be unreliable."

"How do you know that? He told you he had to help a friend fix his car. Is it so hard to believe that he may have actually done that?"

Alex thought about the possibility that Nathan had told the truth. She also thought about their break up a decade earlier. She could still remember how she felt when she heard that Nathan had a little too much fun at a friend's party. She confronted him about it and he admitted to getting oral from a dancer there. Heartbroken, she split up with him right then. For those next few days, he called her day and night, trying to see if they could work things out but her anger and hurt would not allow her to hear him absent of judgment.

After numerous calls and emails from Nathan, Alex grudgingly agreed to listen to him in person for two minutes. He said he would call her that night to let her know when she could expect him. That night came and that night went. Not only did he not call but he never came by. She hadn't seen or heard from him again until…the gas station. He seemed so happy and cheerful, walking over to her car—as if that night never happened.

Thinking about the breakup took her breath away and made her eyes sting. She steadied herself on the inside and responded to Izzy.

"What if I can't trust him?"

Izzy stopped mid slurp. "Then, I guess you have a decision to make. Either you're going to give this a chance wholeheartedly or you're going to run the other way." Izzy pointed at her. "But be careful which way you go, Alex. You really need to follow your heart."

Alex grimaced. Gerard said follow her gut, while Izzy was telling her to follow her heart. These seemed like two different ideas. Trying to do both would certainly cause her a lot of distress. Since Nathan sent her the flowers, she didn't even know what her gut wanted her to do. She only knew she didn't want to look like a fool.

Her heart, however, was another story. Sometimes it seemed that it had stopped reacting. Like maybe it only sat in her chest for decoration, while it allowed her head to take over all her decisions. It wasn't that she opposed letting her heart lead but she really didn't know where to begin. Her heart hadn't done much for her in a long time. It had become much easier to think her way through life—making practical decisions along the way. All things emotional and romantic took a back seat. How was she supposed to all of a sudden start thinking with her heart now?

She looked over at Izzy licking the ice cream off the back of her hand. The two women lived very different lives and, in some ways, Alex couldn't imagine being Izzy but she had to admit one thing: she admired her friend's resilience. Over the years, Izzy had become the poster child for heartbreak and romantic disenchantment but no matter how hard she'd get knocked down, she got right back up on the same horse all over again. Alex considered herself a strong woman but she didn't know if she had Izzy's type of strength.

"What do you propose my heart is telling me to do?" Alex asked.

"I don't know. Only you can answer that question. But the fact that we're having this conversation must mean something."

Izzy faced Alex. "You only talk about a man when he means something to you. You should give this thing with Nathan some more thought."

Alex took a deep breath to overcome the wave of anxiety that hit her at the thought of talking to Nathan again. She swallowed it down and gave Izzy a weak smile, while nudging her along.

"Why?"

"Let's say I have a good feeling about this." Izzy smiled wider.

"Better than you had about Phillip," Alex said.

"Ha! Way better than I had about Phillip." The women laughed and walked into Donovan's shoe store.

•••

After her girls' day out with Izzy, Alex headed home. Darkness set into the Southern sky. As she approached a grocery store, she remembered there were a few things she needed to pick up. She made a quick turn at the next light into the store parking lot. Once parked and inside the store, she reached into her purse and grabbed her brief list. She walked in the store and picked a shopping cart. Before she could get down an aisle, her cell phone rang. She shuffled through her purse for the phone and finally reached it at the beginning of the third ring.

"Hello?"

"Hey. Whatcha doin?" her mother asked.

"I'm in the store picking up a few things." Alex placed her purse in the basket and started to walk.

"At this time of night? What did you have to get?"

"Only a couple of items. I missed some things the last time I came."

"That's because you don't write a list. I've told you to sit down and create a list before you go to the store. Like talking to myself."

Alex rolled her eyes. As usual, it never took long for her mother to start nagging her about what she should have been doing.

"Anyway, Ma...I have a list now and I'm here to pick up a few things. Did you want something else?"

"Yes. I was planning to go to the movies this weekend. Do you want to go?" her mother asked.

"I guess. What were you planning to see?"

"I'm gonna see *The Arc* with that actress, Roxie."

"You usually don't go to see her movies," Alex said, surprised at her mother's selection.

"I heard it received good reviews. I hope they're not exaggerating because she's in the news right now."

"I don't know but that's fine. Let me finish grabbing the things I need."

Alex ended the call with her mother and continued to stroll down the aisle. She ended up on the condiments side. Alex saw the salt and stopped. Flashbacks of her last argument with Phillip ran through her mind. *Gosh, have I really waited three weeks to buy the salt?* Alex's brow furrowed. How could she expect herself to manage taking care of a child, when she couldn't even remember to buy a seasoning?

Alex reached over and picked up the salt. On top of the weight of her sadness, the twenty-six-ounce box felt heavy. Yet, she managed to hold it in her arms long enough to place it in the basket. After picking up a few more things that were on her list, she went to the register and paid for the merchandise, barely noticing the friendly cashier's greetings.

Once she reached her car, she threw the plastic bag holding her few items in her passenger's seat and dropped into the driver's seat. Alex cranked the car but stopped short of shifting into drive. A tear welled up and spilled over the rim of her eyes. She blotted it with the back of her hand only to have another tear fall over. This time, she reached into her arm rest and pulled out a napkin. For a minute, she buried her face in the napkin, allowing the tears to flow.

Something was happening to her. For the first time, she felt a pull toward change. She could not accept Phillip as the end of it all. She needed someone more supportive and he wasn't even a nice guy. She had to refocus and create some type of improvement in her life. She hated feeling sorry for herself.

When she dabbed the rest of the water from her face, her cell phone rang. She sighed and picked it up without looking at the caller ID.

"Hello," she mumbled.

"Alex? It's Nathan."

Alex sat up and cleared her throat. "Hello, Nathan. How are you?"

"I'm good. I'm glad I was able to reach you. Did you get the flowers I sent you?" Nathan asked. His voice harbored a mixture of panic, concern and relief. Between the busy work day and her chitchat with Izzy, she didn't think to call him back about the flowers. *Ugh, that's real polite, Alex.*

"Oh, yes. I did receive the flowers," she said.

"Good. Did you like them?"

"Yes, they were very lovely. I meant to call you back but—"

"It's okay. Listen." Nathan paused. "I completely goofed up our date last week but I'd really like to see you again."

Alex's heart raced with anxiety. The moment of truth had arrived. She thought about her urge to transform her relationships. She also considered Izzy's advice, trying to force those thoughts to overpower her own fears of getting played like a checkers game.

As if Nathan could read her mind, he spoke again. "I really think we should talk about some things."

Alex rubbed her forehead, wondering if she would regret this. "Okay. How does Saturday sound?"

CHAPTER 15

A lex reached into her office mailbox and pulled out a few envelopes. One was a big brown envelope from a company she didn't recognize. Curious about it, she opened it right then. While she read the contents of the envelope, Mr. Sims approached her.

"Morning, Alex."

She turned quickly. "Morning, Mr. Sims."

"How's everything?"

"Awesome. Another busy day."

He nodded. "That's true. How's it going with the fair?"

"I've generated a lot of interest with employers. Several are in the pipeline. We should be moving forward any day now."

"And how is Dan doing?"

That's a good question. Although she had vowed to get with Dan on their game plan, Alex hadn't quite done that yet. Dan hadn't reached out to her either. They hadn't even spoken since the meeting—where they both received the bad news that they'd be working together. She hadn't been avoiding the inevitable; she completely forgot. She had to handle this immediately.

"I think he's doing well," Alex said.

"You think? Have you all gotten together to work out details on how the fair is going to run?" Mr. Sims asked.

"Our schedules have not allowed us to meet officially but we will be hashing everything out right away.

He frowned. "Okay. Well, make sure that you to link up as soon as possible. I expect you both to be prepared to report on the progress at our next meeting."

"And we will be hundred percent ready. You have my word," Alex said.

"Good. I'll see you later, Alex." He smiled and walked away.

Alex stuffed her letter back into its large, brown envelope and made a beeline to the elevator. She pushed the button for the third floor and practically sprinted off the elevator when it opened there. She dashed through the sea of cubicles to look for Dan's desk, which turned out to be no easy task. After spinning around in circles for a couple of minutes, she stopped and turned to the young woman with the name "Bernice" on her cubicle.

"Do you know where Dan Reece's desk is?" Alex asked.

"When you turn right here, I believe it's the second one on the left," Bernice said.

"Thank you," Alex responded as she walked around the corner and looked to her left. There she found a cubicle with Dan's name on it. He, however, wasn't in it.

"Great." She glanced around, hoping to see him somewhere talking to a coworker. No such luck. She then stepped into his cubicle and grabbed a post-it and a pen and scribbled a note for him.

Come to my office as soon as possible. It's an emergency!

She signed her name on it and stuck it on his computer screen so that he wouldn't miss it. Alex rubbed her hands together. She felt a little better knowing that she'd taken action to get them on track.

Alex went back up stairs to her office, dumped her mail on her desk and waited for Dan to meet her. She didn't sit there doing nothing; she continued coming up with ideas for the fair, answering questions for her staff and analyzing reports but, in between all of that, she kept looking at the clock, wondering when Dan was coming. She hoped he planned to come. It would not look good on either of them if they weren't able to cooperate for the sake of the project. Alex was not about to lose her job because Dan had an ego problem.

She spotted the time on the clock again. Eleven thirty-two a.m. *I refuse to let him leave for lunch before seeing me. I'll call his desk and if he doesn't answer, I'll have him paged.* Right after Alex picked up the phone to dial his extension, she heard a knock at the door.

"Come in," Alex said.

Dan slowly opened the door as if he wanted to make sure he had permission to enter. "Did you leave a note for me?" he asked with uncertainty in his voice.

"Yes. Come in." She placed the phone back into its holder.

Dan stepped into her office and closed the door behind him. He took a few steps in and stood in the middle of the floor. Alex tooted her lips upward.

"Come on. Why are you creeping in here? My note may have been a little startling but nobody's gonna bite you." She laughed.

Dan smiled a little. "I know. I guess it's...well, you've never asked me to come to your office before." He looked around. "It's all right."

Alex nodded. "Thank you. Please, have a seat."

Dan obeyed. "So, um, what was the emergency?"

"I ran into Mr. Sims this morning and he wants us to be prepared to talk in detail about our progress. So, I wanted to meet with you and get a handle on what we're working on together, as well as separately."

He nodded. "Okay."

"In terms of the fair, what are you working on now?" Alex asked.

"I looked at a few venues for it and got some prices. I can get them for you if you'd like to see them."

"Actually, that's fine. We'll be holding it at the Rockford Center. I've already checked it out and they have the space we need for an event of this magnitude."

Dan sat back in his chair and crossed his arms. Alex could tell that he didn't like the fact that she'd already decided on a location without consulting him but that was too bad. She, unlike him, couldn't afford to wait around for the day of the job fair to arrive and then look for a venue.

"I thought you were working on employers," Dan said.

"I am."

He sighed. "If you have everything under control, then what do you need me for?" Dan sounded even more irritated as he spoke.

I don't. Mr. Sims thinks I need you. "There are still a lot of things that we need to nail down."

"Like what?"

"In order for the job fair to go off the way that we want, we need sponsors pronto. You know a lot of people because of the contacts you constantly have to make. I wanted to know if you could take on everything having to do with the sponsorships."

"Yeah, I do meet a lot of people." Dan sat up in his chair and pushed his chin out. "Okay. I'll do it."

"Great! Do you already have people in mind?" Alex turned to her notebook to write down Dan's responsibility.

"Yes."

"Really? Who?" Alex asked.

"You'll see." He smiled wide.

A knot formed in Alex's stomach. *You have to trust your team member.* She cleared her throat. "Okay. Well, call anyone you know that might be interested in investing in something as important as this."

"Oh, I'll work it out. I mean, we'll work it out."

She smiled. *Baby steps.* "Good. I'm confident that this will be a breeze for you."

"Thanks, Alex."

Dan stood up and bounced out the door. Alex smiled. She'd done the right thing—giving Dan a chance to show what he can do. Something told her he would not disappoint. However, she planned to find some potential sponsors and keep them in her back pocket, in case he did drop the baton. Leaning back in her chair, she decided to break for lunch.

CHAPTER 16

When they were making plans, Alex requested a relaxed evening out but Nathan insisted on making it an official "date." She knew one thing; she refused to get all dressed up like she had done before. Their last failed date made the second time he'd let her down. She had to command herself to think positive and believe there wouldn't be a third time. Just in case, Alex opted for a pair of blue, boot-cut jeans, a white, buttoned shirt with a black body shaper under it, a black, stone-studded belt and silver heels. She conveniently swept her hair into an up do.

Before she could check her thinly applied makeup, her doorbell rang. She raised her eyebrows. *Is he really early this time?* When she walked downstairs and peeped through her door hole, she saw that he had arrived early. Refusing to get too excited about this one instance of good behavior, Alex unlocked the door and opened it for him.

"Hey, Alex!" Nathan wore a lavender sweater with gray slacks. He stepped past the threshold and hugged Alex—firmly but gently. "Um. You look great. I'm so happy to see you again."

The smile on his face matched the look in his eyes. Warm and sincere. She wanted to fall into the soft place that his expression promised to her but Alex preferred to keep her guard up. She reached for her leather jacket. "Thanks. Are you ready to go?"

"Sure."

When they pulled out of her driveway, anxiety hit Alex like a Mack truck. She suddenly realized that she didn't know his plans for their "date." She turned to Nathan.

"So, where are we going?" Alex asked.

"To the Landing. I thought we might have dinner down there and go for a walk."

"Do you have reservations or something?"

Nathan turned to her and smiled wide. "Yes."

Alex frowned. "What are you smiling about?"

"I see you haven't changed much."

"I hope you have." The comment slid out before Alex had a chance to wheel it back in. The moment she said it, she wished she hadn't. Sure, she might be a little ticked that he'd stood her up a week ago. Even more bothered about him standing her up ten years ago, but if they had any hope of enjoying the evening, she would have to remain cordial.

Alex rushed in to fix her comment. "I mean, I'm sure you've changed a lot."

Nathan brushed off her comment, as if he hadn't thought twice about it. "How was work today?"

"Fine." Alex looked outside the window.

"How has the year been treating you so far?"

"Good."

Nathan nodded. "Is it better than last year?"

She sighed. "I don't know. It has its hiccups."

"Really? Like what?"

"My company is going through some changes. They want us to come up with ways to increase recruitment numbers. We have to make our own effort. Whoever they are not satisfied with, that person will be let go."

"What?! Whoa!" Nathan turned right at the green light. "Have you already started?"

"Yes."

"And?"

"It's coming along. I have to work with Dan." She rolled her eyes.

"Who is he?" Nathan asked.

"Let's just say he's not the sharpest pair of shears."

"Aww. Well, just because he's not the sharpest guy doesn't mean that the job fair won't be a success. Maybe you can offer to help him on areas you think might be difficult for him."

"If he listens," Alex said.

"He will. Anybody can see that you know what you're doing, even a dim shear."

She chuckled.

"Is there anything I can do to help?" he asked.

She shook her head. "Nope."

"Well, let me know if that changes."

After a couple more blocks, Nathan pulled into Rucker's Italian Cuisine and Grille. Nathan opened the door for Alex and they walked inside. The host led them to the back where they sat at a button, leather sofa that surrounded a half-circle table.

"What would you like for a beverage? We have an excellent red wine selection." The host motioned toward the bottles of wines to the table beside their couch.

"I'll have water for now," Alex said.

The host nodded and placed the menus in front of them. "And you, sir?"

"I'll try the red wine."

While the host poured the drinks, Alex found herself staring at the country style paintings and brick décor.

"Do you like it?" Nathan asked, following her gaze.

"Yes. It's nice."

"Good." He leaned forward and placed his hands on the table. "So, tell me what else has been going on in your life, besides fighting for your job?"

Alex glanced down at Nathan's large hands. His hands always fascinated her. They looked like they could toss a boat across the ocean. Yet, it amazed her how hands so big could handle her so gently. Afraid that he would notice her staring at them, she turned her attention to the menu and answered his question.

"Oh, you know. Work," Alex said.

"There's got to be more to your life than that."

She looked up at him. "What's going on in your life?"

"I asked you first." Nathan smiled.

She rolled her eyes and turned the page on the menu.

He chuckled. "I'm not trying to give you a hard time. I'm only trying to figure out why no one has snatched you up yet. I'm lucky but I'm not that lucky."

Why does he have to do this? Alex smirked. "Why hasn't anybody snatched you up?"

"You first," he insisted.

She didn't know what to say. She'd told herself that marriage had taken a backseat to her career. While her job did sometimes require longer hours, she didn't know if that was the full truth. Alex thought that if she'd met the right man she'd be married already. However, believing that her career caused her singlehood made her feel like she had some control over the situation as opposed to the powerlessness she'd felt lately. *If I really had control, would I have ended up with a jerk like Phillip?* Her chest tightened as she fought back feelings of self-pity. She couldn't allow Nathan to think her life had fallen apart since they had broken up years ago.

"Maybe I haven't been ready to be snatched up," she said.

Nathan nodded. "Are you ready now?"

Yes! Alex practically screamed in her head but knew better than to say that out loud. She nodded slightly. "Maybe. Your turn!"

He laughed.

"I wasn't gonna let you forget," Alex said.

He licked his lips. "I know you weren't." He leaned back in his chair. "I guess I haven't had the right person in my life."

"Are you sure it's not because you were playing all this time?"

The easy smile that had danced on Nathan's lips a few minutes ago faded from view. His eyes narrowed and the corners of his mouth pulled his face downward. "No, it's not that."

Alex sipped on her water, aware of the change in his mood. "Do you want to be snatched up?"

"Doesn't everybody?" he asked, taking a sip of his wine.

Alex and Nathan retained eye contact for a few seconds before the waiter returned to take their orders. Nathan's eyes were like transparent pools of water. They seemed to relay a sincere desire for love and happiness but Alex issued herself a warning. She'd been here before and had it all blow up in her face.

By the time their food arrived, they had lapsed into lighter conversation. They even managed to share a laugh or two. For a while, she forgot about her anger toward him, their missed date and the awful ending to their relationship from years ago. She focused on enjoying the evening.

When they finished their meals, they strolled through the center of the complex, passing a mime juggling, a group of people with matching family reunion shirts and a local band playing on a stage. By the time they reached more store fronts, the loudest noises had dissipated. The clocking sound of their shoes hitting the brick pathway became more prominent and isolated.

"Did you like dinner?" Nathan asked, breaking the sound of their footsteps.

"Yes, it was good. I should go there more often. How did you hear about them?"

"I have a friend who used to be a sous chef there. I used to go by and he would hook my ex and me up."

For some reason, the mention of his romantic past rattled her nerves but she pretended to not care. Instead, she nodded.

"What about you? When was your last relationship? For real," Nathan said, leaning her way.

Alex's discomfort started from the pit of her stomach and spread across her face, to which Nathan immediately noticed.

"I'm sorry. I didn't mean to pry. If you don't want to talk about it, that's fine."

"No, it's okay." It really wasn't. She preferred to put it behind her but, since he felt like sharing, she feared appearing standoffish, if she didn't do the same. Besides, the evening had been going so well. Shutting down now would ruin the positive vibe.

"My last relationship ended a few weeks ago," Alex said.

"Oh, I'm sorry. I didn't realize it had been so soon. What went wrong?"

Alex shrugged. She really wanted to forget about Phillip. He reminded her that she had a long way to go before she could reach her dream of a husband and kids. A stable homelife. She never felt more like a loser than she did right then. Still, Alex came up with the most general answer she could. "We wanted different things."

"Like what?"

"I wanted to succeed in life. He wanted me to be Mary Poppins," Alex said, looking up at him.

Nathan's eyebrows nearly reached his hairline. "Was it that you didn't want a family or…" he looked down at the sidewalk, "was he the wrong guy?"

"He was the wrong guy," Alex whispered.

Nathan nodded in apparent approval of her answer. "I know what you mean. When I was with Clarissa, I felt like she wasn't the right person for me but I hung in there and tried to make it work. Looking back, I probably should have let it go long before I did but then, I wouldn't have my little man." He smiled. "I love him, even if his mother is nutty."

"Yeah," Alex said. They stopped in front of a railing and faced the water. Red, white and blue lit up the Hudson Bridge and the water below it. As Alex gazed out at the scenery, Nathan turned to face her, as he took a deep breath and let his words rip.

"Alex, I'm sorry for the way things ended with us," he blurted out.

She hoped she appeared calm on the outside because she shook on the inside with the sound of each word. She didn't know what to say or if she should say anything. When she opened her mouth, her throat threatened to close on her. Unaware of her internal struggle, Nathan kept talking.

"I…I know what I did was wrong but I was young and still out there, you know?" He looked at Alex only partially waiting for an answer. "I knew that, um, you were special and that I really cared about you but I didn't know how to love you. I was still going through things."

Alex continued to stare off into the water, motionless. Nathan moved closer to her. "I always wished I could have another chance. When I saw you at the gas station, it was like God was whispering to me or something." He laughed softly. "You're still one of the most beautiful people I've ever met. If I had another chance, I would treat you better."

Alex shut her eyes and covered her ears.

Nathan frowned. "What?"

Alex took a deep breath. "I'm confused."

"Why?"

Her chest heaved up and down, struggling to contain her volcanic emotions. "Where is this coming from all of a sudden?"

"It's not all of a sudden. I've always felt this way. I want you to forgive me for what I did. I need you to forgive me, Alex."

Alex rolled her eyes before she had a chance to stop herself.

"What's that about?" Nathan asked.

"That's about you, waiting ten years, until you happened to run into me at a gas station to let me know how you feel. You couldn't have told me this when you called me that night?"

"What night?"

"The night that you were supposed to come by and talk to me." Alex raised her voice.

Nathan's eyes scanned the ground, searching for the answer. He turned back to her. "You were angry with me. You told me it was over."

"Right. And then I allowed you to talk me into meeting with you to discuss our relationship. But you never came. You never called. You never came. You disappeared."

Nathan's mouth dropped. He closed it and opened it a couple of times before uttering anything. His words were soft. "I... I thought you didn't want to have anything to do with me. I thought that if I showed up, you would only tell me to leave. I figured 'what's the point?'"

Alex trembled, inside and out. She had hoped their conversation would go a lot smoother. Then again, she'd never really imagined this conversation all the way through. She took in a chest full of air. Then, she released it in jagged breaths. She could feel herself losing the little control she had left.

"The point is you left me hanging." She closed her eyes. "Even though I'd called it off, I felt...unwanted when you didn't even call me to tell me that you weren't coming," Her voice broke. "And I haven't been able to understand how you could be so up-beat, like nothing ever happened."

With her last words, a hot tear slid down her face.

"Aww." Nathan sighed. "Alex, I didn't know."

He reached over, gave her a hug and led her to a bench nearby. Nathan wiped her tears and pushed a strand of hair away from her face. "I never meant to make you feel that way. I kinda went on with life, thinking that you'd never get over what I did. I should have come by. It was selfish to leave you hanging that way."

Alex covered her face in disbelief and embarrassment. She felt as naked as a jay bird. Since so much time had passed, she'd thought she had gotten over this—at least to the point where she could talk about it without getting emotional—but obviously she hadn't.

A sob escaped her throat. Nathan wrapped his right arm around her and squeezed her. After he held her for a few more minutes, Alex finally lifted her head and sniffed. Nathan stared into her eyes.

"Are you okay?" he asked.

She nodded. "Yes, I'm fine."

"I'd like you to accept my apology. I'd like for us to try to work through this. Can we do that?"

Alex looked up at Nathan's clear and kind eyes. She saw patience and compassion. For the first time in several years, she felt free. Not because Nathan said the right things. The toxic emotions that were rumbling beneath the surface for so long had spilled over and left her body. She could now see the opportunity to change and it was time to take it.

"Yes." Alex nodded.

Nathan smiled and held onto her, as they sat in silence.

CHAPTER 17

E ven though Alex didn't feel like it, she made herself go to the office an hour earlier than usual. While it required extra effort to wake up earlier to get there, she appreciated being one of the few people in the office and she reveled in the quiet. It gave her time to think. Today was the day of the big meeting. Mr. Sims expected her and Dan to report their progress to him and they had to be on point. Luckily for Alex, she'd been keeping pretty steady notes on her progress with the employers and the call center but there was one problem lingering: confirmed employers for the job fair. She'd made contact with at least a dozen companies but, so far, no one had signed on the dotted line. If she could get one of them to participate, it would be much easier to get the other companies on board.

As she sat at her desk occasionally sipping her hot tea, she tried to focus on her outline for the meeting but that proved difficult as she went in and out of her notes. Her date with Nathan began to occupy her thoughts. Since their cathartic conversation, she'd been floating. They finally got to say things that needed to be said and they were going to try and rebuild their relationship—something she never thought would happen.

Thinking about their renewed relationship gave her a warm feeling inside. *I guess Izzy was right. I did need to follow my heart.* She only hoped that things turned out better this time. Alex closed her eyes and willed her mind to stay in the moment instead of trying to figure out the future. When her cell phone rang, it startled her. She grabbed the phone and answered.

"Hey, Alex," Nathan said.

She smiled. "Hi. I was just thinking about you."

"Oh. That must be why my ears were burning." He chuckled.

"I think that's supposed to happen when I'm talking about you." She laughed.

He sucked his teeth. "Same thing."

She laughed again. "No, it's not."

"All right, all right. I didn't want to hold you up. I wanted to catch you before you got to work and wish you a good work day. Try not to stress out."

"That's really sweet. Although I will be stressing, I appreciate it."

"You shouldn't. Everything's gonna work out."

"Yeah, we'll see after this staff meeting today. I don't know what Dan is doing. I hope he has it together because, depending on how we present, my boss is either going to praise us or give us the boot," Alex said, browsing through her meeting outline.

"I'm sure it's not going to come down to that. You'll be fine."

Before Alex could respond her office phone rang. "Oh. Nathan, I have to go. I'll talk to you later."

It was still a little early for Alex to be there. She couldn't imagine who would be calling her at this time of morning. She and Nathan said their goodbyes and she quickly picked up her phone.

"Hello. This is Alex."

"Hello, Ms. Carter. This is Edward Allen from PharmScope. How are you?"

She sat up in her chair. "Mr. Allen. It's a pleasure to hear from you. I am very well. What can I do for you?"

"I wasn't sure if you were in yet but I thought I'd give you a ring to update you on our decision."

Alex closed her eyes and said a silent prayer. "Oh, okay."

"I spoke with my staff about your proposal during our last meeting and they gave me their feedback. With all things considered, everyone here agrees it would be beneficial to participate in your fair."

She wanted to jump out of her chair and do a cartwheel but she managed to control her jumps and yelps long enough to respond to Mr. Allen. "That's wonderful. We look forward to helping you find as many candidates as possible."

"We'll settle for fifty."

Alex and Mr. Allen chuckled. "No problem. That I can do."

"Okay, then. We look forward to working with you."

"Same here."

Once they hung up, Alex allowed her excitement full expression. "Yesss!"

She turned back to her outline and added PharmScope as the first employer. Her prayers had been answered. As soon as the meeting was over, she would be on the phone with all of the employers, gently pushing them to sign on before all the spaces are taken. She smiled while putting the finishing touches on the outline. She hit print and walked over to her printer. After four copies, the machine stopped and displayed an error message that she had run out of paper. She looked for more paper in her drawers. When she didn't find any, she grabbed one of her outlines off the printer and went to the copy room to finish her copies.

Alex had walked halfway down the hall when she found herself passing Mr. Sims.

"Morning, Mr. Sims," she greeted him.

"Morning, Alex. Just the person I wanted to talk to. Are you and Dan prepared for the meeting today?"

"Absolutely. Looking forward to it. I'm actually printing off some copies of my presentation now."

"Good. I would like for you two to meet me in my office in thirty minutes."

"Okay. Is there anything wrong?"

"Not at all. I'd like to get a feel for where you guys are with it now."

Oh snap. "Sure. Does Dan already know about the meeting or should I let him know?"

"No. You can call him and have him meet us in my office."

"Will do. See you in thirty minutes."

Alex dashed to the copy room, made her copies and sped back to her office. She flopped down in her chair and dialed Dan's extension. He answered after two rings.

"Dan. I'm so glad you're there. Mr. Sims wants us to meet him in his office in twenty-four minutes. He wants a preview of our update on the job fair," Alex said, almost breathless.

"Oh. Why?" Dan asked.

"I don't know and I wasn't going to ask. Are you ready?"

"Yes, of course. I was born ready."

Alex rolled her eyes. *You'd better be.* "Okay. I'll see you there."

Less than half an hour later, they were walking into Mr. Sims' executive office.

"Come in," Mr. Sims motioned with a smile.

Dan and Alex followed his directions. They sat across from his desk and waited.

"So," Mr. Sims folded his hands on top of his desk. "I called this meeting with you two specifically because I wanted to gauge where you are with the job fair. See what type of response you're getting. You know, figure out if you needed any additional support."

Alex nodded. "I appreciate that, sir."

"As do I. Yesterday, I was telling someone how we are given so many opportunities to grow and excel at this company. The agency really does support its employees in a big way," Dan said.

Alex had to fight the urge to roll her eyes. They weren't there to brown nose; they were there to convince Mr. Sims that they'd made progress.

"Thank you, Dan. Now, tell me about the employers. Have any of them expressed an interest?"

Alex smiled. "Yes, PharmScope said that they look forward to participating."

"Okay. Any others?" Mr. Sims said.

"Several other companies are on the verge of saying yes. I will be following up with them today. I should have at least three to four more on board by the end of next week," Alex said.

"And what part is the call center going to play in this?"

"They will use the database to identify qualified candidates. I will personally review their choices with them before they make the call."

"All right. Make sure you stay on that." Mr. Sims turned his attention to Dan. "How are the sponsors coming along?"

"Good," Dan said.

"Have you gotten any yet?" Mr. Sims asked.

"Not yet."

Alex wanted to crawl into a ball. How could Dan come into this meeting knowing that he hadn't made an ounce of progress? What was he waiting on? She took a deep breath and tried hard to hold her tongue.

"Who are your prospects?"

"Drink Soft, Mobile Roller, to name a couple."

No wonder he hasn't landed any sponsors. Those companies were too big. It would take months to get them to pony up any cash. They need more local and regional companies to cut down on the time needed to get a decision. *Thank goodness. I know a few people.*

Mr. Sims frowned. "Those companies can take months to make a decision. Do you have a backup plan?"

"I don't think I'll need to. Getting those bigger companies will decrease the number of sponsors we need," Dan said.

Alex faced Dan. "Yes, but we will find ourselves with no money for the venue, food for the employers or other expenses." She couldn't take it anymore. She had to say or do something to keep them from looking like complete dodo birds.

Dan squinted at her.

She turned back to Mr. Sims. "When I first started planning the fair, I contacted a couple of local chain restaurants to get a feel for how things would go. They were quite receptive. I can reconnect with them again and let them know that the opportunity is available," Alex suggested.

Mr. Sims rubbed his chin and stared at her. "Okay. If they're willing, we should hop on it swiftly."

Alex nodded and smiled.

"Well…" Mr. Sims checked his watch. "That's about all I have. I have a phone conference before the meeting. Is there anything you two want to add about the fair?"

Dan and Alex shook their heads.

Mr. Sims stood up. "It looks like you all are off to a good start. Continue to work together and nail down as many details as you can as soon as you can."

"We will." Alex nodded.

On that note, Dan and Alex stood and exited Mr. Sims' office. When their boss closed his door, Alex dropped her shoulders in relief. "Whew! That was close. Glad we pulled it out."

"We? The next time you want to show off in front of our boss, why don't you let me know. You don't need me around for that."

Dan stomped down the hall. Alex watched him in confusion.

CHAPTER 18

F ive o' clock couldn't come fast enough. Alex kept her promise to Mr. Sims. She called all the companies she had spoken to prior to PharmScope agreeing to participate. She was right; companies were more eager to get involved once they knew another major employer would be there.

Alex finally felt like the job fair was moving forward but she didn't like the way she and Dan were working together. After their issue in Mr. Sims' office, he'd avoided her all day. She couldn't understand the problem. Dan dropped the ball and she picked it up. Isn't that what team members are supposed to do? That's what she thought. She truly didn't understand his anger. Alex was willing to give him the rest of the day to cool off but tomorrow, they would have to get back on one accord because she refused to fail.

She fell in her car seat, closed the door and laid her head back on the headrest. Her eyes were burning. Probably from waking up earlier than usual today. Alex slowly opened her eyes and cranked up her car. She drove down the street with her mind fixed on home. When her phone rang, she snapped out of her zombie state to see Nathan's number on the phone. She managed a weak smile. Half of her felt excited to see his name; the other half wanted to go home and hit the bed.

"Hey. How did it go today?" Nathan asked.

"Good and bad."

"Really? How?"

"I've had two new companies to sign on for the fair but Dan isn't speaking to me."

"What?"

"Never mind. It's not important. How was your day?" Alex asked.

"Pretty good. I had the day off. What do you mean, it's not important?"

"I don't want to bore you with the long story over the phone."

"Then, why don't you come over for dinner and tell me about it?" he asked.

Alex yawned. "Excuse me. I don't know, Nathan. I kind of want to go home and fall out right now."

"You need to eat before you go to bed."

"I should be fine if I'm not hungry."

"Nope. You'll wake up in the middle of the night wanting to eat."

"Um." Alex liked the idea of seeing him again but the closer she got to home the more she could hear her bed calling her.

"At least come by and get a plate."

"Then you'll complain about me eating and running." Alex chuckled.

"I'll let it slide this time."

"Fine. I'll come over for dinner."

Nathan gave her directions to his house and she followed them. She pulled up to his red brick home nestled in a nice little cul de sac.

Alex walked up to the door and rang the doorbell. Nathan answered with a big smile.

"You made it." He leaned over and gave her a big hug. "Come in." She stepped in and walked down a couple of steps into the living room. It was complete with a large rug over a wooden floor and antique-like furniture. The setting fit Nathan's personality—warm and homey.

"Very nice. Did you decorate it?" she asked.

"Yes."

Alex raised her eyebrows. Nathan laughed to himself. "Don't tell me you don't think a man can decorate his own house?"

"Now, now. I didn't say that. I don't remember you being Martha Stewart. That's all."

They both laughed. He walked over to her and planted a kiss on her lips. "I'm almost finished cooking. Do you want something to drink?"

"Yes. I need a little help waking up. Do you have tea?"

He sucked his teeth. "Do I have tea? Of course, I do."

He took her hand and led her toward the dining room. While she sat down, he fetched a glass and tea for her.

"So, you wanna tell me why you're beefing with your coworker?" Nathan asked.

"Because he's incompetent."

"Ouch."

"Seriously, he showed up at our meeting with no results. He hadn't done anything."

"Did he try?" Nathan walked out of the kitchen with her tea. He handed it to her and then went back to the kitchen to check on his sauce.

"Sort of. He's trying to get sponsorships from big companies but as my boss and I both pointed out, we don't have time to wait for their money. He doesn't see it that way so we don't have any sponsors yet."

"I don't get why he is mad at you."

"Because he thinks I showed him up at the meeting. All I did was say that I would contact some restaurant owners I'd already talked to."

"Um."

"What?" Alex asked.

Nathan hesitated as he stirred his sauce. "Well, you could have waited until after the meeting and then recommended that he call the people you mentioned, especially since it was originally his responsibility."

"Why? I stepped in because he's not doing his job."

"That's my point. You stepped in. Men have fragile egos. We don't want to look like chumps in front of women or our boss. He came up looking crazy in front of both."

She rolled her eyes. *Men.* She didn't know if she'd ever understand them. Dan liked to strut around the office like a peacock but when it came down to business, he seemed to be all thumbs. How was that her fault?

Alex played with the cloth placemat at the dining room table. "So, what am I supposed to do about it?"

"Who has the higher authority in your company?" Nathan asked.

"Me."

"Then you're going to have to take the leadership in this situation."

"I already am. I'm doing pretty much everything."

"You know as well as I know that leadership isn't about doing everything. It's also about delegating. You do that all the time anyway. Do that with him to make him do a better job." He smiled. "Go ahead. Give him that womanly touch."

Alex frowned. "Ugh. Whatever. I don't have time for that."

Nathan doubled over laughing.

Alex shook her head and stood up. "You are so silly." She walked over to his stove, looking over the pot. "Are you done yet?"

He raised an eyebrow. "Oh, we're ready to eat now. A while ago, you wanted to go to nap town. Now you're ready to chow down."

She leaned over and muffled her laugh on his shoulder. "I'm awake now."

"Um hmm. Here." Nathan reached for a wooden spoon and dipped the end of it into the sauce. "Try this and tell me if you think it's done."

Alex blew on the spoon a few times, then, wrapped her lips around it. She tasted the mushrooms and little chucks of meat in the sauce. It was pretty good.

"I think it's ready," she said.

It didn't take long for Alex to begin devouring the spaghetti and meatballs, especially after she added shredded cheese over it. She was happy she decided to come there instead of going home and jumping in her bed. As they sat next to each other at the table, it warmed her heart to see him again. She smiled, while she sucked up a single strand of spaghetti.

"What are you smiling about?" Nathan asked.

"I was wondering when you started cooking," Alex said, refusing to acknowledge her bliss.

"When I had a son. He can't eat McDonald's all the time."

"I know that's right. *We* can't eat that all the time."

"Nope."

"How did you learn?"

"Why? You want me to teach you?" He smiled.

Alex picked up her fork and held it like she intended to stab him.

He laughed. "I picked up a few recipes from my mama, the Internet or the bookstore. That's all."

"Like that, huh?" Alex asked, staring at him and taking another bite.

"Yeah. I'm not studying recipes on my lunch break or anything."

Alex chuckled and covered her mouth.

"I started out making things for him but it evolved. If I think of something I might want to make, I find out how to make it," Nathan said.

"That's cool. Now I know who to call when I need to cook something."

He sucked his teeth. "Man, I don't know everything."

"Sure," Alex mocked.

Nathan's home phone rang. He stood up. "See. That's why you can't tell people nothing."

Alex laughed.

He picked up his phone and answered.

"Hello...Hey, Man. What's up?"

He looked over at Alex. "Um...Nah, I have company...Yeah, yeah. Call me later though... All right. Bet."

Later. Was Nathan planning to go somewhere? It wasn't like she intended to stay the whole night but it was a weekday. She wouldn't expect him to be out, if he had to go to work the next day. Where were they going this particular day?

Nathan hung up and moved back to his plate at the table. "Sorry about that."

Alex nodded. "Friends wanting to go out?"

"Huh? Oh, yeah."

"How long have you guys been friends?" Alex sipped water now.

"Well, I've know A.J. about nine or ten months."

She nodded. "Is he attached or married?"

Nathan shook his head. "He told me he had a quickie marriage one time. The thing was over in thirty days." He snickered and bit into a piece of bread.

"Wow," Alex said.

"I'm not surprised," Nathan said in between chews.

Alex raised her eyebrows. "Why not?"

"Well, how do I say this?" Nathan asked, looking up at the ceiling. "A.J. isn't exactly the type of guy that a woman can settle down with. He's my boy but he's got a lot of play in him."

Alex nodded. "Do you still have a lot of play in you?"

Nathan stared into her eyes. "No."

"Oh. Well, how are you able to hang with someone who's not focused on settling down if you might be ready to settle down?" Alex rested her chin on her palm, waiting for his answer.

"Well, don't you have friends whose lives are different from yours?"

Alex nodded and shrugged.

"I don't like to judge people. However they live is fine with me. I know what I want." Nathan focused his attention back on his plate.

"And what do you want?" Alex wasn't intent on aggravating Nathan. She wanted to know where he stood. He acted like he'd changed—grown up—from the days that he ran around with his friends doing whatever but she wanted to make sure. She was in no mood for surprises with him.

"I want what any regular man wants: a rewarding career and a family."

"How many children do you want?"

Nathan threw his head back and laughed. "What is this? An inquisition?"

Alex smiled. "Well, how am I gonna know if I don't ask you?"

He held up his hand. "Fair enough, fair enough. I want three kids."

"Any gender preference."

"Two boys and a girl. Hey. Didn't I mention this to you before?" Nathan squinted his eyes and pointed at Alex.

"Just checking. You have a good memory."

He shook his head and finished off his plate. Alex had finished her plate. She sat at the table studying him. At this point, she had to see the situation through; she wanted to try their relationship out again and figure out where they were headed but her mind insisted on staying sharp to any changes. *I sure hope he's sincere.*

CHAPTER 19

Alex stood in front of the snack machine, pondering which snack to buy. She shouldn't have been buying anything but she had a light breakfast and her stomach wouldn't stop reminding her of that fact. She bent down midway to get a better look at the selection. Alex heard footsteps. She turned around to find Mr. Sims approaching her. She sent him a readymade smile.

"Hello. How is everything, Mr. Sims?" she asked.

"Morning, Alex. Everything is good. How are you?" he asked.

"Excellent."

"I was talking to Dan about the job fair yesterday and he didn't seem as enthusiastic as you are. Is there a reason?"

I'm getting really tired of Dan. She couldn't seem to get away from him. "I think he's having some problems with the tasks."

"Oh. How are you all working through it?" He crossed his arms.

Looking at his face, Alex could tell Mr. Sims had a pretty good idea that she and Dan weren't getting along all that well. Whatever she said next, she had to inject a certain level of truth into it so she didn't seem like she was playing him for a fool. "We are still having some difficulties but we're trying to figure out the best way to work together."

"Well, if I may make suggestion," Mr. Sims said.

"Of course, sir. Any help you give would be appreciated."

"Try to be on each other's side. We have noted several times how important it is for your ideas to benefit our numbers but you all do have to work together. In a chain, wherever the weakest link is, that's what needs to be fixed. Your discord could affect your fair. I'd sure hate to see that happen."

"It won't happen, sir. I can assure it."

He shrugged. "Maybe it won't. Fix your team and make sure it doesn't."

Great. First, Nathan. Now, Mr. Sims. It seemed like everyone was telling her to accommodate Dan, which irked her inside. She'd worked her butt off to get where she was. Why did she have to baby him? Why didn't he have to figure things out like everybody else? At the risk of thinking like a little kid, she really did think it was unfair.

"Yes, Mr. Sims."

Her boss walked away. She grabbed a small bag of chips and went back to her office, trying to think of how she would approach Dan. She couldn't stand the idea of kissing his butt. However, Alex did need to work with him. Knowing that Mr. Sims was watching them so closely, made it even more imperative that she make amends.

She devoured her chips, wiped her hands and grabbed her tablet off her desk. She took a trip to Dan's floor. When she reached his desk, he was sitting in his chair conversing with a coworker. The coworker spotted her approaching and stopped talking. Dan followed his gaze. Alex saw Dan's whole demeanor change. The lighthearted, carefree expression he had while talking had disappeared. It had been replaced with a steep frown. As if his coworker had been made aware of Dan and Alex's contention, he lowered his head and walked the other way.

Dan turned toward his computer.

Okay. I know you see me coming so don't even act like you don't.

"Hello, Dan. How are you?" Alex said once she'd reached his desk.

He glanced over his shoulder. "Fine. How are you?"

"I'm good." She paused. *Here goes nothing.* "May I talk to you for a minute?"

He cleared his throat. "I'm kind of busy. Can it wait?"

Alex leaned over his desk. "No."

Dan stared up at her and sighed. "Okay."

"Why don't we go somewhere else?"

He stood up and motioned for her to lead the way. Alex led him to the break room on his floor. No one was there to listen in on their conversation. She pulled out a chair at the table and sat down. Dan followed suit.

She placed her tablet on the table and crossed her hands over it. "First, allow me to apologize if I did not present a united front with you when we met with Mr. Sims. I was simply concerned with making a good impression on him so that we would look like we knew what we were doing. I didn't mean to make it look like you didn't know what you were doing."

"But you did," Dan said, leaning in.

Alex took a deep breath to steady her mind and contain her initial reaction. "I understand that. The main thing is we have to work together and I would like for us to make a concerted effort to do so because our tails are on the line."

"I can't afford to get fired. Alimony is already messing with my pockets."

She didn't know what to say to that. Afraid to pry, she let the comment slide with a generic comment. "Yeah, I hear those can be challenging."

Dan snorted. "You don't know the half of it. I don't think we were married long enough for me to pay her spousal support but that didn't stop her from getting it. And...ooh...child support." He shook his finger. "Don't get me started on child support."

He hung his head. For the first time, Alex could see the stress and strain wearing on his face as opposed to the haughty smirk he often wore. She had mixed emotions about his admission. She was intrigued that he had a family unit. Although it had fallen apart, he still possessed more than she did. Instead of pressing about the job fair, Alex wanted to ask him questions about his family, balancing home and his child, likes and dislikes of parenthood but, even in her wish for information, it wasn't the right time to ask him these things. So, Alex nodded, again stumped on how to respond to his rant.

"Sure, I took care of her but she's perfectly capable of taking care of herself. She's lazy, is all." Dan stared off at the wall, almost like he could see his ex-wife in the off-white paint.

What did I step into? Alex thought quickly of a way to get him back to the task at hand. "Right. Well, this is exactly why we must work harder at making sure this fair goes off without a hitch," she said.

Dan thought about it. "You know what? You're right." He waved his hand. "I probably overreacted a little after the meeting. I hope you accept my apology as well." He extended his hand to her for a shake.

Her mouth dropped. *An apology? Now this I did not expect.* She recovered and extended her hand as well. "Apology accepted."

He smiled. "Great!"

Alex returned his smile.

"Now I brought down a list of the things that need to be done. I've checked things I'm taking care of, like the employers and supervising the call centers efforts to find candidates. Which of these other things are you willing to do?"

Dan stared at the list. "I'm definitely going to keep at the sponsorships."

"Okay. I will give you the names and numbers of the people I met at the beginning so that you can go over the details with them." She handed him a sheet of paper with local restaurant owners' contact information.

He lit up. "Thank you."

They sat together for the next fifteen minutes and divvied up their responsibilities for the next few weeks. When they finished, not only did Dan look happier but Alex felt better about the situation. She was proud that she'd figured out a way to relate to him about the fair. Even though they were still polar opposites, she could see them creating the best job fair ever.

CHAPTER 20

"All right, Alex. It's your turn," Nathan said.

Alex agreed to go bowling for fun and to spend time with Nathan. She had very little interest in the activity because she had very little skill in it. Still, she figured being with him would be worth the embarrassment of throwing gutter balls. That wasn't quite the case.

She walked up to the line of balls and grabbed a heavy green bowling ball. When she stepped to the edge of the lane, Nathan gave her a kiss on the forehead. She shifted her attention to the polished wooden floors in front of her and held the ball to her chest. She took a deep breath, then, let the ball go. The ball wobbled down the lane. It seemed to take forever getting to its destination. At times, Alex was afraid that it would stop in the middle of the lane, which would be extremely embarrassing. She was no pro bowler but she still didn't want to look too bad in front of Nathan. After what seemed an eternity, the ball reached the end, knocking out three pins in its wake.

Nathan clapped and hollered. Alex turned around, where Nathan stood. She scowled. "What are you clapping about?" she asked.

"You did good." Nathan blinked and smiled.

She rolled her eyes. "Yeah, right."

"Really! C'mon. We all have to start somewhere. Right?" Alex understood his desire to encourage her but it was only annoying her, especially considering that he had already skunked her on their last game.

"Your cheery attitude is starting to get on my nerves," Alex said.

Nathan cracked up laughing. "What? I'm proud of you."

"Aren't you supposed to let me win these things? Isn't that the unwritten rule? Thou shall let your date win games like bowling and putt-putt golf," Alex said.

"If I did that, you would never learn how to play. What are you gonna do if your company goes bowling one day? You could end up making your team lose and your coworkers would be angry with you."

"I'd tell them to get over it."

Nathan shook his head and grabbed a ball. He brought it up to his chin before swinging it backwards and rolling it forward. Alex watched his ball glide down the center of the row, as if it had been predetermined. It wiped out all the pins.

"Yess!" He shouted.

"This is sickening," Alex said.

He leaped over to her and hugged her while smothering her with kisses. She giggled under his outpouring of playful affection. Nathan sat down beside her and threw his arms on the back of the seats.

"What is work like these days?" Alex asked as she leaned back against the seat.

"It's cool. More of the same. Customers with attitude. Mad at the world about nothing," Nathan said.

"I know the feeling."

"C'mon. You deal with executive people at your job."

"That doesn't mean they can't be nasty, especially when they're caught in the wrong. Fingers start pointing so fast it'll make your head swim," Alex said.

"Yeah. This week, I had this lady come in and she was so angry because the service tech told her she needed new brake pads and routers. She wanted to know why she couldn't get the pads and nothing else. I had to explain to her that she had waited too long to buy new ones. Therefore, she needed the routers, too. No matter how many times, how many different ways I tried to explain it to her she continued to say she didn't understand."

"I hate it when people do that. They want to blame you for something they neglected to do," Alex said. "How did you end up resolving it?"

"I finally ended up giving her the pads free on the condition that she paid for the routers."

Alex frowned. "Why? It was her fault."

Nathan shrugged. "Sometimes it's easier to give the person what they want than to keep going around in circles."

"Is that what customer service is about?"

"Sometimes."

Alex shook her head. "It's like handling children."

"You want children at some point?" Nathan asked.

She hesitated. Her immediate reaction was to agree quickly but she didn't want to sound too eager. Alex had kept her inner thoughts about having children to herself. She didn't want to scare him off with her enthusiasm. "Of course."

"Then, see it as practice." He smiled.

"I'd prefer to have the real thing," Alex said.

She suddenly thought about her longing for a family. She looked over at Nathan and imagined him as the father of her children, a thought she found hard to brush aside. Alex figured he'd be as warm, caring and thoughtful as he was with her. He had a knack for putting her at ease that would no doubt prove helpful in calming a screaming child. She wondered if it was too soon to tell whether they would even reach that point. They hadn't been back together for long. Then again, things had been going well. They were getting along. She smiled while thinking about the possibility that Nathan could father her children some day.

"When do you want to have kids?" Nathan asked.

"When I've found a husband."

He nodded. "Traditional. That's good."

"What else would I be?"

Nathan shrugged. "You could be traditional or modern. It doesn't matter to me."

"Are you traditional?" Alex asked.

He hesitated. "In some ways, yes. In other ways, no. Although I didn't marry my son's mother, I'm trying to teach him traditional values."

"Hmm. I think many people are." Alex turned to face him. "That reminds me of this actress who recently conceived her child through artificial insemination. There's this big to do about it, you know? She went about it unconventionally but, to me, the thing she wanted—a baby or family—was quite traditional."

"Umm. She must have been pretty determined. I don't know if I would take it that far."

"No? Well, she said her relationships didn't work out. So she felt like she had to go it alone," Alex added.

He shook his head. "She may have felt that way but everybody has a bad relationship from time to time. I'm sure she had more options. Nobody has to have a child all on their own like that."

She crossed her arms. *Another one.* Nobody saw the reasoning behind Roxie's choice. The actress simply felt the need to start thinking strategically before time ran out, which in Roxie's case meant considering all her options.

"What makes that any different than a person who becomes a single parent the natural way?"

"I don't know too many people who are single parents on purpose. It kinda happens that way through various unfortunate circumstances."

Unfortunate circumstances. Right then, she couldn't think of anything more unfortunate then living out her life alone simply due to bad relationships. Everyone deserved happiness and many times that happiness came through rewarding relationships. Alex wanted to have a full life with people in it. Though she hated comparing her life to that of a celebrity, it comforted her to know that someone else had taken responsibility for creating their own personal happiness. It helped her feel that there were a variety of choices and roads to contentment for her.

But Alex would have been ecstatic if she didn't have to look any further for her happiness. Her eyes penetrated Nathan, searching for some glimpse of their future together. "Well, let's hope we don't have any more unfortunate circumstances."

CHAPTER 21

A lex twirled the phone cord around her index finger while her call center lead searched his report for information. They had a little less than two weeks to get everything together for the job fair. The good news was that they'd signed on seven companies. The bad news was that Alex had some concerns about the call center reps and their method of choosing potential candidates. Although she had given them basic requirements, their recruitment numbers weren't high enough for her. There had to be over twenty thousand people registered with Priority One Recruitment Agency. Why were they only pulling two hundred fifty-eight job seekers?

"Brian, this is what I want you to do. From now until I tell you guys to stop, I want you to send me a compiled list of the candidates they are pulling at the end of every day. I need a daily Excel spreadsheet of the job seekers' names, phone numbers, type of experience, and rather they have a misdemeanor or felony," Alex instructed.

"Okay. Since the current number isn't what you're looking for, do you want them to hit a certain number by the end of the day?" Brian asked.

"If you would like to set a number for them, that is fine. I'll say we definitely need a higher target. Time is winding down. The fair date is right around the corner. They will have more people on their lists or the whole call center will have to work overtime because this fair must succeed," Alex said.

"I understand. I think they are getting caught up on the criminal background. Some are shying away from people who have charges. Do any of the companies have leniency on that issue?"

Alex saw this as sticky subject. She preferred they have no criminal background because some of the companies they were working with could be a little funny about it. She also understood that no one was perfect and some people—when given the chance—could shine, regardless of their rough past.

"There are a couple that may be a little more open than others. It's the type of thing that has to be taken on a case by case basis. Have them fill their list with people they believe are qualified. Make sure they note any problems with their background. After you send me the first report today, I will come over and meet with you all tomorrow at..." Alex stopped talking to browse through her calendar. "Ten-thirty. This way we can navigate who's a good pick and who's not together. Okay?"

"All right. Sounds good. I'll let them know. Thanks."

Alex dropped her phone back into its receiver and exhaled. She needed to go through their candidates and make sure they were qualified. She'd made some pretty high promises to PharmScope, as well as the other companies that were now on board. The candidates had to be well screened and ready to work. No excuses.

She clicked on her computer software and attempted to generate a report based on job seekers with ten years sales experience. Maybe she would save the report and compare it to the names the call center reps were submitting as a way to double check their efforts. While she scrutinized one job seeker's credentials, she heard a rapid knock on her office door.

"Come in!" Alex said.

Her door opened and Dan burst through it. He sounded out of breath and appeared eager to share his news. Since they'd come to a consensus about their tasks, he was more cooperative and friendlier to Alex. He was also more comfortable. A month ago, he would have never come to her office uninvited. In all honesty, she wouldn't have let him but lately they were like new people to each other. She appreciated the camaraderie.

"Alex!" He stepped in and closed the door behind him. "You won't believe this."

"What?"

Dan flopped down in the chair facing her desk. "I was able to get us media coverage for the fair."

Alex's eyes widened. "Really? How did you manage that?"

"One of my sponsorship contacts knew a reporter at WULX news station. He kindly gave me the number to the reporter. After I talked to him for a few minutes, he agreed to cover the fair. Isn't that great?"

"That's awesome. It could be another draw for the companies. Does he need anything from us?"

"Only mere basic information about the company. I asked the PR department to send him a press kit. So, everything is set to go." He smiled.

Alex returned his smile. "That's great news."

"How's everything going on your end?" Dan asked.

"It's moving. The call center reps are going to send me a list of candidates every day and I'm going to meet with them tomorrow morning to make sure they understand what we're looking for," Alex said.

"Oh. Need any help?"

"No. I'm pretty sure I've got it covered. The hardest part was getting the companies on board. Now that they are signed up things should work out fine."

"Good." Dan nodded.

An uncomfortable silence lingered in the room. Alex began to tap her pen in her hand. To the outside person, their unease would appear to come from nowhere but, for Alex, the cause for it was quite apparent. Besides Dan's little outburst about his divorce woes, they'd never had much to say to each other outside of work but this was different. They were actually cordial, which meant they should be able to engage in conversation about their lives, in general—a difficult task for Alex.

She was so used to separating her personal and professional life she didn't know how to approach chit-chatting at work. She really didn't trust anyone with her personal information. Alex had no time for gossip and preferred not to be the subject of it.

In this instance, Alex didn't fear Dan gossiping about her; she really wanted to ask him questions about his life, particularly his child. Since she wanted to have a child sometime in the near future, she wanted to ask him about his experiences and routine. How did he balance a kid and work? *Just start talking Alex.*

She cleared her throat. "So, how is everything else?"

"It's going."

"How's your child?" Alex cringed inside. That didn't sound normal to her.

"She's fine. I talked to her yesterday. She's looking forward to seeing a puppet show with me," Dan said.

She smiled and leaned forward. "Cute. How old is she?"

"Six going on thirty."

"Uh oh. Sounds like you have your hands full." Alex chuckled.

"Oh, yeah. A couple of weeks ago, she told me she wants to be an astronaut and a chef."

Alex raised an eyebrow. "Ambitious. Wants it all. My kinda girl."

He shook his head. "You women are all the same. You always want it all."

"I resent that." She eyed Dan. "Is it hard relating to a girl?"

"I'll put it this way. She keeps me on my toes."

"Did you always want to be a father?"

He shrugged. "I don't know. I didn't give it much thought until after it happened." Dan cocked his head to the side. "Are you planning to have a kid?"

Aware of all of her questions, she suddenly became self-conscious. Alex wanted it to be a conversation, not an interrogation. She leaned back into her chair and swatted his question away. "No. I think it's great that you have such a close relationship with your daughter."

Dan nodded but eyed her with a hint of suspicion. "Oh, okay. Well, let me get back to work. Call me if you need anything.

He stood up and exited Alex's office. Like many others, having a child "happened" for Dan. Meanwhile, she hadn't been so lucky. *Maybe that will change now.* She and Nathan seemed to be back on track. Whenever she thought about him, she had a warm and fuzzy feeling inside. She felt good about the direction they were headed. They might have a chance at marriage and kids. Although it had become her habit to avoid placing bets before she saw all the cards, she really wanted to believe that this time would be different because it simply had to be.

CHAPTER 22

On a lazy Saturday afternoon, Alex vacuumed her living room and dining room. She didn't feel like it but it was time to do so. Amidst the loud noise of the vacuum, she used that time to think. Alex told herself she would run over the tasks she needed to complete for the job fair but her mind ended up wondering about Nathan.

It hadn't been that long since they'd gotten back together but she wondered if he'd thought about marriage. She remembered considering it the first time they dated but, after the party fiasco, she obviously changed her mind. Nathan had so many qualities that appealed to her. Qualities that made her feel safe and loved. She hated to admit it but she hadn't found anyone else that made her feel that way.

Alex imagined being married to him. Life would be easier. She'd have a man around the house to help with things. That would make her mother happy. She would also be done with going on date after date only to find that the man was rude, a deadbeat or chauvinistic. Or even more she'd have no chemistry with him. That was the hardest for her. With Nathan, she'd have the emotional support and compatibility she couldn't seem to find anywhere else.

The doorbell rang and interrupted her thoughts. Alex shut off the vacuum. When she approached the door and peered through her peephole, she saw Nathan. She smiled wide.

"Hey," Alex said, when she opened the door.

"Hey." Nathan stepped into her foyer and gave her a hug and a kiss.

Alex could feel heat rush to her face. She briefly dropped her head for fear that he could see or feel it.

"I wanna take you somewhere," Nathan said.

"Where?"

"It's a surprise," Nathan said.

Alex looked down at her sweatpants and T-shirt. "How will I know what to wear?"

After a short pause, Nathan said, "Dress comfortably. Not this comfortably."

She sucked her teeth. Nathan laughed.

"You're not gonna do something crazy like take me hiking, are you?"

He laughed. "No, but trust me."

"Okay."

They walked down the hall. Nathan went into her living room and flipped the television to ESPN. Alex proceeded upstairs to find something to wear. She lucked out with a green sleeveless, V-neck romper. She topped it off with silver sandals and a green bracelet. After swooping her hair into an up do, she trotted back downstairs to find Nathan engrossed in the day's sports scores.

"Are you ready?" Alex asked standing beside him.

Nathan did a double take. "You look great. Perfect." He rubbed her leg. "Can I finish watching this one part right here? It'll only be three minutes."

Alex shrugged and sat down on the couch adjacent to him. Three minutes turned into fifteen minutes. Every update led to another one. Finally, she stood up.

"Either we are going or I'm going to go back upstairs and change back into my sweatpants," Alex said, placing her hand on her hip.

His eyes widened. "Okay, okay." He reached for the remote and cut the television off. Alex grabbed a sweater and set her alarm.

Once they were in the car, Nathan pulled on his sunglasses. They pulled out of her driveway and rode down the street. "So, where did you say we were going again?" Alex asked.

"I told you, it's a surprise," Nathan said.

"Can't I get a hint?"

"Look behind you."

She glanced at the backseat and saw a blanket, some champagne and a basket. She smiled.

"A picnic," she said. "That still doesn't tell me where."

He looked at her over his sunglasses.

"What?" she asked.

"Do you not know the meaning of surprise?" he asked.

"Yes."

"What is it?" He turned his full attention back to the road.

"It means to do something for someone that is unexpected."

"Good answer. Now you know why I can't tell you," Nathan said. "On another note, how's everything going at work?"

"Great. Seven companies have signed on for the fair and my call center staff is scheduling candidates to participate. It even looks like we're going to get some press for it," Alex said.

"That *is* great. And how are things with the guy you said you had trouble working with?"

"Dan? Yes, it's much better now. We are actually able to get along."

"Oh. What changed that?"

"Well, I took your and my boss's advice. After that meeting that went bad, I went to him and apologized and showed him a list of things we needed to do. He took it well. We divided everything up and our interactions have been good ever since."

Nathan nodded. "I'm glad I could help. My bill will be in the mail next week."

"And I'll be sending it right back to you."

They both laughed.

She sighed. "But seriously, I do want to thank you for listening to me. I really appreciate it."

"Anytime." Nathan squeezed her hand.

When they approached their destination, Alex could see that Nathan had kept his promise; he didn't take her hiking but nature did factor into their day out. He pulled up to a park overlooking the St. Johnson's River. Once he put the car in park, he jumped out and opened the car door for Alex. He then reached into the back seat to pick up the picnic basket.

There was only a subtle breeze floating off the large trees. The contrast from the usual February chill offered a preview of Spring. The leaves had already begun their transition from dusty brown to lush green.

As the sun peered between the trees, Alex removed her sweater and opened the car door to place it back inside. Her sleeveless outfit bared her toned arms.

They found a place to sit and spread out a blanket to set their utensils out. While she helped him, Alex marveled at Nathan as he set out the silverware and napkins in order. They used to go out on picnics but she didn't remember him being this meticulous about them before.

Nathan caught her staring at him. "What?"

"Nothing. Watching you fuss over the silverware. I don't remember you being so detailed about it," Alex said.

"I think you're worth the extra effort, don't you?" He winked.

Alex tooted her lips upward.

Nathan sat down across from her. "Besides, I like doing things for you."

He reached into the basket and pulled out a bottle of champagne and two long stem glasses. He filled one glass and handed it to her. Then, he filled his glass halfway and set the bottle down.

"Why didn't you fill your glass all the way?" Alex asked, eyeing him.

"I thought I would graciously let you have most of the bottle in case you wanted to really throw down."

"I don't drink that much."

Nathan held up his glass. "I want to make a toast to a wonderful woman who continues to make great strides in her career. Alex, you can never be replaced."

She smiled and they clinked glasses. They both took a sip.

Nathan put his glass down. "So, besides knocking them dead at the office, what have you been up to?"

"Oh, not much."

"You don't hang out with your family? How's your mother?"

"The same."

"Aww." He chuckled.

"She recently dragged me to my cousin's baby shower."

"How was it?" he asked.

She sucked her teeth. "I don't even want to think about it."

He frowned. "Why?" Nathan crawled next to her and stretched his legs out.

"Because it was rowdy. There was an argument, someone threatened to call the police."

"Police? Nobody got hurt, did they?"

"No. They made a lot of noise. That's all." Alex took a sip of her champagne. "I spent part of the time talking to my cousin's husband."

Nathan reached into the basket and handed Alex her ham and cheese sandwich on wheat bread. "How did you...?" Alex asked.

"I remember." He smiled at her. Nathan reached in and grabbed his turkey sandwich. He unwrapped it and picked back up with his questions. "What did you guys talk about?"

Alex didn't know how to explain her conversation with Gerard. She remembered how he had told her to be cautious with Nathan. Technically, he was only looking out for her best interest but she still didn't know how he would take it. She took a deep breath and shook her head. "I don't really want to talk about it. I shouldn't have mentioned it."

"Why?"

She rubbed her arm. "Because he wasn't exactly convinced you would be good for me."

Nathan raised an eyebrow. "What? Okay." He sat his sandwich back down. "Start from the top."

She sighed. "He asked me if I was seeing anyone lately and I mentioned you."

He smiled. "That's good. Go on."

"Well, I told him that we were just reconnecting. He inquired why we broke up in the first place and I shouldn't have, but I told him what happened. He told me to be careful about you."

Nathan placed his hand over hers and nodded. "Alex, I understand where he's coming from."

"You do?"

"Yes. I commend him. He's only trying to look out for you. With that said..." Nathan moved his finger under her chin and gazed into her eyes. "All I want to do is love you. That's it. I have no ulterior motives."

A warm feeling rose within her. She loved it and hated it when he said things like that. It felt like a dream come true for him to say that he wanted to love her. She hoped those words were the truth. Her future with him depended on it. She shivered at the breeze that hit her.

He put his arm around her. "Are you okay?"

Alex nodded. "Yes." She knew what she wanted to say next but she struggled with the words. "It's just that. Contrary to my family's belief, I want to be a wife and a mother in addition to being a career woman." A simple declaration, simple desire yet somehow she couldn't resist the shame of even wanting those things, especially at this point in her life. She sometimes wondered if she were supposed to accept the life she'd been leading as her fate and dismiss her dreams of love and motherhood. "It's only getting later in the game but I don't think it's too late. I could do it and do it well," she said, hitting her fist on her thigh for emphasis.

"Sure you could."

"You think so?" Alex asked. She stared into his eyes trying to determine his sincerity.

"I know so. Okay? You're smart and capable. Any man would be lucky to have you as a wife and any child would be happy to have you as a mother."

She rolled her eyes. "I wish someone would tell my mother that."

"Hey. Don't let it get to you. You decide what you want out of life and you make it happen. No one can decide what will happen for you."

"That's what Izzy keeps telling me."

"Izzy! How is that girl?" Nathan asked, laughing.

"She's good. Her usual optimistic self." Alex smiled.

"Well, you should consider what she's telling you and stop letting other people's opinions bother you." He snapped his fingers. "I know what you need."

"What?"

"A distraction. My friend is performing at Spears later this week. Why don't you come with me?"

"Never heard of that place," She shrugged. "But I guess I'll come."

"Great. And as far as everything else, let me know when you're ready to knock out that baby."

Alex laughed and playfully pushed Nathan away. She couldn't believe how things had progressed. A couple of months ago, she had broken up with Phillip—a bad match for her—now she sat in a park next to Nathan—an ex she'd written off years ago. She marveled at the way things had changed in such a short period of time.

"I'm hoping my husband will take care of that. Thank you."

"So am I," he said, reaching for his glass to take a swig. "So am I."

CHAPTER 23

Alex was growing tired of seeing her dishes stare back at her. Out of shear willpower, she ran water into the sink and poured dish detergent in it. As she dumped some plates and pans in there, it dawned on her that it had been a little while since she'd talked to her best friend. *I'd better call and check on her.*

She dialed Izzy's number and waited for an answer.

"Hello?" Izzy said.

"Hey! How you been?"

"Oh. You know. Dealing with kids and a new job. How have you been? I thought you'd disappeared off the earth."

"I'm sorry. I've been swamped at work," Alex said. She really felt bad that she'd deserted her friend.

"Among other things. How's it going with Nathan?"

"Pretty good. By the way, he says hi."

"So, have you two set a wedding date yet?"

"Ha ha. Very funny."

"All right now. You think I'm joking. Watch what I tell you. He'll be popping the question any day now."

"I don't know about all of that but we *are* off to a great start," Alex said. She turned off the faucet and grabbed the dishcloth.

"What's the problem? Don't you want something more with him?"

"Of course, Izzy. I would love to be married to him and have a child with him."

"Wow."

"What?" Alex stopped washing a cup.

"That's the first time I've ever heard you admit to wanting to marry and have kids with Nathan."

"So?"

"That is a major breakthrough."

Alex sucked her teeth.

"It really is. You guys really must be hitting it off."

"Well, yeah. There's that and the fact that I don't have forever. I'm only getting older. I need to get clear about what I want and start to move toward it. I want to marry. I want kids."

It took a lot for Alex to admit out loud that she wanted her relationship with Nathan to evolve into marriage. She wouldn't say it if she didn't feel like the sentiment wasn't mutual. With the way he'd been treating her, she figured he had to feel the same way.

"I hear you and you'll get it with Nathan. I joke a lot but I really do feel like he's the one. You're about to get exactly what you want."

"I hope so."

• • •

Five floors up, Alex's office flaunted a wide view of the city's hustle and bustle. Like every weekday afternoon, cars sped down the highway to and fro but Alex remained transfixed on the hills in the distance. Their majestic serenity called to her through her window. She smiled. *I wonder what Nathan is doing now.* Shaking her head back and forth, Alex spun around in her chair and willed her brain to return back to the call center's list. She and Dan were supposed to meet with Mr. Sims again at 9:45 a.m. She tapped her pen on the desk while she scanned her notes and the names of potential candidates for the job fair. After Alex arranged for the call center to send her a daily list of their candidates, the numbers improved. They were now almost up to four hundred.

Alex, however, would not halt their efforts. She had them continue searching through the agency's database for people that fit the companies' qualifications. Alex had given them a few days to come up with more candidates for each company. She would hold another meeting with them to review their picks on Friday morning. She could have held it that day but she didn't feel like it. Honestly, Alex couldn't focus and her staff needed to see her as her usual self— determined and professional, not distracted and uninterested. But overall, they were on track to have the job fair on the appointed date. That kept her from feeling too bad about her current attention span.

She stopped tapping her pen on her desk. *I can't believe this.* Before reconnecting with Nathan, she would have worked late nights and brought work home—sometimes falling asleep with the papers spread across her bed. Now, she couldn't wait to go to that club with him and she didn't even like clubs. She continued to fantasize about what their life would be like if they married and had children. She bet he'd be a good father. He already had the practice with his first son.

She sighed. Her pride tried to keep her from taking their relationship too seriously but her heart knew different. She had fallen for Nathan all over again.

Alex glanced down at the clock on her computer. She had ten more minutes to go before time for the meeting. Hovering over her list, she refocused on the burning issue that hadn't been addressed for the job fair: money. She had given the sponsorship task over to Dan and she'd even given him the names and contacts of people who might agree to it but she hadn't heard his update on that yet, which made her a little nervous.

Although Dan had been going above and beyond since they started actively working together on the job fair, the sponsorship was a sore spot in their last meeting with Mr. Sims and she didn't want that to cause another rift, especially since she and Dan had recently learned how to work with and respect each other. She also had to take into account that the food and the venue would cost money. They could not charge unemployed candidates a fee to get in. Their agency would have to get sponsors. They desperately needed Dan to come through with this.

At 9:40, Alex knocked on Mr. Sims office door. He answered promptly.

"Morning, Alex." Mr. Sims motioned for Alex to enter.

"Morning, sir. How are you?" She stepped inside the immaculate office.

"Wonderful."

A minute or two later, Dan showed up with tablet and pen in hand. He and Alex nodded to each other as the meeting began.

"Well, it is good to see the both of you here today. I trust that all is going well."

"Yes. It is," Alex said.

He nodded. "Tell me about your progress on the job fair."

"The venue is set and ready to go. We have seven companies on board to participate and they are really excited about it. The call center is sending a daily log of the people they are referring to the job fair. So far, we have almost four hundred candidates recruited."

"Excellent. That is really good news," Mr. Sims said with a smile. He faced Dan. "What about you, Dan?"

C'mon, Dan. Don't mess this up.

"Well, the fair is shaping up to be exciting and catching a lot of attention. We have a news station and a couple of newspapers that are planning to cover the event," Dan said.

"Oh, okay. I didn't expect that," Mr. Sims said.

"Me neither, but people were waiting for something like this," Dan said.

"Where are we with the sponsorships?" Mr. Sims asked.

Alex held her breath while waiting for Dan to respond.

"Very good, sir. We have four sponsors and one more pending. They are also eager to be a part of the event," Dan said.

Yes! I could kiss you, Dan.

Mr. Sims smiled wider than Alex had ever seen him smile before. "Now, we're in business. Will you have enough to cover the expenses of the job fair?" Dan returned his smile. "I'm certain of it. As a matter of fact, Alex and I planned to meet later today to hash out all the expenses."

Mr. Sims slapped his desk. "Well, you two have truly outdone yourselves. You are putting together a quality event that will benefit several different sides and I commend you.

"Thank you, sir," Alex and Dan said in unison.

"Keep up the good work. Let me know if you need anything." Mr. Sims stood from his chair.

He walked them to the door with his hands around both of their shoulders.

After he closed the door behind them, they turned to each other and smiled.

"You did good," Alex told Dan.

"So did you," Dan said.

CHAPTER 24

shouldn't have agreed to come. As Alex and Nathan rode down the street, she nervously tugged at her pink and black dress. Looking out the window, she wondered how long they had to stay at the club. It wasn't her favorite place to be and she didn't know how she would keep from going stir crazy. The last time she went to the club she was accosted by a man with stinky breath. She couldn't imagine going through that all over again. Perhaps the chances of that happening again were slim; Nathan would be at her side. Certainly, no man would approach her with him standing there. The thought made her smile but only for a minute.

"Are you okay?" Nathan asked, peeking over at Alex.

She faced him. "Yes, of course. I'm fine."

"Are you sure?"

"Um hmm. Why do you ask?"

"Do you remember when you were a little kid and your mother yelled at you or whipped you before getting in the car for a ride? You'd spend the car ride looking out the window, with a sad look on your face."

"Yeah?" Alex frowned.

"That's what you look like right now."

She sucked her teeth.

"I'm serious. C'mon. What's wrong?" Nathan asked.

"I don't really like clubs," Alex said.

"Okay," Nathan said.

"I'm not a club person, I guess. It's noisy. People grope each other on the dance floor. Some people have sex in corners." She squirmed. "It's not my thing."

Nathan nodded. "I got you. Those things can happen but they don't happen all the time. And it depends on which club you go to."

She shrugged. "I wouldn't know. I don't like to visit any of them."

"I know what the problem is."

"What?" Alex asked.

"I've been picking places for us to go but I haven't been giving you the opportunity to choose. You should choose the next place." He stopped at a red light. "Where do you wanna go?"

Alex looked around. "I don't know right now."

"Well, pick a place and that's where we'll go next. From now on, we'll switch off. You choose a place. Then, I'll choose a place. Does that sound like a plan?" He put his foot on the gas as the green light came on.

"Yeah."

"So, do you know where you want to go yet?" Nathan asked.

"No."

"I know where I'm gonna take you when it's my turn."

"Where?"

"To a little club outside of Orlando. They play salsa and other types of Latin music." He turned the corner. "I think you'll like it. The place has an amazing atmosphere and you won't have to worry about anybody 'getting it' in the corner, the bathroom or anywhere else on the premises." He smiled at Alex. "Does that sound good to you?"

Alex smiled and shook her head. "Yeah, that's fine."

"In the meantime, I promise to make tonight up to you later." He winked and licked his lips.

Nathan pulled in front of Spears, a large, brick building with an electric blue sign. Cars lined the walls, while people straggled into the club. As Nathan drove around looking for a parking space, Alex could hear the thuds from the bass heavy music inside the building.

"What type of music does A.J. perform?" Alex asked.

"Hip hop," Nathan said, still rubbernecking in search of a parking space.

Alex nodded. She needed some way to keep herself occupied tonight. Although she didn't mind listening to it on occasion, she wasn't really a hip hop kind of girl. The funny thing was she didn't remember Nathan being a hip hop kind of guy.

She turned to him. "When did you get into that type of music? I thought you liked Jazz and R&B."

"I do. I just try to support my friend."

"Oh. Well, you're a good friend."

Nathan smiled at her. "Ah, here's one."

Once Nathan finished parking, he jumped out of the car and walked around to open the door for her. She stepped out and adjusted her dress. Nathan closed the door behind her and pressed a button to lock it. As they began walking toward the club, Alex noticed that the zipper on her small, silver purse wasn't closed. She fell out of step with Nathan, as she struggled with it. Nathan hit three steps ahead of her, then stopped after noticing her absence at his side. He turned around.

"What, what are you doing?" Nathan asked.

"I'm trying to close this thing up." The purse finally gave in to her pressure.

Nathan stepped back and grabbed her left hand. He gently pulled her up to speed with him. "Don't do that. Never walk behind me," he whispered.

"What?" Alex narrowed her eyebrows and looked up at him.

"Always walk beside me or in front of me. That way I can see if someone is coming at you."

Alex stared at him, stunned. Her feet were still moving but she couldn't feel them. One half of her thought he was overreacting. But the other part of her was touched that he cared about what happened to her. No man had ever said that to her before. She didn't think any other man she dated cared where she walked.

Deciding to drop the issue, she shook her head. "Fine."

The closer they got to the club, the louder the thuds became. If Nathan hadn't been holding her hand, she probably would have darted back to the car but, with her hand securely placed in his, he led her up to the door.

"Nathan Chestnut!" Nathan shouted over the thumping.

The bouncer checked the list. He nodded and unhooked the rope to let Nathan and Alex in. When they entered the club, the loud music reverberated through her core. Ironically, it wasn't as unbearable as Alex thought it would be. The truly loud music awaited them beyond the arch a few feet away. There were people scattered, talking and drinking. There were several black leather booths aligning the wall. A bartender stood behind a bar taking orders and chatting with patrons. A few people sat in the booths, where the electric blue sign illuminated their hair. Alex had begun looking for a place to sit down, when Nathan tugged her toward the arch.

"I think A.J. is in here," he said.

When they stepped through the arch, a much higher level of noise rushed toward them. People were shouting the words to the song, which Alex couldn't hear. Luckily for her, it didn't last long. The audience cheered. Then, the host strode onto the stage.

"Coming to the stage is one of the coldest artists I've seen in a long time. Put your hands together for my man, A.J.," the host shouted.

Nathan clapped and hooted along with the crowd.

In a black studded, T-shirt and faded black, urban jeans, A.J. came out on stage. He bobbed side to side to the music and the audience bobbed with him. A.J. rhymed into the microphone and he actually sounded like someone Alex would hear on the radio, if she wanted to listen to his type of music. He wasn't bad.

After a few minutes of flowing, he ended his set to cheers. The host came back to the stage.

"Give it up for A.J."

The crowd cheered again, Nathan whistled. Alex found Nathan's support of his friend endearing. Although the two men were obviously different, he valued his friendship with A.J. enough to support his dreams. Having a friend like Izzy, she could understand and appreciate why he insisted on being there. She followed Nathan's lead and applauded A.J.

Nathan turned back to her. "Wasn't that great? I told you he was good." He smiled.

Alex returned his smile. "Yes, he did a really good job."

"C'mon. Let's tell him we're here."

Nathan grabbed Alex's hand again. As they waded through the crowd, she tried hard not to bump into people because some of them were moving on the dance floor, while holding their drinks. Her dress cost $212—too much money to be ruined by vodka and cranberry juice. Nathan spotted A.J.

"A.J.!" Nathan cupped his hands over his mouth to tunnel the sound of his voice. "A.J.!"

A.J. turned in the direction of Nathan's voice and smiled. "What's up, man?" The two men moved toward each other and man hugged.

"Watching you do your thing up there. Great job, man. The audience was feeling you."

A.J. looked around. "Yeah, there were a few ladies feeling me, too. I'm trying to see which one I can take back to the 'mot' later."

Alex scowled. *Is this who he calls a friend?* The saying "birds of a feather flock together" came to mind as she watched them interact. She began to wonder what this said about Nathan. Up until then, he seemed like he'd changed from the guy she remembered. The guy who seemed more interested in chasing women with his friends but what if he hadn't changed at all? Was Alex making a fool of herself by giving him another chance?

Her eyes drifted to the floor as she thought of the worst possibilities. Nathan broke from his pow wow with A.J. and glanced Alex's way. He quickly reached out and moved his arm around her waist to pull her into the conversation.

"A.J., this is my lady. I told you about her."

"Yes. Hey, how's it goin'?" A.J. shot her a crooked smile.

Alex nodded. "Good. Congratulations on your performance."

"Thank you."

"I'm gonna go get a drink. Do you want me to bring you anything back?" Nathan asked Alex.

She shook her head. "No."

Nathan leaned into her and whispered into her ear. "I'll be right back." He rubbed her back as he left.

Alex nodded again, trying to remain confident and unfazed. A.J. lit a cigarette, inhaled the nicotine and faced upward to blow the smoke out.

"So, what do you do?" A.J. asked.

"What?" She frowned.

"For a job? What do you do?"

"Oh. I'm a recruitment manager."

"Cool. You help people find jobs, huh?"

That's the idea. "Yes," she responded.

"So, how did you and Nathan hook up, Clarissa?"

Alex frowned and put her hand on her hip. "Clarissa? That's not my name."

"Oh, my bad. That's the last woman he told me about."

Nathan had introduced her as the woman he'd told A.J. about but she didn't remember him saying her name. Perhaps he was confident that A.J would know her. It didn't make sense for Nathan to leave that open for him to make a mistake, if he'd been seeing another woman. And not just any woman—his son's mother. But then again, why didn't Nathan say Alex's name? It's not like he didn't remember it. They had a long history.

The more she thought, the more confused she became. She scanned her memory for clues that Nathan had been dishonest but she couldn't find them. He almost always answered his phone. When he didn't, he promptly returned her calls. They went out regularly.

"Oh, well." A.J. leaned closer to her. "What are you doing later?"

While he broke into laughter, Alex's blood boiled. She didn't want to stay there another minute. She looked around for the front door. Before she could take one step toward it, Nathan popped back through the crowd.

"Hey." Nathan smiled at them.

Alex looked the other way.

"Yo, Nathan. I gotta split, man. I got some people I need to see before they leave," A. J. said.

"All right, dude. I'll see ya later," Nathan said.

A.J. nodded. "Nice meeting you." He shot Alex a twisted smile and disappeared into the crowd. While Nathan spent the next few minutes nursing his drink, Alex quietly nursed a wound—a wound that increased by the second.

On the ride home, Alex stared out the window in silence, similar to the way she had done on the way to the club, except this time she didn't talk much. She muttered an occasional "um hmm" when appropriate but returned to her thoughts and hurricane of anger.

"Did you enjoy the show?" Nathan asked, looking at her.

"Um hmm," she said.

"A.J. did a great job. He'll be on the radio in no time. I told you he was good, right?"

"Um hmm."

"Did I tell you how great you looked tonight?"

"Um hmm."

"We passed a restaurant. Do you want to stop and get something to eat?"

She shook her head. "Uh uh."

"What about a walk on the pier?" Nathan asked.

"Uh uh."

"Is everything okay?" he asked, frowning.

Alex glanced at him briefly. "Yeah, everything is fine."

"Then, why are you so quiet? You haven't said much since we left Spears."

"I don't know. I guess I don't have anything to say right now."

"Yeah but were you even listening to anything *I* said?"

"Yes."

"What did I say?"

Alex sighed. "You said A.J. did a great job tonight and that he had a shot at getting onto the radio."

"And?"

"That I looked really good tonight." Alex rolled her eyes.

Nathan tooted his lips to the side. "Lucky guess."

They pulled up to her house and Nathan turned off the car. He scanned her up and down, then, turned his whole body to face her. "Seriously, Alex. What's wrong? Did I do something?"

Alex stared ahead. Before then, she had become confident in her relationship with Nathan, believing that they were going to have a better go at it this time. Since her conversation with A.J., that confidence had been shaken.

Did he still have feelings for his son's mother? It was possible. After all, she and Nathan hadn't been back together *that* long. They hadn't officially talked about a future together. She didn't even know if he had considered building a life with her. Suddenly, she felt stupid for jumping the gun on their relationship—expecting more than was being offered but she had to address this Clarissa issue.

She sighed. "No. Well, sort of. I don't know."

"What do you mean?" Nathan asked.

"Are you still seeing your son's mother?" Alex blurted out.

Nathan jerked his head back as if he'd been jabbed in the face. "No! Where did you get that from?"

She inhaled. "A.J."

Nathan stared forward and shook his head. "No, Alex. I'm not seeing her anymore."

Alex focused on her hands to keep from looking at Nathan.

He turned back to her. "You believe me, don't you?"

Alex forced a smile and nodded.

"Listen. I'm sorry. Okay? This won't happen again." He reached for her face, pulled her closer and gave her a kiss on the lips. As their faces parted, his eyes penetrated hers, searching for recognition of his effort to make peace.

"Okay." She grabbed her purse. "I have to go."

"Really?" Nathan asked, surprise escaping from his voice.

"Yeah, I'll talk to you later."

Alex opened her car door before he could think about jumping out to open it for her. Once she stood outside of the car, she leaned down, waved and closed the door behind her. She walked up her front steps, trying to push out images of the surprise and disbelief on Nathan's face. She tried to tell herself that he couldn't care less about her concerns, even though the look on his face and the ten minutes he sat outside in his car said different.

CHAPTER 25

For about five minutes, Alex sat at her desk and stared at her computer. She saw the screen but was not focused on the words. She kept thinking about the night before, playing the events in her head over and over. Although she'd tried to brush it off, she had a hard time finding a reasonable explanation for the incident with A.J. She continued to lapse into a trance every few minutes.

They have a kid together. Why wouldn't he still want a relationship with her? It was more than he and Alex had together. History didn't quite cut it up against creating a life with someone. She thought about having a kid with him but maybe she thought too soon. Maybe her desperation made her see an opportunity where there wasn't one. If that was the scenario, she had no one to blame but herself.

She felt a pain in her chest. *No. Please, don't let that be it.* Her office phone rang and she blanked rapidly. Startled, she fumbled with the phone.

"Hello?"

"Ms. Carter? Will you be able to make it to our meeting?" Brian, her call center lead, said.

Alex gasped. She looked at the clock. She was sixteen minutes late meeting with her call center reps. "Oh my gosh. Uh. I'm on my way."

She scrambled to find a pen, tablet, the agenda and their current report. Then, she dashed out the door. After reaching the group, Alex felt the need to apologize. Usually, she didn't but her behavior felt so out of character for her that she couldn't resist apologizing and offering an explanation.

"Morning, everyone. I am so sorry for my tardiness. I almost forgot we had a meeting today. Please forgive me." Alex set her tablet and reports down on the desk and sat down in the desk chair next to it. "Have I missed anything?"

"No, ma'am. We were counting the number of candidates we've found so far," Brian said.

"All right. Um," She shuffled with her papers. "Where are we?"

"We've counted four hundred twenty candidates."

She nodded. "Excellent."

"Do you have anything to go over with us, Ms. Carter?" Brian asked.

"Uh, yes. I have a few things."

Alex stood back up and cleared her throat. Suddenly subconscious about asserting her authority, she pushed herself to the front of the group. "I want to take the time to thank each and every one of you because without your diligent efforts, we would not have so many qualified people ready to interview with these top companies. So, for that, you all should give yourselves a hand."

The group clapped for themselves.

"As for the day of the fair, I'm going to need some help with registration, set up, checking people in and giving them practical information. I'm going to choose a few people from the center to help with that next week. I don't know who yet but prepare to get a call from me."

The reps looked around at each other, seeming to wonder who would get the call.

"Other than that continue to push forward. We're not quite done yet but we are in the home stretch. So, um… Does anyone have any questions for me?"

They all shook their heads.

"Awesome. Keep up the good work," Alex said.

"Okay, you guys. You can get back to work; make sure you remember to send me your list by the end of the day," Brian reminded them.

Alex nodded and picked up her tablet and report. Brian walked over to her.

"Is everything okay, Ms. Carter?"

She looked up at him. "Oh. Yes. All is fine. Why?"

"You seem a little frazzled; that's all."

She pressed her shoulders back. "Everything is good. You guys are doing such a good job. I'm very excited about the job fair."

"Yeah, the reps are really coming through and I want to thank you for your encouragement. You're tough but fair. Your standards really do help make us better."

"Wow. Thank you, Brian. I appreciate that."

She waved goodbye to them and walked back to her office. Alex's preoccupation with Nathan caused her to almost miss a meeting. She even arrived fumbling and bumbling, which was quite embarrassing. *I can't let that happen again.* Her work had the potential to provide some type of temporary relief from the constant debating in her head but she wasn't going to get an answer to her questions that way. She needed to call Nathan.

Alex went back to her office and sat at her computer. As a couple more hours passed, she continued to pull her brain back into her tasks and out of the club with Nathan and A.J. The only good benefit was that she could hide out in her office to keep anyone else from seeing how frazzled she was. Good thing the job fair was on track for success. If it weren't for Dan, she'd really be going stir crazy. The call center didn't even have any questions for her.

Each time she thought about the noisy club, A.J.'s comment and Nathan's denial, her shoulders drooped at the memory. *I should have stayed home.* Alex shook her head free of the situation and forced her brain to refocus on her work.

When lunch time finally rolled around, she grabbed a couple of things off her desk and searched for a restaurant, hoping she would be able to disappear in the lobby corner or something. She settled on going to the Tutti Frutti Smoothie shop. It seemed like a laid back spot at first but the level of noise increased from the time she first entered the building.

Deciding against the noisy lobby, Alex paid for her peach and mango smoothie and returned to her car. She took a quick sip of the drink and sat it down in the cup holder before leaning back in her seat to think things over. What were her options? She could leave Nathan alone. She didn't need the drama. Getting out early to avoid the hassle seemed like the smart thing to do.

Then again, Nathan said he hadn't done anything wrong. He said he and Clarissa were done. He could be telling the truth. Up until then, they'd made real progress on their relationship. She'd let go of her anger about the way they'd ended years ago. He took her out. He listened to her. He even seemed to dote on her. Nathan hadn't shown any signs of having ulterior motives or playing games with her. Should she really come this far and give up?

She didn't want to give up. Unlike Phillip, Nathan made her happy. He made her feel special and appreciated. After years of trying to find that type of connection, Alex knew that if she let him go, she couldn't expect to experience this again anytime soon.

Alex reached for her iPhone and tapped the screen. She stared at Nathan's number but felt like she wasn't ready to talk to him yet. To be honest, she didn't know what she would say if he answered. Alex decided to send a text. That would give her time to think of what she wanted to say and say it uninterrupted. When the blank white box appeared, Alex stared at it for a second. She finally got her thoughts together and began to type:

Hello, Nathan,

Thank you for bringing me along last night. I hate that it didn't turn out better but I'm glad you were understanding. Anyway, what are you doing later?

Alex struggled with the decision to type more. She decided to keep it short and to the point. She hit the send button and placed the phone back into its holster.

The rest of the day was uneventful. She found ways to keep herself busy. She had to—Nathan didn't send one text back. Every hour, she checked her phone. Not a text, a message or even a missed call. She started wishing she hadn't sent the text in the first place but she didn't see a reason why she shouldn't. It seemed like the nice thing to do. To issue an olive branch. To show good faith. She hoped he wasn't trying to punish her or prove a point. She didn't do anything wrong. Alex reacted to a situation that surprised and upset her.

Five o'clock hit and Nathan still hadn't responded to Alex. By the time she stepped off the building elevator onto the first floor, her mood had tanked. It wore on her that Nathan still hadn't texted or called her back. *Maybe I've blown it. Maybe he's done with me.* On her way to the lobby, she ran into Dan. He saw her and smiled wide.

"Hey. How's it going?"

"Can't complain." Alex straightened her posture to portray her usual confidence.

"Me neither. My car was hit yesterday."

Alex frowned and kept moving. "Are you all right? I thought you said you couldn't complain."

"I can't." They walked past the receptionist, waving goodbye to her. "Check out the rental they gave me."

Dan pointed to a red convertible 2012 Jaguar XK coupe. Although there was a sea of cars on its row, its shiny exterior made it stand alone.

"Whoo! How did you get that type of upgrade?" Alex asked.

"There was a big mix up this morning when I went to get my rental. They didn't have 'my' car ready. The price was wrong. It was a mess. Once I strongly expressed my disappointment in their professionalism, they put me in that little baby."

Alex smiled. "You mean you threatened them."

Dan sighed. "Tomato, tamato. The point is they made up for it." He shook his head. "Isn't she a dime?"

Alex shook her head. "Sure, she is. Have you taken the top down yet?"

"On the way to work." He cheesed and nodded.

She chuckled. "I'll bet you broke every heart you passed."

"I might have heard a few breaks here and there." He laughed.

It amazed Alex the ease in which she and Dan were now able to communicate. Not long ago, she was constantly annoyed with him. As she chuckled at his enthusiasm over the rental car, she wondered why they were ever at odds.

Apparently, Dan had the same thoughts. He broke from his laughter and cocked his head to the side.

"What's wrong with you?" Alex asked, a little self-conscious.

He caught himself. "Oh, nothing. I never knew you were capable of letting your guard down and having a good laugh. That's all," Dan said.

She sucked her teeth. "Well, it's easy when you have someone helping you pull off a big project. Less stress means lighter mood. You're doing a great job with the sponsors and everything." She turned and walked toward her car.

Dan followed. "Thanks but really you seem more easygoing these days. Happy, even."

She stopped walking and looked up at Dan. Before she could respond a horn honked twice. Alex and Dan faced the sound. Nathan opened his car door, stepped outside and smiled at Alex.

Before she could stop it, Alex's face stretched as wide as it possibly could into a grin.

Dan nodded. "So, that's why."

Heat rushed to her face. She covered her cheek as if steam were shooting from her pores.

"It's okay. I'll catch you later, Alex." Dan briefly placed a hand on Alex's shoulder.

Dan walked toward his "temporary" sports car, while Alex waded through the cars toward Nathan. Despite her attempt to look calm, she smiled at Nathan, allowing happiness to overtake her face. When she reached him, he wrapped his arms around her for a strong embrace and kissed her softly—a contradictory yet intoxicating combination for Alex.

"How you doing?" he asked.

"Good. How are you?" Alex asked, looking into his eyes for clues.

"Good. I got your text." He nuzzled her nose with his.

"Is that why you came to my job?"

"Yes. Why didn't you call?"

Alex couldn't admit that she didn't know what to say. So, she lied. "I only had a few minutes left in my lunch break."

"Umm. Do you have time for a movie tonight? The theater, my place, your place?"

Alex could go for a movie but she really wanted to go home, as opposed to sitting in a cold theater trying to listen over loud talking. "We can watch a movie at my place."

Nathan loosened his grip. "Okay. I'll go buy some movie theater popcorn and chocolate."

Alex raised an eyebrow. "Chocolate?"

"Yes. You have to eat popcorn with chocolate. It's a requirement."

"I don't know about that. Chocolate is dangerous to a healthy diet."

Nathan ran his eyes over her size 4 figure. "I don't think you have anything to worry about," he said in a low voice.

Alex returned his earlier kiss. "See you in about two hours?"

"Two hours it is."

Nathan jumped back into his car, while Alex pulled away in hers. She dashed home and squeaked into her driveway. Upon opening the door to her laundry area, she discovered that she hadn't folded the towels she'd washed that morning. Another unwashed load spilled over a basket. For a moment, she thought about closing the laundry door in hopes that he would not notice but she decided against taking the risk that he would see. Not that he was the type to judge her but she still wanted to be prepared for his arrival.

Alex threw the heavy load in the washing machine and took the basket of clean towels for a quick folding. By the time she'd finished folding and changing clothes, she heard the doorbell ring. *Right on time.* She jogged downstairs and opened the door. As he promised, Nathan stood there with movie theatre buttered popcorn and a bag of mini Hershey bars.

"You ready?" He smiled.

"Sure. Come in." She waved him into the house.

About ten minutes later, they sat on her couch flipping through the pay-per-view movies on her satellite dish. They settled on a horror movie. As they watched it, Alex began to regret agreeing to the movie. All the gory torture scenes made her lose her appetite for the popcorn and pile of chocolate on the coffee table. When a scene with someone stuck in a metal head brace popped on the screen, she turned her head in disgust.

"Ugh!"

Nathan chuckled. "Come here." He pulled her into his body and they stretched out on the sofa.

"What? Are you going to be my knight-in-shining-armor now?" Alex asked still covering parts of her face.

"I don't know. I like taking care of you. You should let me do that more often." Nathan's eyes pierced into her eyes as if he were dissecting her soul and examining each part.

"I'm a big girl," she said, diverting her eyes to avoid any further probing from his.

"Everybody needs to be taken care of every now and then." He paused. "I'm really glad you reached out to me today. After last night, I didn't know when I would hear from you again."

"I needed to sleep on it," Alex said.

"Sleep on what?"

"Last night's events."

"But you understood what I said, right? I'm not with Clarissa anymore."

Her nerves jumped at the mention of the other woman's name. Alex knew Nathan would bring this up but she really wanted to put it out of her head altogether and try to forget that it happened. If Nathan said he and his ex were over, she would have to take him at his word and leave it alone.

"Yes, Nathan. I understand." She turned onto her right side to face the screen, signaling her desire to end the conversation. After a couple of minutes watching the movie, a chill hit her and she shook her shoulders.

"Do you want to change the station?" he mumbled in her ear.

"No, it's paid for. Might as well watch the rest of it."

"Not if you don't want to." Nathan ran his hand down her back and slid it around her waist.

Suddenly hyper aware of his touch, Alex sought to maintain her composure. She reached for the remote control and pressed the select button. "There's only thirty-six minutes left in the movie. We should finish it." She replaced the remote back on the coffee table and placed her head back on the couch arm rest.

"Well, I can think of something else to do if you don't really want to watch the movie."

Alex looked over her shoulder at him. "What?"

Nathan maneuvered his hand up her shirt. His warm breath traced her neck while his lips followed close behind. Alex closed her eyes. Not to shun the graphic scenes in the movie but to try and control the wave of emotion rising within her. It wasn't working. By the time his lips found hers, his hands had found the supple mound under her bra. He caressed it slowly, coaxing her out of her usual self-control. Unable to take any more, Alex shifted on her back and pulled Nathan closer to her.

Her heartbeats doubled their normal speed. She shook all over with anticipation and want. The moment of truth had arrived. Nathan was offering her the love that she'd gone so long without. She hadn't felt this type of intensity since they were together years ago. And she could not allow herself to go another day without it.

Alex wiggled out of her pants. Nathan followed suit. She could barely wait for him to finish before enveloping his waist with her legs. Although her squeezes to his back sent clear signals she wanted him right then, he insisted on taking his time. Nathan ran his hands back up her stomach, moving her shirt over her head. He paused at her chest to wind his tongue in circles around her jutted pebbles of flesh.

Unable to wait any longer, Alex clawed at his back until he finally pushed himself inside of her body. She squealed and squeezed him tighter, taking comfort in his long lost familiarity. He responded by rolling his hips in rhythmic motion, as if he could hear a sensual ballad in the distance. His movement drove her into an irrepressible frenzy. Curling her toes, she finally gave in and rode over the edge. Nathan was not far behind.

He momentarily collapsed on her before silently laying behind her on the couch and wrapping his arms around her. As they turned back to the TV screen, Alex made no attempt to concentrate on the movie. Instead, she closed her eyes, preferring to focus on how it felt to lay in Nathan's arms again.

CHAPTER 26

The next morning, Alex woke up to her familiar routine. She did all the same things: showered, dressed, made breakfast with a side of tea but, despite the familiarity, something about this day wasn't familiar at all. Alex walked around the house, to and fro, with a consistent smile on her face. She'd been that way since Nathan left.

All of a sudden, everything was perfect. She felt certain that Nathan loved her and, for once, she could admit that she loved him, too. *Wait until I tell Izzy.* As Alex reached into the cabinet for a tea bag, she chuckled, thinking about her friend's reaction to her revelation. It would be exactly what she wanted to hear.

While the bag soaked in her go-to travel mug, she reached for her cell phone to check her messages. She immediately saw a text from Nathan. She smiled and opened it to read three simple words. *I love you.* She hit the reply button and typed that she loved him too. After hitting send, she returned to her main screen and saw a pop up alert that she was supposed to schedule a follow up doctor's appointment. She hit her contacts button and obeyed her calendar's reminder.

A super friendly medical receptionist answered the phone. "Dr. Nugyen's office. May I help you?"

Alex greeted her with the same pleasant attitude. "Morning. I want to schedule a follow up appointment with the doctor."

"Okay. What is your name?"

"Alexis Carter."

"What's your date of birth?"

"August 21, 1976."

"What are you coming in for?" the receptionist asked.

"I was having headaches. Dr. Nugyen gave me a prescription and requested that I come back in for a follow up."

The receptionist typed for a few seconds. "Which day were you planning to come in?"

"Can I get an appointment for next Wednesday around ten forty-five?" Alex planned to take that day off, since it'll be the day after the job fair. She was sure she could use the break.

"All righty. You're all set for next Wednesday at ten forty-five."

"Thank you."

Alex hung up and went to her mug to finished preparing her tea. When she was ready to go, she grabbed her mug, briefcase and headed out the door. She encountered a little bit of traffic on her way to work but it didn't dampen her spirits. She still rode high from their afternoon together. She strolled into the building, passing Betty.

"Hello, Betty," Alex said.

"Morning. You look really nice today, Alex," Betty said.

"Thank you. So do you. I like your haircut."

Betty raised her eyebrows. "Thanks. I cut it a few days ago. I didn't think you noticed."

"Of course, I noticed. I think it's great. Did you add a little bit of color, too?"

"Yes. There are some highlights in there." Betty ran her fingers through her hair to draw attention to them.

Alex nodded. "I knew it."

Betty smiled, looking self-satisfied. "Oh, Dan wants you to call him when you're ready to go over to the Rockford Center," Betty said, suddenly remembering her message for Alex.

"Okay. Thanks."

Alex quickened her step toward her office. When she sat down at her desk, she turned on her computer and checked her emails. It wasn't anything earth shattering—regular updates. She placed her briefcase in her drawer. She then dialed Dan's extension.

"Hey, Dan! It's Alex. Are you ready?"

"Yeah, I'm ready. I'll meet you downstairs."

Alex grabbed her tablet, purse and keys and walked back out the door. About ten minutes later, Dan came downstairs to join her.

"Are we going in your car or mine?" Dan asked.

"What? And miss the opportunity ride in that Jag? Are you kidding?"

Dan smiled wide. "All right. Let's go."

They pulled out of the agency's parking lot and glided onto the expressway.

"Do you want the top back?" Dan asked, hovering a finger over the button.

Alex shook her head. "No. Not now. Maybe when we're on the street. Can't have messy hair when I'm talking to the director at the center."

"Right. Right," Dan nodded in agreement. "So, how is everything?" A smile tugged at the corner of his mouth.

"Everything is good." Alex glanced over at him. "I'll be glad when this job fair is over. It feels like we've been working on it forever."

"Yes, it does. The good news is it'll all be over soon and you can spend more time with the guy."

"What guy?"

"You know the one that was in the parking lot."

Alex remembered Nathan outside her job. She also thought about their time together after that. Heat rushed to her face as she realized that Dan was looking at her waiting for an answer. *I hope he doesn't read minds.*

"Oh, him," she said, choosing not to elaborate. "Well, I mean it'll be good to be able to relax for once."

"True but the guy? Uh, what's his name?"

Alex sighed. "Nathan."

"Nathan. You are dating him, right?" Dan asked.

Alex squirmed in her seat. The conversation made her uncomfortable. "We've known each other for a long time."

"If you're not dating, you should be. You guys look pretty cozy together. Plus, he's making you happy."

"How do you know my happiness has anything to do with him?"

"The same way I know the sky is blue. I look at it," Dan said.

She rolled her eyes. "Whatever."

Dan paused for a couple of seconds before speaking again. "You're tough and everything but it's okay if you love him, Alex."

She stared at Dan.

He continued as if unaware of her. "Sometimes we, ambitious types, work so hard in the office that we forget what's really important to us. We forget what we really want." Dan faced her. "I'm saying don't be afraid to want something else."

Alex looked away. It was strange to hear Dan talk this way. Because of their office rivalry, they hadn't shared many deep conversations. To be honest, she never thought he was a deep person but she was wrong and his insight proved it. His words seemed to come from a deep, dark place, alluding to a few not so fortunate experiences. She felt like his words were for himself, as well as for her.

She appreciated the advice but, despite his effort to reach out to her on a personal level and her persistent afterglow, Alex had to stay mindful of the fact that she was talking to a coworker. She still felt the need to be professional, even if they were having a comrade moment.

Alex swallowed. "I won't."

A few short minutes later, they arrived at the center, a large, beige structure with four columns at the entrance. They walked into the center and went to the main office to see the director. He pointed Dan and Alex to the area of the center they would be using. They viewed the rooms they would use during the job fair and considered the lay out for the set up.

"Okay. So, we can put the registration table out front. That way as soon as they walk through the door, the table will be the first thing they see," Alex said to Dan.

"That sounds good. We can also put the biggest sponsor's banner in front of the registration table," Dan added.

Alex nodded. "We need to figure out where to put the other banners."

"Right. Let's go ahead and determine which company will get which room and how we're going to arrange the tables and chairs," Dan said.

They walked toward the other rooms and decided where they would put each employer. Alex had a good feeling about the job fair. Seeing the center made its success real for her. She felt like the fair would not only save her job but set her head and shoulders above the rest of the managers. After identifying where they would hold lunch for the employers, the two migrated back to the car.

Once Dan put on his seatbelt, he turned to Alex. "Well, do you think we can pull all this off in a few days?"

She faced him. "We'd better."

CHAPTER 27

A lex stumbled through her laundry room and dropped her briefcase. She desperately wanted to kick off her shoes but before she could lift one foot, the phone rang. She hobbled over to the cordless and answered.

"Hello?" She sounded rushed.

"Hey, Baby. What's up?" Nathan asked in his usual casual, positive tone. She smiled wide, wondering how he did that. Every time she talked to him, he had a way of sounding as if nothing ever bothered him. Life was smooth sailing. It was an attitude that she secretly envied and one that made her love him even more.

"Oh. Nothing, really. I walked in the door a couple of minutes ago."

"You left a little late today, didn't you?"

"A little. My boss decided to come into my office five minutes to five and hold a thirty-minute conversation." Alex shook her head. "But that's okay. It's getting close to time for the fair. He constantly wants details."

"Oh. I've been thinking about you all day," Nathan said.

Alex sat down at the table. "I've been thinking about you, too."

"I want to see you. Are you up to doing anything tonight or do you want to chill out?" Nathan asked.

Alex's pulse quickened at the thought of spending more time with him. "I can stand some distraction. What did you have in mind?"

"Uh uh. You have to choose, remember?" He laughed.

She tooted her lips to the side. "Right." Alex thought for a few seconds. Then, she snapped her fingers. "There's a local art gallery downtown that holds art shows a few times a week. Why don't we go there?"

"Oh, okay," Nathan said.

"We don't have to go there. It's a suggestion."

"No, I'm cool with seeing the art gallery. I've never been. When should I pick you up?"

"Give me an hour," Alex said.

"All right. I'll be there."

•••

Even though the viewing was free and the skyline looked great, Alex was surprised how many people were there. There were a few more cars there than usual. Still, Alex and Nathan managed to find a parking space fairly close to the door.

As they reached the bright lights and music from the gallery, Alex saw a room of at least thirty-five people inside. They stepped inside and were greeted with a room full of chatter. The white wall and the white floors created the perfect contrast to the art displayed throughout the room. They walked around and listened to the different descriptions of the paintings. When they got to the sixth painting, Alex couldn't resist running her fingers over the rough exterior. After marveling over the painting, she happened to glance over at Nathan and saw him looking around. To her, he looked bored. She nudged him.

"Are you okay?"

"Yeah, I'm fine. Why?" Nathan asked.

"I don't know. You look kinda disinterested. This is a great painting. Look at the colors. Even though there is a roughness to the texture, the blending of the reddishness of the sky and the light blue in the water make it very gentle and beautiful. Don't you think?" She turned to him.

He moved closer to her and nuzzled her neck. "I think you're gentle and beautiful."

Alex chuckled and covered her mouth. "C'mon. Focus on the painting."

She grabbed his hand and led him toward the next painting. "See, look at this one. Don't you like it?"

He put his arms around her. "It's nice."

"Why is it nice?" Alex asked, looking up at him.

"Because it has nice colors with the textures and paper," he mumbled.

Alex shook her head and laughed. "You are pitiful."

He hugged her tighter, while burying his face in her neck. Warm and fuzzy feelings rose within her. All of her incessant doubts seemed to be gone but they were still there. They were at rest like a sleeping giant.

"Nathan! What's up, man?"

Alex and Nathan heard the loud greeting. They turned around to see where it was coming from. A man approached wearing jeans, T-shirt and sneakers, a tad bit underdressed for an art gallery.

Nathan broke from his embrace with Alex. "Hey, Eric. How you doing?" He shook hands with him.

"Man, I'm cool. Whatchu doing out here?"

"Ah. Hanging out with my lady." Nathan pointed at Alex. "Eric, this is Alex." He turned back to her. "Alex, this is Eric. We used to work together."

Well, there's something he did different. He included her name in the introduction. She didn't remember him doing that when he introduced her to A.J. She supposed he'd learned his lesson but, as she observed the difference in each man's wardrobe—Eric's outside casual choice opposed to Nathan's business casual attire—she wondered about Nathan's friends. From A.J. to Eric, how could they be so different from him?

When she thought about A.J., her good mood started to deteriorate. She wondered if he'd talked to him since the incident. Were they still close friends? How would that impact her and Nathan's relationship?

"Hello." Alex nodded a greeting to Eric.

"Hey. How's it going?" Eric said.

"Good," Alex responded.

"All right, man. I won't keep you long. I'll let you two be," Eric said, shaking hands with Nathan.

"Cool. See ya later," Nathan said.

Eric waved and walked off. Nathan turned his attention back to Alex. "Now where were we? Oh, you were telling me how pitiful I was for not knowing the first thing about art."

"Um. What are the odds of us running into people we know here, huh? I don't know anybody else that likes art enough to go to a gallery," Alex pondered out loud, while staring at the painting.

He shrugged. "Eh, I don't think Eric likes art. He happened to be here. That's all. Plus he knows a lot of people in this area."

"Do you know a lot of people here? Have a lot of friends?" Alex asked. She faced him, her once pleasant demeanor giving way to the sleeping giant inside of her.

"I guess. I mean, I've been here for most of my life, minus college. It's hard not to get to know different people all over the city. Don't you?" he asked.

"What?"

"Have a lot of friends?"

"Not really. I keep my friend circle small and tight. That way I can avoid drama and confusion." She eyed Nathan.

He nodded. "I suppose with women that's a bigger issue."

Alex placed her hands on her hips. "With women? And men don't have similar issues?"

"No."

"So, how do you describe what happened with A.J.?" she asked.

"That was an unfortunate situation, which I've talked to him about."

"And what did he say?" Alex crossed her arms.

"He said it was a misunderstanding."

She scowled. "You believe him?"

Nathan sighed and ran his hand over his head. "Listen. Don't worry about that situation. It's not gonna happen again."

"But you're still friends with him?" Alex asked. She shouldn't have been surprised but she was disappointed. Trusting him would be difficult knowing that the two men were still thick as thieves.

"Yeah. What's the problem?" Nathan asked, sensing her distress.

"The problem is that we're going to have a hard time building this relationship when there is someone around intent on sabotaging it. Why don't you see that? Why can't you see that you're going to have to cut him loose?" While this may have been a bold statement, Alex felt justified in saying it. It was necessary to address it because she didn't want a repeat of ten years ago.

"Wait a minute, Alex. You can't tell me who I can and can't be friends with."

"But your 'friend' tried to cause problems for us."

"And I said I dealt with it."

Alex shook her head. He still didn't get it. "What if it happens again? Are you gonna deal with it again?"

"Yes," Nathan said, staring her in the eye.

She turned back to the painting and pursed her lips. "Well, given our history, that's not good enough."

"What about our history?"

Reluctant to go there, Alex hesitated in answering him. "We have a history of friends getting in the way."

Nathan stepped beside her. "That was a long time ago. You said you forgave me."

"I do but I don't want history to repeat itself," Alex said.

Nathan's tone and demeanor changed. He lowered his voice. "Then, you're gonna have to trust me."

Alex maintained her strong stance but deep inside she was hurt. It's like she saw a Mack truck coming but couldn't push her and Nathan's relationship out of its path. On one hand, she respected his desire to be a loyal friend. She also understood that he wasn't the type of guy to take someone telling him what to do. On the other hand, she had a hard time seeing a happy ending to this situation. Her discomfort grew as she thought about the type of games A.J. probably had up his sleeve. It sickened her. She didn't know how she would compete with him on that level. Nor did she know how she would keep Nathan focused on their relationship instead of the foolishness.

Her gaze fell from the painting to the floor. "You're making it hard for me to do that."

CHAPTER 28

T he disagreement Alex and Nathan had at the art gallery worried her. She was even more worried about the fact that they hadn't spoken in a few days. In her heart, she wanted to call him and try to hash out their differences. She missed the whirlwind they were in. She missed talking to him almost every day about how they missed each other and how they were so glad to have found each other again. Although Alex had been reluctant to believe in their relationship a second time, she found herself giving in to the happiness their renewed union created.

Now her newfound bliss had been threatened and she didn't know how to recover. She asked herself was it worth it to take the risk of repeating the same thing all over again? She believed Nathan to be a good guy. His actions, however, were either naïve or conniving. He had to know that A.J. meant them no good.

But when the clock hit 4:00 a.m. on February 23rd, Alex didn't have the option of worrying about those things. It was the day of the job fair. She knew the event would go well because she and Dan put a lot of preparation into it. She also knew that she would have to pull her attention into the fair and away from Nathan—at least until the afternoon passed.

She quickly dressed and piled a few boxes and bags into her car. After swiping a bacon, egg and cheese McGriddle from McDonald's, she arrived at the Rockford Center way before others. Between bites, Alex pulled decorations, numbers and other things she needed out of the boxes. A few call center reps arrived to help Alex arrange the tables, signage and check-in forms. She then briefed them on their responsibilities and answered their questions.

A staff of four suited professionals walked in carrying briefcases and two medium-sized boxes.

She greeted them with a smile. "Hello, I'm Alex."

"Hi, Alex. I'm Bela and this is Harper, Felicity and Kennedy. We're here to recruit for PharmScope."

Alex reached out her hand to shake each of theirs. "It's a pleasure to meet all of you. We are so happy you could be here. This is going to be an awesome job fair."

"Me, too. A lot of people have asked us about it," Felicity said.

"Same here. Let me show you where you all will be setting up."

Alex walked them toward the second room from the entrance. She and the reps had placed six chairs in each room to make sure they had enough for recruiters. The PharmScope recruiters placed their boxes on the table and began arranging their laptops and pens. Alex proceeded to brief them on the number of candidates they were expecting and the way the agency planned to handle the crowd. Harper opened the box with several plastic bags but did not remove the contents.

"Where is the nearest restroom?" Harper asked Alex.

"Right next door." She pointed.

"Great."

Alex heard multiple footsteps outside. Dan's voice followed. She peeped around the door and found him introducing himself to a few other recruiters that had arrived.

"I'll be right outside. If you all need anything else, please let me know," Alex said to the PharmScope staff.

"Hey, Dan," Alex said once she stepped outside.

"Hey. I see you already have the reps set up. That was Continuum International. I showed them to the room across the hall."

"Good. Where are the banners?" Alex asked.

"They're in my car. I'll go get them now."

Once Nathan and Alex retrieved the banners from his car, they hung them up. Meanwhile, more employers trickled into the conference center. She and Dan switched off in preparing the recruiters for the onslaught of people coming their way. By the time the last employer arrived, potential candidates had lined up outside awaiting the conference center doors to open. Alex trotted over to the rep's table and flipped through the check in sheets. She also made sure the reps had enough numbers for each candidate.

"All right, you guys. Showtime."

She opened the doors for the candidates and they filed in. They hurried over to the table where the reps verified their names on the check-in sheets and handed them a number matching their number on the form.

The candidates underwent an interview with their appointed employer. If the employer found them interesting, they were given a background check and a urinalysis. Those that passed all three—interview, criminal check and test—were given a date to report to the employer's office for training.

Before the candidates left the center, they checked back out at the reps table and reported if they received a training date from the employer. Some candidates left the center very happy; others left very angry. Alex kept tabs on the hired count all day but, as the relentless heat from the early afternoon gave way to more subtle warmth of the sun, she begin directing her attention to winding the event down.

While the last group of candidates exited the building, Alex stood outside on her final task—lunch. Since Dan did such a good job securing sponsors, finalizing the center and putting out fires during the fair, she thought she'd take over making sure the pizza arrived for all the employers and agency staff. It turned out to be harder than she thought because the pizza delivery guy hadn't arrived.

Alex held her cell phone to her ear and repeated the same directions over and over again trying to guide him but he kept passing the same bank building. He'd put her on hold for the fourth time. *If he would listen to me, he wouldn't be lost.* Alex breathed a sigh of relief when she saw the delivery guy's dark blue sedan turn the corner.

Finally.

Once he set the pizza, cinnamon sticks and soda in one of the front rooms, the employers filed in and swiped a few slices. Alex gave them about fifteen minutes and then she headed back to the lobby, where the call center reps from the agency were helping to break down signs and move tables back to their original place.

Alex smiled at them. "How's it going?"

"Good," the reps said in unison.

"Where did you want these tables?" the shorter one asked.

"You can push those up against the wall. They'll be out of the way there."

They followed instructions.

"Fantastic. Well, you guys have done an excellent job. Thank you for coming out to help with the physical labor." She chuckled.

"No problem," the taller rep said.

"Come on to the back and get some pizza." Alex motioned for them to follow her.

As the pizza disappeared, the employers begin to leave, also. The agency staff hurriedly cleaned up so they could go home. Pleased with the outcome of the four hundred fifty candidates present, Alex felt like she and Dan had done a good job. She grabbed her bags of spare supplies and walked toward the exit. Halfway there, she ran into Dan.

"Hey! You're ready to go?" he asked. "Gotta a hot date?" He raised his eyebrows twice in rapid succession.

She smiled and tooted her lips to the side. "No. I'm tired."

"Me, too but that doesn't mean I'd skip a trip on Operation Love Boat. You gotta stay motivated." He snapped his fingers.

Alex laughed.

"How are things on that front?" Dan asked.

Alex had managed to go the whole job fair without thinking about Nathan. It sucked that Dan had to bring that up but at least the fair was over. She smiled to try and cover up her sadness. "It's fine. Thanks for asking. Look. I'm gonna head on out of here."

"Do you need some help?"

"No. I got it."

"All right. Well, I'll catch up with you later. And great job," Dan said, throwing her the thumbs up.

"You, too."

Alex stepped outside and rounded the corner. As soon as she neared her car, her cell phone rang. She sighed. She couldn't answer it and carry the bags. She unlocked her car and placed her bag on the back floor. Once she climbed into the front seat, closed and locked the door, she checked her phone, hoping to see Nathan's number. She saw Izzy's number instead. Disappointed, she hit the screen to dial her back.

"What's up, girly?" Izzy answered.

"Not much. How's it going?" Alex asked.

"Fine now that I'm home. Finished wrapping an up do. I thought it would take forever and the girl was so impatient."

"Well, it's only been a couple of months since you started doing hair professionally. It'll take time to get used to it."

"Yeah, I guess."

"Other than that, how's it going? Is it everything you thought it would be?" Alex asked, cranking up her car.

"It's cool. I love the freedom and the money."

"I'll bet. You're already racking up a big clientele."

Izzy chuckled. "I'm still working on it. The salon is fairly new. Anyway, what's going on with you?"

"My job fair is officially over."

"Yay! How did it go?" Izzy asked.

"It was excellent. We managed to get a lot of candidates and make it look easy."

"Congrats. What are you doing to celebrate?" Izzy asked.

"Sleeping," Alex lied. She had every intention of calling Nathan as soon as she returned home.

"No, you won't. You're coming to this new club with me."

"What club?"

"I can't remember the name right now but the rest of the salon is going over there after work tonight. And we should go."

"Don't you think they only expect you to show up?"

"No. Everybody's inviting people."

"I can't stay out late tonight. I have a doctor's appointment in the morning."

"Alex, you're coming."

Great. I'm really not in a partying mood. Realizing that Izzy wasn't going to let up, Alex mentally searched her closet for something to wear. She settled on a purple dress with matching purple and green shoes. She hoped this night would be more bearable than New Year's. Clubs really weren't her thing but maybe this one would be different. She could even leave early.

"Give me a couple of hours to get ready."

B y the time Alex pulled into her garage, her energy was low. She lacked enthusiasm for the night ahead of her. She enjoyed hanging out with her friend but Alex felt like she had some unfinished business to take care of first. After she pushed the remote to let her garage door down, Alex pulled out her phone and dialed Nathan's number. The phone rang and rang until his voicemail came on. She hung up. She wanted to talk to him, not leave a message for him to ignore.

She sighed and gathered her purse and box to take inside of the house. Before she could step outside the car, her phone rang. Alex set the box down and grabbed her phone. It was Nathan. She put her finger on the screen and slid it down.

"Hello?"

"Hi, Alex. You called me."

"Yes." She paused for a moment, suddenly drawing a blank on what to say next. "How are you?"

"I'm all right."

Alex cleared her throat. "Nathan, I'm calling because I wanted to talk to you."

"Yeah. I was thinking about calling you today," Nathan said.

Well, why didn't you? "Izzy and I are going somewhere shortly but, afterward, is it okay if I come over?"

"Sure."

"Okay. I'll be there later tonight," she said.

When they hung up, Alex felt a little bit better. She didn't know how her talk with Nathan would turn out but they had to get a better consensus on the relationship. Maybe he only saw this as a short-term affair. She did not see it that way. She was thirty-five. Alex had no time to play around and, though she didn't want to put pressure on him, she certainly wanted and needed to know where she stood. Alex picked up her purse and a box of job fair supplies. Temporarily pushing the situation out of her mind, she went in her house and proceeded to get ready for her night out with Izzy.

•••

Alex's heart almost stopped when she saw the neon lights and brick building. She and Izzy pulled up to Spears, the same club she and Nathan had gone to a couple of weeks ago. The same club where she met A.J., his unsavory friend. Alex looked around as if searching for an escape route.

"What's wrong?" Izzy asked.

"This is the club."

"Yeah, the new one I was telling you about. Remember?" Izzy asked.

"No. This is the one Nathan took me to. You know the one where A.J. performs."

"Oh!" Izzy covered her mouth. "My bad, Alex. You never told me the name of it."

"I didn't remember. Great. What if he's here?"

"We're in luck. There aren't any performers scheduled tonight. Just a DJ," Izzy said.

"I don't know, Izzy." Alex wanted to believe her but, as she glanced over at the building, a gnawing feeling developed at the pit of her stomach.

"He's not here. This isn't a night for amateur performers. The only music played will be off the record. It'll be fine. C'mon, let's go."

Izzy popped out of the car and Alex slowly followed her. While Izzy bopped along carefree, Alex's mind ran down the list of worst-case scenarios. A.J. could end up seeing her across the room and confront her in front of everyone for snitching to Nathan about his slip up. She hated to cause a rift between the two friends but she wouldn't tolerate A.J. in her face either. Steam rose under Alex's face as she thought about the possible altercation. *Wait. Don't jump to conclusions. 1...2...3...*

Izzy interrupted Alex counting to five. "So, other than the A.J. issue, how are things going with you and Nathan?"

Alex's mood softened but only a little. "Um, it's kinda tough right now," she responded, trying not to allow herself to lapse into worry.

Izzy caught a glimpse of her friend's hesitance. "Why?" She sucked her teeth. "Don't tell me A.J. put that much of a damper on your relationship cuz he's not worth it."

"After that issue, we seemed to have come to terms with everything. We seemed okay but we fell out the other day." Alex sighed. "I don't know."

Izzy stared at her. "Every relationship hits a tough spot. This is yours but it's not time to give up. Not yet."

I can't believe it. What made Izzy so sure that everything would work out? Nobody can be that optimistic. Alex rolled her eyes. "I appreciate your support but this isn't exactly a slam dunk."

"No. I'm telling you, Alex. Nathan is the one. Watch what I tell ya." Izzy wagged her finger at Alex.

"What does that even mean?"

They approached the door where groups of people were scattered around talking. The big burly man behind the rope stared at them. "We're with the salon party," Izzy said as she showed her ID. He scanned the list. After spotting Izzy's name, he moved to the side to let them in. They entered the club and Izzy faced Alex to resume the conversation.

"It means that he's it. He's the man you'll marry."

"I still don't understand what has happened to make you so sure I should marry him."

"I don't know. Maybe it's the way you light up when you talk about him. Or maybe it's the fact that he's been so persistent in getting you back. Please tell me you can see this, Alex," Izzy said, rubbernecking through the crowd to find their party.

When it came to Nathan's gestures, he had impressed and affected her, though she didn't want Izzy to know it. She was still trying to keep her head above water with him. His presence soothed her Type-A soul and she enjoyed being with him but they had some serious kinks to work out of their relationship. She had no way of seeing whether they were headed down the aisle.

"I see his flowers, picnics and heart-to-hearts as a step in the right direction. A chance to see where things are going," Alex said, trying hard to maintain some objectivity. Deep down, she hoped that they would be able to work through things when they talked later.

Izzy chuckled. "Wow. You are amazing…And in denial. I want you to take notice soon." She playfully nudged Alex. "See? That's why I hate you. You always get what you want."

Laughter erupted from a group to their left. Alex and Izzy turned to see two women licking salt off the back of their hands and taking shots, while another three cheered.

"Thank God for babysitters. Right, Portia?" the loudest one asked.

One of the women who took a shot nodded.

"There they are," Izzy said, smiling and pointing.

They walked over to the booth. The loudest woman saw them approaching and smiled even wider.

"Hey! Glad you made it." She stood, towering over Izzy to give her a hug.

"Melinda, this is my best friend, Alex. Alex, this is Melinda. She's the owner of the shop."

The two women hugged. "It's good to meet you. Please, come join us," Melinda said, motioning toward the group with her burgundy nails.

Izzy and Alex sat down with the women.

"Why don't we go around the table and have everyone introduce themselves?" Melinda suggested.

The introductions started from the left with a woman dressed in yellow. "I'm Jill Thompson, I'm a stylist and I'm single."

Alex cocked her head to the side. She never understood that. What would make a woman talking to a group of women introduce herself as single without being asked? Out of all the things she could say about herself, Jill made sure they knew she was single. *What are we supposed to do? Introduce her to somebody.* Alex listened to the rest of the women describe themselves in similar terms: single, married, divorced. When her turn came, Alex cooperated so she wouldn't seem standoffish.

"I'm Alexis Carter. I'm a recruitment manager and I'm single."

For the next hour, the women, including Jill, Melinda, Karla, Ursula and Portia, drank alcohol and laughed at each other's raunchy jokes. Alex slowly nursed a Strawberry Daiquiri, preferring to stay lucid in case she needed to drive. By the way Izzy giggled exces-

sively—a telltale sign that she'd reached a "higher" state of mind—
she would probably need to take over driving duties.

The women were pleasant but Alex's mind kept drifting away to
Nathan. She wondered what he was doing. Unable to resist the
urge to find out, Alex excused herself to find a restroom. She could
go and then call Nathan before returning to the group.

"Excuse me. I'll be right back, you guys," Alex said, standing up
from the table.

As she walked toward the restroom sign ahead, she saw a long
line coming out of the door.

"Aww, man," Alex said.

The bartender looked up at Alex. "I don't know why they're
waiting in that line." He pointed upward. "The sign says there's
another restroom on the other side."

"Where?"

"Walk straight behind those tables and make a left at the booths
against the wall. It'll be down the hall on your right."

"Thanks."

Alex followed the bartender's instructions. She quickened her
step as she thought about hearing Nathan's voice again. She rounded
the corner near the booths only to run into a taller frame. She
leaned back against the wall to regain her footing.

"Ooh. Watch out. You all right?"

Alex stood up straight to answer and looked right into A.J.'s
face. Her stomach flip flopped. She saw red. "Yes, I'm fine." She tried
to brush past him before he could say anything else.

"Hey. Wait a minute. Haven't I seen you before?" A.J. asked.

Alex cringed. *Deep breath.* "I don't know what you're talking
about." She moved to the side again.

He held his hand out. "Yeah. You're the one messing with my

boy, right? I met you a couple of weeks ago. You came up here with Nathan."

She sighed. "Yes. I was here with him."

"Hey! What's up? You guys here now. I didn't see him."

"He's not here."

He leaned forward and spoke low. "You here with another dude? It's okay. I'm no snitch. Unlike you."

Alex scowled and placed her hand on her hip. She didn't trust him. As a matter of fact, she would probably have to call Nathan to make sure that A.J. didn't spread lies to him first. This is exactly what she was trying to tell Nathan. As long as A.J. was in the picture, they will have difficulty growing their relationship.

He held his hands up. "That's cool. I thought you might wanna keep your options open while your boy is preoccupied." A.J. looked her up and down.

"Why are you bothering me?" Alex asked.

He shrugged. "Cuz I hate to see such a pretty woman being played."

She squinted at him. "You don't know what you're talking about."

"Oh really? Then, why isn't he here with you now? He has to be somewhere. Right?"

A.J. pulled out his iPhone. He opened the camera function and ran through the pictures. When he reached one, he expanded it and showed the picture to her. It was a picture of Nathan all smiles with Clarissa and their son.

"Maybe he's over there," A.J. whispered.

At first sight of the picture, Alex's eyes stung. They stung so bad that they became blurry. She had a hard time focusing but it didn't matter; she knew what she was seeing. Struggling to recover, she took a deep breath.

"What is this supposed to mean?" Alex asked.

"What do you think it means?" A.J. asked. "Listen, why don't we stop wasting our time? Say you and me let bygones be bygones, get out of here and go somewhere we can get to know each other better?" He traced her sleeve with his finger.

Alex swallowed back nausea. She pushed past A.J. and all but sprinted to the restroom. She couldn't believe what she had seen. Here she'd believed that she and Nathan were getting somewhere in their relationship and all along he had other plans. She stopped in front of the bathroom mirror and placed her shaky hands on the light beige granite counter. How could she be so stupid?

Alex panted and broke out into a sweat. She grabbing a paper towel and patting her face, trying to calm the quake in her stomach. She pulled out her phone and dialed Nathan's number. It immediately went to his voicemail. *Again. I guess now I know why he's not answering.* He and Clarissa were probably together. She squeezed her eyes shut and tapped her fingers on the counter top as she waited for the voicemail to beep.

"Nathan. I can't believe you. I can't believe I fell for this again. You said you'd never do this to me again. Thanks for making a fool out of me. You're a real jackass."

She ended the call and leaned against the wall.

CHAPTER 30

Even in her tipsy haze, Izzy sensed something had gone wrong when Alex returned to the table. Alex played it down and excused herself for the night. Izzy ended up leaving with her but the two didn't talk much in the car. Alex focused on driving Izzy home, where she picked up her car and went home.

That night, Alex showered and laid in her bed awake for hours thinking about Nathan. She kept telling herself to go to sleep so she would be able to get up for her doctor's appointment the next day but she couldn't help thinking about the picture of Nathan sitting happily with his son and his ex. Or current. Alex pondered everything he'd ever said or did for her, looking for clues of his deception. When she thought about it, he did take a while to call her after she gave him her number. But he did eventually call. Then he stood her up on their first date. He did, however, make it up to her with flowers and another date. Earlier that evening, he didn't answer his phone but, then again, he did call her right back. And, of course, there was tonight at the club when she called him and he didn't answer. He must have been with her then.

Who was she kidding? Their relationship obviously had no potential. He'd lied to her. She could never trust him. In fact, she would have to break it off with Nathan. The very thought made her eyes well with tears of sadness. Although they were in the early stages of their reconciliation, she really did believe that they could work things out.

By the time Alex finally stopped thinking and fell asleep, her alarm clock buzzed her out of her slumber. She slapped it silent and peeked over her covers to see that the time was eight-thirty. She wanted to scream at the idea of having to get up but she had to make it to her appointment or pay the cancellation fee.

After scrambling two cheese eggs and downing some V8 Splash, Alex grabbed a book and headed out the door for the doctor. The sun beat down as if it was angry and Alex immediately began paying the price. The heat from the pavement engulfed her exposed legs as she stepped into her car. Even though the AC worked perfectly fine, it still felt awfully muggy for a February morning.

When she reached the St. Nicholas Medical Center, she searched for a place to park in the newly paved parking lot. She was grateful to find a spot so close to Building B but feared that it wasn't for visitors. There was no machine to dispense a ticket and no parking attendant to take her money. She didn't feel like paying for a parking ticket but she didn't want to drive all the way to the other side of the building to park in the garage, where she knew she would find a parking attendant.

Choosing to cast her fate to the wind, she turned her ignition off and opened her car door. Grabbing her purse, she walked as fast as she could in two-inch heels to Building B. Dr. Nguyen's waiting area seemed fairly light. *Good. Maybe I can get in and get out.* She walked across the light green carpet to sign in at the little, sliding window. The receptionist sat chopping it up with one of the medical assistants. Alex signed in and sat in one of the chairs. Since the coffee table to the right of the room had outdated magazines scattered all over it, she ignored them in favor of the book she brought with her.

Alex spent several minutes going in and out of her book before the nurse opened the side door and called her to the back.

"Ms. Carter?"

Alex pushed her book back into her purse and stood up. Once the nurse closed the door behind them, she began with the usual.

"What brought you in today?"

"I'm here for a follow-up on the headaches I had a few months ago."

"Are they better?"

"Yes, I haven't been popping any Ibuprofen or anything. I think I've improved."

"Have you started any other types of medication?" They walked into a small room with a sink and a scale.

"No," Alex said, sitting down next to the blood pressure monitor. She reached for her cell phone and turned it off.

"When was your last menstrual cycle?"

"Uh…" She shrugged. "About two and a half weeks ago."

"Which day?"

"It started on Sunday." Alex knew they always asked that question. She should have figured an answer beforehand but she never did.

The nurse took her blood pressure, temperature and weight. Then, she escorted Alex to another room where she told her the doctor would be in shortly. Alex pulled her book back out and read it until Dr. Nguyen came in, examining her chart.

When he looked up at Alex, he smiled as if she were an old friend. In some ways, she might be considered one. He'd been her doctor since she was fifteen years old.

"Hello, Alexis! How's it going this morning?"

"It's good."

"How's your head?"

"It's fine. I only had one headache a while ago after exercising for an hour on my treadmill. Other than that, no problems."

"How long did it take to subside?"

"Maybe forty-five minutes. It was morning and I hadn't eaten before exercising. So, it was probably hunger."

"But there were no other instances?"

"No."

He nodded and scribbled something in her chart. "It sounds like you're getting over the headaches but I will double check to make sure nothing is wrong."

Dr. Nguyen pressed his stethoscope to her back and instructed Alex to inhale and exhale. Then, he shed a small light in her nose and ear. "Everything sounds and looks good. The headaches were probably your body's way of telling you it's time for a little one." He chuckled.

Alex shook her head. Dr. Nguyen was the only person who could joke with Alex about being unmarried and childless. Somehow, he kept it from sounding like chastisement. It made her feel like somebody still believed she could become a mother. After her short laugh, she turned somber.

"I'm working on it, Dr. Nguyen."

"Oh, really? Are you with someone now?"

"Yes. I mean, no. Well, sort of." Alex sighed. She scooted to the edge of the little bed, "Dr. Nguyen, it's only getting later. If my relationship doesn't work out, what are my options?"

He placed her chart on the counter and took a seat on the rolling stool beside the bed. "You can still have a husband and children," he said.

She grimaced. "Yes, but in case the husband thing doesn't materialize, what else can I do?"

"Are you asking about artificial insemination or in vitro?"

"Yes."

Dr. Nguyen raised an eyebrow. "I'd rather your relationship work out."

You and me both. She ran her hand over her hair in frustration.

"Both procedures have varying success rates. Many times as low as five percent. You can still make it happen on your own," he said.

"I just thought I'd ask." Alex frowned.

He shot her a gentle smile and stood up. "To be honest with you, it would be easier for you to have a baby with someone you already know as opposed to searching for a donor *and* having the procedure."

She sighed. "Great."

"In the meantime, make sure you eat a little something before your stationary marathons and the next time I see you, I'll expect to hear that you're pregnant." Dr. Nguyen winked and exited the room.

How am I supposed to do that?

CHAPTER 31

When Alex walked outside the doctor's office, she stuck her hand in her purse in search of her cell phone. Once she retrieved it, she turned it back on and saw that Nathan had called her back three times during her doctor's appointment. She started to call him back but opted to disregard his calls. All the back and forth on the phone would be futile. If they were going to end their relationship, it was better to do so in person.

So, Alex threw her phone back into her purse and got inside her car. She reluctantly pulled out of the parking lot. Heaviness fell upon her. Her impending drive to Nathan's house felt like the end of a dream. The dream that one day she would have a husband and a child. She felt like he was her last hope—her last ditch effort to make that dream a reality. Now, as she pulled onto the expressway, she realized that she had to wake up and deal with the situation in front of her.

Nathan clearly had other priorities or concerns that didn't include her. Why else would it take him so long to call her back? She knew why. He was preoccupied with his ex. She had to fight off all memories of the warm moments they'd shared together in order to let him know that she would not be mistreated. That sounded easier than it actually was but, as Alex pulled into Nathan's driveway and turned off the ignition, she knew that she had to give it her best shot.

Instead of hopping out of the car, Alex sat, shaking. Dread filled her stomach. Looking at the door and knowing what she planned to do gave her so much anxiety that she could barely think straight. She'd been down this road so many times. Hoping for things to work out only to look disappointment in the face one more time. Tears rose to the surface of her eyes but she refused to let them fall. She had to face Nathan with dignity and self-respect.

Alex took a deep breath and looked at Nathan's house. Her heart sank as she thought things through. She could feel sweat gathering under her pores. She didn't know how to address everything without showing the same anger she had the night before but she had to figure it out. Exiting the car and walking to the front door, she sniffed and swallowed the lump forming in her throat. *C'mon, Alex. You can do this.*

When she reached the door, she knocked, holding back her earlier dread. She knocked on the door again. Within a few seconds, Nathan opened it. His eyes widened at the sight of her.

"Alex! Where have you been? I tried calling you," he said.

Seeing his face and hearing his voice caused anger to rise up within her again. She closed her eyes and tried to focus on the reason she came—to peacefully call their relationship off. *Breathe.*

"Are you okay? Why don't you come in?" He opened his door all the way and motioned for her to step in.

"Yes," Alex said, finally opening her eyes. "Uh, no. I mean, yes, I'm fine but can we go somewhere else?" She swallowed and tried to gain some control. She glanced up at the expectant look on his face.

"Sure. You want to go for a walk or go to a restaurant?"

"A walk is fine."

Nathan stepped back into his house, grabbed his keys and locked the door behind him. They strolled off his driveway and onto the sidewalk. Alex prepared for the next thing she would say but Nathan beat her to the punch.

"Sooo, what was up with that message you left me last night?" Nathan asked.

"I was upset," Alex said.

"Clearly. But what about?"

"About you and your half-hearted attempts to rebuild a relationship with me," Alex said.

Nathan shot laser beams at the pavement.

Alex sighed. "I don't think this is working out."

He turned to her and frowned. "I don't understand where all this is coming from. What do you mean?"

"I think that we should cool it." Her voice threatened to break but she forced her words out.

"Why? Because I'm still cool with A.J.?"

"No, because I don't want to keep trying to make a relationship work with someone who hasn't moved on from their past relationship."

He stopped walking. "But I told you that's over. I'm not seeing my ex anymore. The only reason we talk at all is for my son."

"I feel like you still have some unfinished business with her."

He shook his head. "This doesn't make any sense. Where are you getting this from?"

Alex thought about mentioning the picture but she didn't want to give him another chance to defend it. She didn't want this to go on and on every time something happened. *Enough is enough.*

"It doesn't matter. This is over." Alex raised her voice.

Nathan reached out and grabbed her hand. "Alex, listen to me. Don't do this. Are you sure there isn't something else I can do, we can do?" he asked.

She shook her head no.

He rolled his eyes. "This is unbelievable. If I was still into my ex, why would I go through the trouble of getting back with you?"

Alex narrowed her eyes. "I'm trouble now?"

Nathan sighed. "That's not what I meant."

"Since I'm so much trouble, maybe now you should go back to what you already know," Alex said.

As soon as the words escaped her, she quickly covered her mouth. *Someone you already know.* Dr. Nguyen's words began to come back to her. When she asked him about fertility treatments, he said it'd be easier for her to have a baby with someone she already knew. She knew Nathan. She could ask him to father her child regardless of whether they were together or not. *Why hadn't I thought of this before?*

She had to admit that it seemed farfetched and a little outlandish—the idea that Nathan would turn over his sperm to her like it didn't matter—but what else could she do? She'd been fighting a battle that it didn't appear she would win. She couldn't compete with the mother of Nathan's son for his affections. If he wanted her, Alex had no choice but to let him be with her. Maybe she could still salvage some part of her dream with a request for a child.

Alex fixed her lips to say what she wanted to say but a block stood between her brain and her mouth. She found herself thinking about what he would think and how he would respond. How could she expect him to give her this favor? Yet, she had to ask. It may be her last chance to get anything she wanted.

"I'm sorry, Nathan. I shouldn't have made that last comment." She paused. "It is hard to believe that you don't have any feelings for her anymore but I shouldn't have made that comment. There is, however, something you can do for me."

Nathan zeroed in on her. "What?"

Alex closed her eyes and blurted it out. "Give me a baby."

She stood still, afraid to open her eyes. She couldn't imagine what Nathan must have thought of her question and she couldn't bear to see his expression. *Wait. This is childish. I'm a professional. I can do better.* She decided to count to 5 and open her eyes. *1...2...3...4...5.*

She opened her eyes to see Nathan's blank expression. The little girl in her wanted to run and hide but that's not who she really was. Suddenly, the image of the actress Roxie popped into her head. She thought about Roxie's calm confidence during her interview. The actress remained proud of her decision, regardless of how it looked to others. Alex straightened her posture, stuck out her chest and looked Nathan straight in the eye.

"This might sound like a strange request but I was thinking. I'm not getting any younger and I want some things in life. I already have a home, a great job, good money. I want a chance at having a family and, even though we aren't working out, I was hoping..." She paused. "You would be willing to help me with that."

Nathan ran his hand over his face. "Wow."

"What does that mean?" Alex leaned forward, analyzing his face in search of an answer.

"It means...wow."

"Nathan, you don't have to do anything. Okay? I mean, you do but once it's here, I can take care of it," Alex added. The more she talked, the more confident she became in her request. She didn't want him to get bogged down in the details. She preferred to keep it simple. Maybe that would increase the chances that he would go along with it.

"Whoa! What are you saying? That you want me to give you the seed and disappear."

Alex stalled. She really wanted his cooperation. *Please don't be difficult.* "Well...what would you prefer?"

"If I'm gonna make a child, I would want to be a part of his or her life."

"In what capacity?"

A small, sarcastic laugh escaped Nathan's lips. "In every capacity."

Part of her wanted to roll into a ball over this new dilemma. She wanted to avoid being hurt by Nathan again but she wanted him to help her have a child. If he were to give her a child, he would want to stick around. She didn't know how she would handle that. The constant reminder of what she couldn't have might prove too much for her.

On the other hand, how was she supposed to walk away from the opportunity now? This might be her only chance to have a child. She had to push her emotions to the side to get what she wanted. She just wished it wasn't so hard.

She placed her hands over her eyes and squeezed them to hold back the tears. "Okay. So, what would you want in order to agree to this? What has to be in place?"

He stammered. "I... I would have to get visitation to start."

Alex sucked in a chest full of air and exhaled. "What else?"

"I'd want to bring the child around my family. I'd want the child to know its brother."

"Basically, you want a hand in the child's upbringing?"

Nathan frowned. "Well, yeah. Why wouldn't I?"

Alex turned to face ahead but he grabbed her arm.

"Wouldn't you want a father for your child?" Nathan asked.

"I don't know. If it has one, great. But if not, I can handle it."

He shook his head. "That's not fair."

Alex scowled at Nathan and shook her arm out of his grasp. "What are you trying to say?"

Nathan put his hands up. "I'm only saying that it's not fair to the child or you."

She rolled her eyes.

"You deserve a man that will be there to take care of and protect you both. Not donate his sperm and walk away."

Alex stared Nathan in the eye. "I'm going to do this. With or without you."

He stared back at her and bit his lip. "You're serious, huh?" he asked, in a low voice.

Alex crossed her arms.

He paused before answering. "All right. I'll do it."

CHAPTER 32

Although Nathan agreed to give her a baby, Alex felt unsettled about it the next day. She thought she'd be jumping up and down, feeling like she'd won some kind of victory but that wasn't the case. Nerves had replaced the determination she felt the day before. Unlike her usual go-getter attitude, she hadn't thought her spontaneous request all the way through. She just knew she wanted to do it. Now that she started this, she had to figure out how she and Nathan were going to pull it off.

Alex brushed her hair back in front of her dresser mirror, thinking about when they should conceive. It should probably be as quickly as possible to keep him from changing his mind. Now for the bigger question: how were they going to conceive? They hadn't talked about it yet and she didn't quite know how to broach the subject. She could go to the doctor and ask to be artificially inseminated but it seemed pointless. She'd be spending a lot of money to do something she could no doubt do for free.

But how would she get past the emotional element? Having sex with Nathan again would conjure up emotions that she'd rather bury. Even though she'd called off their relationship, she still wanted to be with him. Alex stared at her reflection in the mirror and shook her head. *Sticky. Sticky.* Her phone rang. She walked over to answer it.

"Hey, Alex." Nathan's somber voice came through the phone.

Alex frowned. "Hi, Nathan. Is something wrong?"

He cleared his throat. "No, um. I wanted to talk to you. Can you come over for dinner tonight?"

"Why?" A lump formed in Alex's throat. She sat down on her bed. "You're not..." She swallowed. "Changing your mind, are you?"

After a pause, Nathan responded. "No. I don't think so."

"You don't think so?" Alex raised her eyebrows.

"How are we gonna do this? What are we going to tell your family? My family? I said I would do it but this is kinda bugging me out."

Oh no. Alex gripped the phone tighter. Sure, she'd asked for a strange favor but she couldn't afford to have Nathan back out now. He couldn't. He gave her his word he'd do it. She had to make sure he went through with it. That's all she had: his word that he would help her become a mother. As scared as the situation made her, the negotiator in Alex had to come forth.

"Nathan, don't worry about it. Our families will take our lead. If everything is okay with us, it will be okay with them."

"Yeah," he mumbled.

"What time do you want me to come over?"

"Eight o'clock."

"Fine. I'll be there. You'll see. There'll be no problems."

Alex hung up with Nathan, determined to make a plan. She needed some talking points that she could use when she met with him. What were the advantages of him doing this? There were plenty of benefits for her but she couldn't think of many for him. The main thing is that he would be helping her. If he cared anything about her, this should be a plus. What were the disadvantages? For one, Alex wanted complete control. Maybe she should draw up a contract of things she's willing to compromise on and have it notarized. That might put him at ease. *I'll bring that up tonight.*

•••

As the orange street light cast a soft light over her car, Alex noticed the peaceful quiet of the neighborhood. It gave her an opportunity to think about what she wanted to say to Nathan first once she walked inside his house. She had to be prepared for all his doubts and objections. She'd gotten him to say yes. Now, she had to keep his answer yes.

You might as well get on in there. It's not going to get any easier. Alex opened her car door and stepped out. She smoothed out the blue and white Tessi Cotton Paisley skirt she'd matched with a white top. She'd put a lot of time and nervous energy into picking out clothes. Catching a glimpse of herself in the car window, she wondered if she had over dressed. Then again, she figured she couldn't go wrong with Ralph Lauren.

She rang the doorbell and Nathan answered after a couple of minutes. His eyes roamed over Alex quick enough to stay on pace but slow enough for her to notice them.

"Hey." He leaned forward and gave her a soft but firm hug. "Come in."

Nathan touched her arm and she turned right to see two lilac candles lit in the middle of his dining room table. Their radiant glow stretched over two place settings, a bottle chilled in a silver bucket and a crystal tray with chocolate covered strawberries. A long stem red rose lay beside one of the settings.

"Please." He motioned toward the dining room.

Her nerves kicked in. All of a sudden, her carefully laid out plan seemed useless. *What is he doing?* She wished she could figure it out but, right then, she couldn't call it. "What is this?" Alex asked with a little bit of panic creeping into her voice.

"A little something to de-stress from the day."

"Really, Nathan? What happened to 'we need to talk?'"

He chuckled at her imitation of him. "I sounded a little bother-some over the phone this morning but I'm calmer now. Don't I look calm?"

Nathan turned around, giving Alex a full view of his black slacks and crisp, white shirt. He looked a flawless blend of dressy and comfortable. He always did know how to put himself together well. "Yes." Alex nodded.

"Great. Let's have dinner." Nathan pulled out the seat for her and slid it back under her. He picked up the rose next to her table setting and handed it to her.

She smiled. "Thank you."

He smiled back. "You're welcome."

He walked to the kitchen and grabbed their plates. Steam floated above their steaks. He placed a plate in front of her and sat across from her with his plate.

"Looks good," Alex said.

"Thanks."

After picking up her knife and fork, Alex immediately dug in—to the reason she came. "So, what did you want to talk about?"

"Whoa! Wait a minute. Let's enjoy dinner. Chat a little. We have plenty of time to talk about everything else." He smiled.

She furrowed her brow, confused. Over the phone, he wanted to talk about their decision to have a baby. Now, he wanted to shoot the breeze. She didn't know what kind of game he was playing but she sure wished he would tell her what the rules were.

She fidgeted. "Okay. Fine." She blew on a piece of steak before biting into it.

Nathan nodded. "I didn't get to ask you yesterday but how did the job fair turn out?" He bit a piece of his steak.

Alex glanced over at his plate and couldn't help noticing the way he ate. Unlike Phillip's need to cut every single piece before taking a bite, he cut one or two pieces before sliding some on his fork. She smiled at the difference between the two men. "It went really well. We had over four hundred candidates show up. The employers looked pleased."

"I'll bet they were. That's awesome. I guess you and the guy don't have to worry about any layoffs."

Alex shrugged and sipped her Pinot Chardonnay. "I don't know. I'm not sure if we're out of the woods yet but the job fair's success was a major plus."

"Are you still concerned about it?"

"No, not really. It's the nature of the beast. I mean, corporate world."

He laughed. "Well, I know you'll come through."

She frowned. "How do you know that?"

"Because you're smart and you know what you want. A woman like you can't ever lose. And even if you started to lose, all you have to do is call me and I'd be there for you." Nathan's eyes penetrated her eyes as if he were reading her soul like a book. She looked down at the table, suddenly uncomfortable with his unwavering attention.

"Are you gonna argue with me?" Nathan asked.

"No." She took a sip.

He chuckled. "I didn't think so."

Unable to hold it back any longer, Alex inquired about his phone call. "What was the phone call about today?"

He dropped his fork back on his plate. "I knew you couldn't avoid it for long."

"You called me and said we should talk. I'm trying to get you to talk."

"What's the rush?"

"I want to make sure that…we're still gonna do this. That you'll still help me." Alex's voice dropped at the end. She didn't know what she would do if he changed his mind.

"Don't worry. I'm sorry if I gave you a scare today. I was sitting at my desk and thinking things over." He shrugged. "I had questions."

"Like what?"

He paused before clearing his throat. "What if you found another man and he and I start beefing? Would you take my child away from me to keep him happy?"

"No. Nothing like that would happen."

"How do you know?"

"Did it happen with Clarissa?" *Dang it, mouth.* As soon as she said that, she wished that she hadn't. His face fell. She had a hard time reading it. She didn't know whether he felt anger or hurt. She guessed a little of both.

"Nathan, this is an unconventional situation but I don't want you to have any concerns." She reached over and placed her hand on his. "I won't keep you from being in the child's life." She felt his energy lighten at her reassuring gesture.

They finally finished off dessert and Alex helped Nathan move the dishes to the kitchen.

"Do you want the rest of these strawberries?" she asked.

"Um, nah. They're yours." Nathan wiped his hands on his dish towel.

"Please take at least some of this. I can already feel the fat pockets filling up on my thighs."

Nathan sucked his teeth. "Whatever. You don't have no fat pockets nowhere."

Alex raised her eyebrows. "Yes, I do."

"No, you don't. Believe me, I know."

She shook her head, as if to shake off Nathan's intimate knowledge of her anatomy. Instead, she searched her brain for a distraction. Something to make their association seem friendly and light. "I saw earlier that there's a movie coming on at nine-thirty. It looked like it might be a good one. Did you wanna watch?"

"No, not really."

"Oh, okay," Alex said, sounding a little deflated.

"A movie is fine but," he said, slowly. "I have a surprise for you." Nathan cut his eyes at Alex.

She stretched her eyes. "What surprise?"

He nodded down the hall.

Alex hesitated, wondering what he had up his sleeve. Nathan nodded again and she walked toward the hallway, measuring each step. She almost turned back around to ask him for more details about the surprise but stopped at the sight of rose petals on the wooden floor. The petals formed a straight line from where she stood to the last room on the left. Butterflies formed in her stomach, as she followed the trail. Alex inched toward the bedroom door and pushed it open.

The petals that led her to the room ended at a large rose petal heart on the king-sized bed. She stepped in farther and opened her mouth to talk but no words came out. Alex caught her breath when she realized what this meant. *Nathan intends to make the baby tonight!*

In the midst of her surprise, she didn't hear Nathan walk into the room and close the door behind him. He grabbed her hand. She turned to face him.

"You know it's ironic that you asked me about having a baby." He backed her up. "Do you remember when you used to fall asleep at my place and when you woke up, I was always watching you sleep and you would ask why?"

"Yeah. You told me you liked memorizing my face in case somebody kidnapped me." She rolled her eyes.

Nathan chuckled. "That was partially true. The other reason was…" He cupped her face with his hands and positioned it upward so that she would look up at him. His eyes pierced her eyes like laser beams. "I was imagining our baby with your eyes." Nathan kissed her eyes. "Your nose." He kissed her nose. "Your lips." Instead of kissing her lips, Nathan ran his tongue from the bottom to the top of her lips.

The wet sensation of his tongue over the center of her lips sent her senses into shock overdrive. In that moment, her feelings for Nathan—feelings that she wanted to deny—caused an avalanche of intense passion. She stared up at the towering force of emotion, knowing that she could not hide from it or outrun it. Even if she wanted to leave, she could not now.

She hadn't expected them to try for a baby that night but Alex was relieved to know that he hadn't changed his mind. Still, her feet remained rooted to the floor for more than the baby. Despite her attempts to develop indifference toward Nathan and dump him *again*, she had to face facts; she really did want him.

He backed her up to the bed and slid his hands up her skirt. Chills ran down her spine as he pulled her panties to the floor. She fell backwards onto the bed but her mind and her body stood at complete attention, anticipating what came next.

At first, Nathan's kisses were soft and subtle. He planted them on her inner thigh, slowly moving upward. He eventually moved to the middle where his tongue began dancing around her button. Alex's earlier, internal upheavals had almost made her forget how attentive he could be to her physical needs. While Nathan demonstrated his intimate knowledge of her, she whimpered, twisted and turned uncontrollably.

Nathan pulled away before she could completely lose it. Somewhat frustrated, Alex began removing his clothes. They'd come too far not to close the deal. She wasn't worried about his supposed relationship with his ex or their broken past. Her mission consumed her full attention. So, she rolled over and placed herself on top. He humored her tender touches and passionate kisses but quickly put her on her back again.

Alex's eyes narrowed as she searched his face for reasoning. Without saying a word, Nathan brushed the hair away from her eyes and looked deep into them. He pushed her left leg over his shoulder. As he pushed himself inside her, Alex closed her eyes and let go.

CHAPTER 33

Quiet darkness gave way to the sound of pots and pans banging. Light cut through the room like razors through the window blinds. Alex popped up in the bed with her eyes stinging from the rays. The smell of fried turkey bacon took her nose hostage. She swung her legs over the bed and realized she had no clothes on. She quickly shoved her legs back under the covers and pulled the foreign sheets up to her neck. Little lines of worry set up shop across her forehead as she tried to remember how she'd gotten there. Then, the night before came back to her. Nathan. Dinner. Chardonnay. Flowers. Bed. Along with the flood of memories came a new set of worries.

Last night sealed Nathan's promise to help her get what she wanted: a baby. But after such a passionate night, Alex expected complete awkwardness between them. The truth was even though they'd made an arrangement, the previous night didn't feel like an arrangement; it felt more like an invitation. Despite her attempt to reject their reconciliation, Nathan seemed to be opening his arms to her, consistently welcoming her back to him.

Alex stifled a smile. Some part of her felt giddy about the current direction of their relationship; another part of her still fretted over his potential loyalty to her. She closed her eyes and willed herself to stay in the moment. Alex willed herself to be happy. After all, the last couple of months had been a little rough on her. It was about time something, somewhere made her happy, even if only for a few minutes.

She heard the microwave beep in the kitchen and wrecked her brain for what to say when she walked in there. Her current excitement did not mean she had to bounce in there like a giggling school girl. She could comment on how good the food smelled but after that, then what? Alex heard more rummaging and decided she'd better go to the kitchen.

Alex took a quick trip to the bathroom, wrapped her body in his terrycloth bathrobe, and then, crept down the hall. She saw Nathan, shirtless in pajama pants, facing the range. He twisted his head to the right, caught a glimpse of her frame and turned. He greeted her with a smile that could melt polar caps. Not the type of smile you give someone you're tolerating for the sake of an arrangement. Suddenly, Alex's worries from a few minutes ago dissipated. She returned a smile to him.

"Morning!" Nathan cheered. He walked over, wrapped his arms around her waist and gave her a long, lingering kiss. His kiss tasted like cinnamon and syrup. Alex smiled, interrupting it.

"What are you smiling about?"

"Couldn't wait for me, huh?"

"I was taste testing. I had to make sure it was right for you." He smiled again.

"Is it?"

"Perfect, if I do say so myself."

"Great." Alex squeezed him and walked over to the stove. Nathan cooked bacon, French toast and omelets. She eyed the food hungrily. "Wow! You're a regular Emeril, huh?"

"I can make it do what it's supposed to do."

She lifted an omelet out of the pan and placed it on a plate. "Have you ever thought about becoming a chef or something?"

"No."

"Why not? You seem to have a real knack for this."

"I might have a knack for it but I don't think I have a passion for it."

"What do you consider passion?" She bit into a piece of bacon.

"When you get up in the morning and can't wait to do something. I don't have that for cooking."

"What do you have passion for?"

"A couple of things, I guess. Helping people," Nathan said.

She nodded. "In what way?"

"I like helping them take care of a need."

"Food is a need." She smiled.

Nathan smiled and shook his head. "Not the need I'm interested in. What about you? Do you have any dreams?"

Alex brought her plate and a glass of apple juice to the kitchen table. "You already know my dream."

Nathan sat down next to her. "Is that all that you want? A child?"

"You don't understand," she said.

"I want to. Explain it to me," Nathan said, sitting down at the table.

"I've always been able to accomplish whatever I wanted to. A family is the one thing that I wanted to do but haven't done. Everything else is pretty much taken care of or at least on the way."

"Why do you want a kid?"

"Because I have to grow and evolve. Live for something other than myself. Being a mother, a nurturer is that next step for me." She shrugged. "A career isn't everything."

Nathan nodded. "I agree but what about love, a husband? You don't want that?"

"Of course, I do. That was a part of the full dream."

"Then, why are you giving up on that?"

A couple of unpleasant emotions hit Alex at once. The first was anger. On some level, she wondered how dare Nathan insinuate that she was giving up on having a full family. She didn't want to let go of her family dreams; she felt like she had no choice. The other emotion that troubled her was sadness. If she had a child on her own, she would wake up day and night to tend to the child alone. The happiness she felt when she woke up in Nathan's bed would only be a memory. She was keenly aware that she would not be getting all that she wanted and it troubled her to the core.

She blinked back her emotions. "I'm not giving up. I'm taking matters into my own hands."

Alex had only eaten two thirds of the food on her plate. Although it was good, talking about where she was in her life and where she was trying to go took her appetite away. Nathan looked down at her plate.

"If you'd waited, I would have brought some to you."

She shrugged. "It's okay. I don't mind coming out to get it."

"What? You don't like breakfast in bed?"

"It's fine but I don't mind getting it myself," Alex said.

Nathan stared at her stiff body language. "Well, here. I'll throw the rest of it out for you."

He reached for her plate but she picked it up before he could grab it. "I got it." She walked into the kitchen and threw it away.

Nathan leaned back in his chair. "So, you don't want someone to ever do things for you or take care of you?"

"I don't mind someone doing things for me but why do I need to be taken care of?" Alex asked, while still scraping food out of the plate.

"Everybody does on occasion. Like when they're sick." He stared at the table. "You should let me do things for you sometimes," Nathan whispered.

"I'm good."

Nathan ran his hand over his face. "Um. What are we gonna do when you're pregnant?" he asked, turning in his chair.

"What do you mean?"

"Are people going to assume we are together or what?" His once lighthearted tone had been replaced with a serious one.

Alex noticed and searched for a response. "Yeah, but we can pretend that we broke up after she gets here, if that's okay with you?" She glanced over at him.

The high that Alex woke up to had disappeared. Instead of riding the sky, her feet were back on solid ground. She and Nathan were back to the situation at hand. They made a deal to go through with something and that's what they were there for. No matter how she felt about the roses and their night together, she had to remember that they made an arrangement. Nathan hadn't forgotten.

He nodded and tapped his thumb on the table. "Okay. Sounds like a plan."

CHAPTER 34

Alex battled the morning traffic with her mind preoccupied. Since she departed from Nathan's house, she hadn't talked to him. She wasn't sure what that meant on his end but she was hesitant to call him. Each time she reached for the phone, she found herself drawing her hand back. At the same time, she almost felt like she should call him. After all, he was doing her a favor. He agreed to help her have a baby. A thought struck her. What if their last time together didn't take? Were they going to go back and keep trying? *There goes another issue you haven't thought all the way through.* Funny. This seemed like such a good idea when she initially mentioned it to him. It was turning out to be harder than she expected.

But did that mean she should quit? Completely give up on her dream to have a child? Alex shook her head. She couldn't. She refused to spend the rest of her life alone with no family. No nothing. Phillip was right. It would get very lonely with her and no one else to care about her. She couldn't do that to herself. She deserved better than that.

Soon she would have to work up the nerve to call Nathan. She'd forgotten her necklace over his house. If she used the necklace as an opening, maybe that would make the conversation flow easier. *I'll call him later.*

Alex pulled into her office parking lot and walked into the building intent on pushing her personal thoughts to the back of her mind. "Morning, Betty," Alex said, only glancing the secretary's way.

"Good morning, Alex," Betty sang. "You're needed in conference room E at ten o'clock."

Alex stopped midstride and turned to Betty. "Why?"

"Because you guys have an emergency meeting."

"Oh, great. Do you know what it's about?"

"Not really." Betty shook her head.

Alex started walking toward the elevator.

"Have fun," Betty chirped in Alex's direction.

She entered her office and dropped her briefcase on the desk. While her computer booted up, Alex reviewed her calendar for the day. The previous day, she'd started making calls to the employers that participated in the job fair. She wanted to thank them for making it a success. She had only been able to call a couple of them yesterday. She thought she might finish up today.

The next on her list to call was Mr. Allen at PharmScope. He had been the hardest to sign on for the fair. When she counted the hires during the event, PharmScope seemed to have hired a large number of people. She wanted to make sure he was satisfied with the end result. Alex picked up the phone and dialed Mr. Allen's number—only half expecting him to answer, given his busy schedule.

"Hello?" Mr. Allen's voice sounded alert at the other end of the phone.

"Mr. Allen. This is Alex Carter. How are you?"

"I'm excellent. I was talking about you yesterday."

"Really?"

"I was telling the staff about how wonderful the job fair went. Everyone agrees that you guys did a magnificent job."

Alex smiled. "I'm glad that you all are pleased. Did you get the fifty candidates you were looking for?"

"Better. We were able to hire seventy-eight."

"That's awesome. Keep me posted on their progress. Let me know if you have any other staffing needs."

"We may be hiring again for a different department in another month or so. I'll definitely give you a call once we are ready to go."

"I'll look forward to it."

Alex hung up with Mr. Allen feeling vindicated. She did what she set out to do. She, with Dan's help, created a first rate job fair to improve the agency's numbers. Alex felt like she could do anything. She smiled and turned back to her computer to check her emails. Her email inbox was still fairly full when the clock struck nine forty-five but Alex needed to cut the reading short in favor of getting to the emergency meeting on time. *I wonder what it's about.* She shrugged and broke away from her computer.

Alex arrived at the conference room with eight minutes to spare. She took a seat while others stood around talking. Perhaps she should have been as social as everyone else but she found her mind wondering back to Nathan. She secretly started tossing around ideas about what to say to him when she called. Despite the chit-chatter, she remained unaware of her own surroundings.

"Hey, Alex," Dan said, dropping into the seat next to her. Before now, Dan would have sat on the opposite side of the table but since they partnered for the job fair, they had garnered respect for each other. He now thought nothing of sitting beside her—his new-found ally.

She glanced over her shoulder. "Hello, Dan. How are you?"

"Good. What about you?"

"I'm well. I talked to Mr. Allen at PharmScope this morning. He was very pleased with the fair."

"That's the general consensus. The sponsors were ecstatic with the turnout. I gave them a free gift card as a token of our appreciation," Dan said.

Alex nodded. "Nice touch."

"Thank you." Dan narrowed his eyes at Alex. "Are you okay?"

"Yeah, I'm fine. Why?"

"I don't know. You look like you have a lot on your mind."

"I'm fine. Really." She shifted her weight in her seat.

Dan leaned toward her. "C'mon, Alex. You can talk to me. It can't be the fair; we did too good a job on that."

She sighed. "I don't wanna talk about it."

"Is there trouble at home?"

She scowled at him and sat back in her chair.

"Wait a minute. Is it the guy in the parking lot?"

"What guy?" Courtney asked, plopping down next to Dan.

Alex thought fast. "One of the HR reps that attended our fair. Yeah, he complained the whole time. Right, Dan?" She squinted at Dan.

"Yes, we had a hard time keeping him quiet but he was a happy camper when we gave him pizza," Dan said, retaining eye contact with Alex.

"Oh. So, the job fair paid off?" Courtney asked.

"Yes," Alex and Dan said in unison.

Courtney nodded. "Cool. Congrats."

Having momentarily satisfied her curiosity, Courtney stood up and darted off to dig into someone else's Kool-Aid.

Alex realized she'd been holding her breath and exhaled. "Let's drop this. Okay?"

"Okay but if you decide that you want to talk about something—anything, I'm here." Dan gave Alex an earnest look.

She nodded, as the meeting began.

"Good morning, everyone," Mr. Sims said. His voice filled the room with an unusual zealousness. "I've called this meeting because we have great news that I couldn't wait to share."

The staff listened, waiting to hear the news. Despite Alex's somber mood, he had her on the edge of her seat. After building them up, he finally told them.

"I'm happy to report that our placement numbers are up twenty-five percent."

Everyone clapped. Mr. Sims raised his hand for them to hold off.

"Much of the increase came from the job fair we held last week. The companies that participated in the fair hired a hundred and forty-six new employees. And the two people responsible for the new hires are Alexis Carter and Dan Reece!"

The staff hooted and hollered. Dan stood up and pulled Alex up with him to bask in the applause. Her pensive demeanor momentarily lifted. As she looked around to see her peers clapping for her, she felt a little more at ease. The concerns she had when she entered the office that morning seemed smaller and more manageable. *I'll work this out. I always do.* Things were headed in the right direction. For once, she believed it. She found herself chuckling as the staff cheered for her and Dan.

CHAPTER 35

After a pretty good day at work, Alex decided to treat herself to a hairdo. Luckily for her, one of the perks of having a friend as a hairstylist was being able to stroll into the shop without an appointment and get serviced quickly. Sure, it wasn't always the nicest thing to do, especially when people were waiting but Alex tried not to hold others up for too long.

She merely wanted to talk to her friend in addition to getting her ends trimmed. One thing was for certain, she wasn't ready to go home yet. As she pulled up to Perfect Hair by Melinda, she realized she wasn't ready to call Nathan either but she planned to do it.

Her nerves began to attack her all over again as she pulled out her phone and prepared to dial his number. She had to swim through a myriad of emotions to resist the urge to put the phone back down.

"Hello," Nathan answered on the fourth ring.

"Hi, Nathan. It's Alex. How's it going?" She cringed at her own inane attempt at cordiality.

"Great," he answered quickly with no apparent enthusiasm. He also lapsed into a strange silence.

Okay. This is awkward. "Good. Um. I have a question. When I came over there, I had on a diamond necklace and I haven't been able to find it. Have you found it?"

"Yes, it's at home."

Alex sighed. "Awesome! I was hoping it would be there. If I'm not there to pick it up today, I'll drop by tomorrow. Is that okay?"

"That's fine. Whenever you want to get it is fine." Another silence followed.

Alex cringed again. The initial hope she had that the necklace would be a good conversational opener had fallen flat. She wouldn't describe Nathan's tone as cold but he wasn't as warm as usual, which made it hard for her to handle him. She didn't know what to say to someone who had always treated her with so much kindness, no matter what the situation. "Um. Okay. So, how's everything?"

"Fine. How's everything with you?"

"Good. My boss recognized Dan and me at a meeting today for the job fair."

"Congratulations," Nathan said.

On that note, Alex didn't know what else to say. She decided to end the conversation for now. "Well, I'll see you later."

"All right. Bye."

With that, he hung up. Alex stared at her phone. *What does this mean?* Why had their interactions become so awkward? It seemed like there was something that Nathan wanted to say but decided against it. Never had their interactions felt so forced. It seemed like the plan that she thought made a lot of sense had produced some other complications.

Alex finally put her phone away and stepped out of her car. When she walked into the shop and saw Izzy, she quietly thanked God for friendships. She headed toward the third chair, where Izzy was working on a weave ponytail. When Izzy saw her, she grinned.

"Hey. Haven't talked to you in a few. What's up?" Izzy asked.

"Oh, girl. Life," Alex said. Her conversation with Nathan remained fresh in her mind and heavy on her heart. She plopped down in the stylist chair next to Izzy.

"We've all got that going on. Things should be easy now that the job fair is over, right?"

"Yeah, that's a relief."

"Then, all is good. However, I did have a question. What happened the other night at Spears? I don't remember much but one minute we were sitting down having a good time and the next minute we were almost at my house." Izzy spun her client around to face the mirror.

Alex sighed and shook her head. "It was crazy."

The client stood up and reached into her pocket for Izzy's money. "I'll call you later this week to schedule my next appointment," the client said as she started toward the door.

"Okay. Talk to you later," Izzy called back to her.

While Izzy put her money away, Alex slid into her chair.

"So, what happened? I was too tipsy to remember," Izzy said.

"When I broke from you guys to go to the restroom, I ran into A.J."

"Oooh." Izzy turned around to face Alex.

Alex spun the chair around to face Izzy. She pointed at her. "I told you we were going to run into him."

"Hey! What were the odds? I figured he had no reason to be there. I didn't know he hung out in the club all the time," Izzy said.

"Well. Apparently, he does."

"What did he say?"

"He hit on me again."

"Naturally."

"He also told me that Nathan is still seeing his son's mother."

Izzy rolled her eyes. "This guy is so getting on my nerves." She sat down on her stool. "How does he know what Nathan's doing?"

"He showed me a picture of them together."

"Him and her?"

"And the child," Alex added.

Izzy raised her eyebrows. "Well, maybe it was a family photo that they took together."

"This didn't exactly look like something they took in a photo studio."

"Then, maybe it's old. And how did he end up with it?"

Alex shook her head. "I don't know. I wasn't trying to stick around to ask him. I wanted to get out of there."

"Aww. Have you told Nathan yet?"

"Not exactly."

"What do you mean?"

"I don't know if it's really worth it to tell him. I mean, he'll probably deny any wrongdoing, right?" Alex asked.

"Yeah, but at least everything will be out in the open. You can't hold that in. You guys have to talk about it or else it'll stay lurking in the back of your mind and you won't be able to move on together," Izzy reasoned.

"That's the thing. Should we be moving on together? If this is going to happen over and over again every other month, is it worth it?" Alex's heart almost broke thinking about the agony of having to relive trust issues with Nathan repeatedly.

"I really think this is the work of someone who is jealous of his friend and wants to ruin his relationship. I don't see this as deception on Nathan's part." Izzy picked up a Styrofoam cup and sucked soda through the straw.

Alex shrugged.

"I know one thing." Izzy stepped off her stool.

"What?"

"I sure hope you don't plan to give up on this relationship."

Alex swallowed. *What would Izzy say if she knew I already had?*

"Seriously. I've never seen you happier. You're smiling more. You look relaxed." She circled her finger around Alex. "And I've known you long enough to know when you're going through changes."

"And what changes am I going through?"

Izzy stopped for drama. "The change of love."

"Oh my gosh." Alex hung her head.

"You know I'm right. I truly believe that Nathan is good for you, Alex. I only hope that you realize it before you make a big mistake."

Alex's mind flashed back to her night with Nathan and their baby plan. From the tone of Nathan's voice over the phone, she wondered if she'd already made a big mistake. She still hadn't told anyone about their arrangement and truth was Alex didn't expect people to understand, not even Izzy. Though they were best friends, Alex didn't want to have to defend her decision. She wanted to go forth with her plans without giving anyone a chance to tell her not to. Despite Izzy's optimism about Alex and Nathan's relationship, Alex only wanted to make sure she made the most of the situation because she couldn't bank on his commitment to her. She couldn't trust her heart or feelings the way Izzy wanted her to; So, Alex had to make the baby plans. And most importantly, she had to keep them to herself.

CHAPTER 36

Alex yawned while she stood in the short line for the copier. Hers had broken and the tech department wouldn't get to it for another day or so. In a way, she didn't mind getting up to walk around; she'd been yawning for the past couple of hours. Good thing she planned to leave right after this quick run. She didn't know how much longer she would hold up. Alex had crossed her arms and faced forward when she felt a tap on her shoulder. Alex turned around to see Romero. *Aww. I'm not in the mood for him right now.*

She stifled her initial reaction and forced herself to greet him with a smile. "Hello, Romero."

"Hello, Alex. How have you been?"

Alex's mind automatically scanned the last few weeks of her life. Although these thoughts took her through a number of complex emotions within a couple of seconds, she betrayed her inner up-heavals with her usual professional confidence. "Great. What about you?"

"Awesome!" He smiled. "I wanted to congratulate you on the job fair."

"Thank you. The caliber of candidates exceeded my conservative expectations."

"Umm. You and Dan really pulled it off. Was it as hard working with him as you thought it would be?" He chuckled.

"No. It actually wasn't. He was prepared and he worked really hard. I was very impressed."

Romero raised his eyebrows and nodded. He stared at her without a word and, for a minute, Alex feared she would have to rebuff another proposed date. She kept talking.

"Surely you know what it's like to work with someone that you initially underestimated. You may have even been a bit of jerk to them," she added.

"Yeah but, according to my girlfriend, I can be pretty hard to deal with anyway." He laughed.

Alex could not resist raising her eyebrows. *Girlfriend. Finally.* She tried to cover her surprise. She could only replace it with relief. "Well, I guess she would know." She chuckled.

As if on cue, the person at the copier picked up their papers and walked away.

"Talk to you later," she said to Romero.

Alex trotted to the machine, finished her copies and darted to her office to get ready to leave.

When she walked toward the front door of the building, she glanced at the lobby clock. *Four thirty-two.* If she hurried, she could get to Nathan's house and pick up her necklace within the five o'clock hour. Alex didn't feel like going to his house after Izzy finished her hair yesterday. She decided to wait and get her necklace today. At least, that's what she wanted to tell herself. She was really postponing more awkward exchanges. She'd been tired all day but she didn't want the necklace to go missing so she figured she'd better pick it up.

All she had to do was go to his house, pick up the necklace, go home, cook, eat and stretch out. It sounded like a plan to her. She briskly walked to her car, balancing her briefcase, purse, mug and car keys.

When she was almost to the car, she pointed her keychain and pressed the unlock button. "Click, Click."

Alex hit the button on her car key chain again.

"Click, Click."

What is wrong with this thing? Every time she tried to unlock her door, it locked back. She exhaled, trying to calm herself down. *All I want to do is get my necklace, go home, eat and sleep.* She placed her briefcase and mug on the hood of her car. Alex grabbed her phone to call Nathan.

He answered with a buzzer sound in the background. "Hello?"

"Hi, Nathan. It's Alex."

"Hey. What's up?"

"I was going to stop by your house to pick up my necklace but I can't. I'm having car trouble," she said, still hitting her unlock button with no success.

"Oh, I'm not home yet. I don't get off until six."

Alex slapped her palm on her forehead. "Oh. Sorry. I didn't realize that."

"What's wrong with your car?"

"When I try to unlock the door, it keeps locking back on me."

"If you unlock it with your key, will it stay unlocked long enough for you to get in and drive?"

Alex tried unlocking the door with the key. It allowed her to open the door and get in. She cranked up the engine.

"Yes."

"Okay. Drive over here to my dealership. I'll let one of the technicians know you're coming."

"But they're not a Lexus dealer?"

"The used part of the dealership sells Lexus."

"I hope it doesn't cost an arm and a kidney." Alex trusted Nathan's judgment on cars but she needed to be prepared.

"I'll take care of it."

Alex breathed a sigh of relief. "Thanks. Okay. I'm on my way."

It started to drizzle as she entered the expressway. Luckily, the roads were still dry and traffic had remained clear. Within thirty minutes, she pulled into Bayside Dealership where a tall, slender man with glasses emerged from a mini office. He leaned over, as she rolled down her window.

"Are you Alex?" he asked.

"Yes."

"I'm Chuck. Nathan asked me to see about your car. What seems to be the problem?"

Alex explained her lock problem. The words spilled out of her mouth so fast she was afraid they were jumbling all together but she had to release her frustration. Chuck seemed to understand her anyway.

He nodded. "You either need a new keychain or there might be a problem with the door latch. Is this the first time this happened?" He inspected the door handle.

"Yes. Well, no. It happened months ago but it went away. I didn't go to the dealership because I hadn't had any other problems and thought they wouldn't be able to do anything about it without seeing the lock stick."

He nodded again. "That's generally the case. I'll take it to the back and figure out which it is. The waiting area is right through those doors. You should be out of here in an hour."

Although she preferred to be a sleep in an hour, she was happy the car would be fixed. Alex smiled. "Thank you."

She grabbed her purse and briefcase before scurrying off to the waiting room. Four black couches surrounded a brown coffee table littered with magazines. Two of those couches were back to back.

CNN blared from the plasma TV. Alex walked around the corner and found an area without a TV—a much quieter space. It housed chairs and a softer couch. Figuring she might as well make good use of the time, she sat in one of the chairs and rummaged through her case.

At first, she struggled to focus. The need to sleep seemed to overpower her at times but, after she purchased a Coke from the vending machine, she could finally concentrate. About forty-eight minutes in, she was deep in thought, reading through the weekly numbers for her team. They were doing even better than usual. While filling in the numbers for her reports, she didn't notice anyone walk into the area.

"Alex."

She almost jumped up in midair.

Nathan placed his hand on her shoulder and sat next to her. "Sorry. I didn't mean to scare you."

"No, it's fine. I was lost in thought. That's all."

He nodded. "Chuck said that it was the keychain and the key latch. So, they've replaced both and it should work now."

"Thank you." She smiled at him.

He nodded. "They're ready for you up front." Nathan stood up and helped her with her briefcase.

When they walked up to the cashier's desk, the cashier informed her of the price. They only charged her for a percentage of the parts, instead of making her pay for the parts and the service. She appreciated Nathan helping set this up for her. If he hadn't stepped in, she would have found away to get her car fixed but it might have taken longer or cost more.

While she paid for the service, she thought about how caring and supportive Nathan was. It reminded Alex of how he'd always treated her. She wondered if things were going to return back to normal for them. Maybe they would be on better speaking terms and better able to work out any differences they had.

She wanted them to get along. At this point, Nathan was the only man she could imagine as father to their child. She could see him picking the child up from school. Taking them to the playground. He'd make a great father. As she thought about his warm personality, she smiled. She wondered if she really wanted him solely as a sperm donor. It would be nice to have him in her life in a more complete way. Maybe she'd jumped the gun letting him go.

Nathan stood beside Alex while she obtained her car keys. His cell phone rang and he answered. He walked off to the side while Alex signed her receipt for the cashier. The lady behind the desk gave Alex a smile and encouraged her to come back. As Alex walked up behind Nathan to thank him again, she could make out his conversation.

"No, Clarissa. I don't have time right now. I can come over later."

Alex's heart dropped down to her stomach. She felt like someone had poked a pin in her balloon. Thoughts of a future with Nathan were obliterated as quickly as they formed. She wanted to think this through but her heart wouldn't allow it. Instead, she reacted.

Realizing that he held her briefcase, Alex grabbed it and brushed past him. She stormed out the glass door.

"Alex! Alex!"

She continued to stomp toward her car. *If I can make it to my car and drive off, I'll be fine.*

Nathan reached her a few steps shy of her car. He grabbed her arm. "Alex? Where are you going?"

"What difference does it make?"

He frowned at her and shook his head.

"Yeah, I don't know either. You couldn't even wait until I left to talk to her."

"She called me. I wasn't aware I was supposed to ignore it."

"You should have, while you were around me. That's rude!"

"What's rude is bolting off like that! You trying to make me look crazy at my job after I helped you," Nathan shouted.

"I didn't ask you to do that. If you didn't want to do it, you shouldn't have bothered."

"Okay. Next time, I won't."

"That's fine with me. I don't need your help."

"That's not the way it looks to me. You're the one asking me to give you a baby."

Alex felt like doubling over at the verbal punch to her stomach but she stood like a stone.

"You agreed." She pointed at him.

Nathan walked closer to her. "After you begged me."

She scowled. "No. You begged me, Mr. Flowers and Picnics. I shouldn't have given in." Alex pressed the keychain and opened her car.

"Like you had so many other choices!" Nathan yelled over her engine.

Alex sped off. Boiling hot tears poured down her face. She dabbed them with the back of her hand.

"What now? What am I supposed to do now?"

She blinked a few times to clear the watery film covering her pupils.

"No man. No baby." She sobbed. "Why does this keep happening to me? Why can't I get this right?"

CHAPTER 37

"**O**uch," Alex said as she placed her fingers to her temples—the point of the pounding inside her head. She'd been suffering all morning. So much so that she'd avoided breakfast and run straight for her prescription. Despite her attempt to medicate, the pain hadn't let up. She couldn't pinpoint anything physical that would cause the headache, unless it was Nathan's words.

They still haunted her, echoing through the walls in her mind. She couldn't believe that he would talk to her that way—as if he'd done her some huge favor with the baby arrangement. Like she needed him. She didn't need him. But then again, she did. Currently, he was her only shot at having a child. There were no other prospects, short of calling up a sperm bank and making an appointment. Yet she, like her doctor, didn't believe that it should come to that. Alex was smart and attractive. Why should her conception be any different from anyone else?

Still, he didn't have to make her feel bad about their plans. It contradicted the supportive and understanding way he'd always treated her. Over the past couple of months, Nathan always made her feel special, even when she doubted the nature of his relationship with his son's mother. So, she couldn't tell whether he was fronting for her or if he'd changed his mind about her altogether. Either way, she'd lost something.

"Ms. Carter?" the call center rep said.

"Hmm?" Alex snapped out of her trance long enough to see the puzzled look on the rep's face.

"Are you okay?"

Alex cleared her throat. "Yes, I'm fine. Why?"

"I was asking what are we going to do about the software? Do you want us to look up the numbers individually since we can't generate a client list?"

"No. Work with the ones you have. I'll report the problem to IT."

"Okay." The rep turned her chair back to her desk and minimized her main screen.

Alex bee-lined her way to her office. She closed the door and searched her drawer for her prescription. Before she could get the bottle open, someone knocked on her door. She shoved the bottle back in the drawer.

"Come in."

Mr. Sims opened the door and strode in with his chest forward. "Alex? I need to see you in my office in five minutes."

Her eyes widened. "What about, Mr. Sims?"

He crossed his hands behind his back. "We've decided to make some changes around here. You need to be aware of them."

What kind of changes? Alex wracked her brain. The changes didn't sound good. Yet, she couldn't imagine why they would be bad. Her team's numbers were better than ever. The job fair had produced many new hires. Their placement numbers had improved. *Are they firing me? No, there is no way.*

She nodded. "Yes, sir."

"Good. See you in five."

He exited the room, closing the door behind him. Alex sat down in her chair and said a brief prayer before migrating to the eleventh floor. As she walked down the corridor, she spotted Dan.

"Sssps! Dan!" Alex whispered. She quickened her step to catch up to him.

Dan turned around. "Alex. What are you doing up here?"

"Mr. Sims came down to my office and asked me to meet him up here in five minutes."

"Same here." Dan shot their boss's door a worried expression. "What do you think this is about?"

Alex bit her lip. "I don't know. No clue. I was hoping you might know."

He shook his head. "This sucks. Do you think we're getting canned?"

This time, Alex shook her head. The sharp pain in her right temple returned and she rubbed the spot. "It doesn't make sense."

Mr. Sims opened the door. He raised his eyebrows when he saw Alex and Dan standing at his threshold. "I was about to go looking for you two."

Both forced a nervous laugh. "We're here and ready when you are, Mr. Sims," Alex said.

Their boss moved to the side and allowed them to set foot onto his thick carpet. Alex immediately saw the president of the agency, Mr. William Stanley, and board member, Mr. Sam McIntosh, in the room. She glanced Dan's way and saw her uneasy feelings reflected on his face. *OMG.*

Despite the twinge of pain in her head, Alex forced her signature confidence to kick in. "Good morning, Mr. Stanley. Mr. McIntosh."

"Morning, Alex. Please. Have a seat." Mr. Stanley motioned toward the chairs across from Mr. Sims' executive chair, which he temporarily occupied.

For a second, no one spoke and the only thing she could hear was the sound of Dan's pants rubbing back and forth from him bouncing his leg up and down. She wished she could put her hand on it and force it still but that would have looked grossly inappropriate.

"How is everything?" Mr. Stanley asked.

"Great, sir. Absolutely splendid," Dan said.

"I've heard. Our numbers are up twenty-five percent now and, for the first time, we have companies chasing us down to work with our staff. That's quite impressive."

"Everyone has been working really hard to improve the placement rates. It's good to see it pay off," Alex said.

"Indeed. The newfound interest in our agency has shown us that there's some restructuring needed," Mr. Stanley said.

Alex's head throbbed so hard she had to briefly look down at the carpet to regain her train of thought. "What type of restructuring?"

Mr. Stanley leaned forward, placing his arms on the desk. "We need to shift some people around. Let some people out of their positions. It's all a part of making the agency stronger, you see?"

Fighting to stay focused, Alex nodded. "Yes."

"Good. Then I'm sure you'll understand that our revisions have to start with you two." He switched his attention to Dan, who sat with eyes as wide as saucers.

"Wait a minute. What are you saying?" Dan asked, allowing a little bit of worry to escape his voice.

Alex ran her hand over the back of her head. *Something's not right. I've got to get out of here.*

"To accommodate our new opportunities, we're promoting Alex to Senior Recruitment Manager and you to Recruitment Manager. Since you worked so well together before, we'll let you guys streamline our efforts to form better relationships with employers. We may even develop a new department around you. Making you the leaders." Mr. Stanley leaned back in the chair, smiling. "What do you think about that?"

"Whoa! That's great!" Dan faced her. "Isn't it, Alex?"

Alex's response was to pass out in her chair.

CHAPTER 38

Alex pushed the key into the familiar gold doorknob. The door opened and the scent of boiled crabs greeted her. It reminded Alex of her childhood, when crab boils were frequent during the summer. Those times fostered a strong love of seafood, which is why she had to come to her mother's house. She said she was boiling crabs and Alex didn't have to be told twice to stop by.

"Mama! I'm here," Alex said.

"Okay!" her mother called from her room.

Alex went into the kitchen, where the crab scent intensified.

"Are you feeling better now?" Alex's mother asked, walking into the kitchen.

Alex grabbed a plastic bag and stretched it in half. She laid a beaten pan on top of it and opened the big, steaming pot beside it. The heat rushed from the pot, after which a clear view of crabs, shrimps, corn on the cob and potatoes emerged. Alex plunged a pair of metal thongs into the pot and pulled out three crabs, several shrimps and a corn on the cob.

"Yes. I don't know what happened. All of a sudden, I had this unbearable headache and it took me out. They let me lay down for a while and a couple hours later I left for the day." Alex shrugged. "But I'm okay."

As she settled the food in her pan and imagined tearing into it, her mother leaned over the pots. "The hotter ones are in this pot."

"These are fine, Ma."

Alex picked up her pan and bag to move to the dining room table. Her mother pushed back the tablecloth to prevent crab juice from flying on it. She was about to sit down and have at it until she remembered that she'd forgotten to grab a drink.

She trotted back into the kitchen and opened the refrigerator. She saw pink lemonade. Alex reached for it, grabbed a glass and poured some in it. She picked up the glass and rushed back to the table to get started.

As she tore into her pan, her mother pulled out a chair at the other end of the table and sat down with a similar pan.

"I know what's wrong. You're not getting enough sleep," her mother said.

Alex shook her head. "How do you know I'm not sleeping enough, Ma?"

"I can see the bags under your eyes. And even when you lived here, you didn't sleep like you were supposed to."

"Everybody doesn't go to bed at nine," Alex said, sucking on a crab leg.

"You don't have to go to bed at nine. Get to bed at a decent hour. Midnight is not a decent hour."

Sometimes Alex swore her mother still thought she was fifteen years old. She took every opportunity to tell her what she thought Alex needed to do, whether she was looking for feedback or not.

Alex opened a crab. "Fine, Ma. I go to sleep late. Therefore, I have bad headaches."

"Yep. But, at least you got over your fainting spell today. With that big house you live in, God knows you need to keep working."

Alex rolled her eyes and pushed a thick piece of crab meat in her mouth. "Yep, that's why I need to keep working. It's not because I enjoy my job. Only for the house."

"Umm hmm," her mother said, ignoring Alex's sarcasm.

"I'm so happy about the promotion, though." Alex slurped the salty, seasoned juice from the crab. "I had no idea it was coming. Poor Dan thought we were getting fired." She chuckled.

Her mother perked up. "Dan? Who's Dan?"

"He's the guy I worked with on the job fair."

"Oh. Did you two go out?"

Alex paused. "Really, Ma?"

"I'm asking! I can ask."

"No. We did not go out."

"Why not? What's wrong with him?" Her mother frowned.

Alex picked up her pink lemonade. "Nothing's wrong with him. He's my coworker."

"So. I had two coworkers that dated and they are married now. I'll bet you don't even look interested when you're around him, do you?"

After taking a swig, Alex put her glass down and turned to her mother. "Why should I? I'm *not* interested in him."

She and her mother peered at each other for a second. Alex opened another crab in her pan, while her mother continued to stare. Her mother picked up her Diet Coke and sipped it, keeping her eyes on her daughter.

"Then, who are you interested in?" her mother asked, noticeably less aggressive than before.

Alex sighed and closed her eyes, wishing the conversation would end. "No one."

Her mother leaned forward. "Now I know you feel like I give you a hard time. And maybe sometimes I do. You're my daughter and I'm always going to care about what's going on with you."

Alex stopped chewing. She hadn't mentioned her reconciliation with Nathan to her mother. She preferred to wait until the relationship picked up more steam and became more stable. It was never fun explaining to her mother why a relationship didn't work out. Her mother always made it her fault.

Since she made the arrangement with Nathan, she still hadn't given much thought to how she would present the situation to her mother. There was no way she could tell her mother the truth. As she sat at the table with her, Alex thought about how to mention Nathan to her mother. Whatever method she chose Alex had to be as careful as possible. Her mother would easily detect a lie.

She remembered when she was fourteen. Her mother told her not to buy a flat iron to use on her hair. Alex went behind her back and bought it anyway, figuring that she could find some clever place to hide it in her room. She decided to stuff it under her bed with a couple of plastic bins she kept there. It worked for a week. Alex came home from school one day to find her mother sitting on her bed holding the flat iron. She was flabbergasted. Out of all the times her mother never looked under her bed, how did she know to check under her bed at that particular time? Her mother grounded her for a week. Ever since then, Alex was convinced she couldn't hide anything from her mother, which is why she kept much of her life away from her. So in most cases, trying to tell her mother about Nathan while avoiding the "arrangement" would be especially difficult.

Still, something about her mother's mini speech dumbfounded her. Rarely, did she ever show Alex this type of patience and consideration. She almost felt like she'd grown up with a nurturing and supportive mother. Almost. Struck curious by her mother's attempt to reach out to her, Alex decided to give her mother the answer she'd been longing for.

Alex cleared her throat. "I was sort of seeing Nathan." She

played with the crab claw to keep from meeting her mother's intent stare.

"Who's Nathan?"

"You know Nathan. We dated about a decade ago."

Her mother scanned the air for recognition until she finally remembered. "Oh! Nathan. When did you run into him?"

Alex shrugged. "A little while ago." She knew better than to tell her mother that they'd reestablished contact more than two months ago. All the patience in the world wouldn't have stopped her mother from blowing her lid over being kept in the dark about it.

"That's nice. I remember you being very fond of him." Her mother cracked a claw. "Why do you say you're 'sort of' dating?"

Alex shrugged and popped a shrimp in her mouth. "I guess we're not all that compatible. Sometimes things don't work out."

"That's unfortunate." Her mother paused. "You should really try to work *this* one out."

Alex could feel her nostrils burning. This was exactly why she didn't like talking to her mother about her personal life. She always had all the relationship advice in the world, even though she hadn't been married since Alex's father left twenty years ago.

"Why, Ma? Because he's my last chance? Because I'm getting older and soon I won't be able to pull them in like I used to? Or is it because eventually nobody's gonna want to deal with someone as stubborn as me?" She was so tired of her mother telling her the worst about herself. She wished for once she could let her be.

Her mother took a deep breath. "No."

"Then, why?"

Her mother stared her square in the eye and let it rip. "Because you're pregnant, Alex."

• • •

This is ridiculous. Ma is overreacting. Alex had a hard time believing she was pregnant. Not because she didn't want to believe it; she had a hard time believing that her mother could tell it by looking at her. *When did she become Miss Cleo?*

Alex pulled her long sweater around her and marched into the cold convenience store. The polite yet stressed look on the store manager's face seemed to acknowledge that she barely caught the store open. Alex nodded to him and made a beeline to the row with the home pregnancy tests. There were several. She didn't know which one to choose. She'd seen a lot of commercials for EPT. Then again, she'd also heard of First Response. All they had was a pack of two for $11.99. *Why would anyone need two pregnancy tests? In case the first one failed?*

She sighed, grabbed the First Response and dashed toward the check out, as a man got in line behind her.

Instead of placing the test on the counter, Alex handed it to the cashier. She wanted as few people as possible to see her with it. The young checkout girl with the nametag that read "Kelly" pushed her glasses on her face, reached for the test and scanned it like it were merely a box of pop tarts.

"Twelve seventy," Kelly said.

As Alex handed her a twenty-dollar bill, her hand shook a little, which perplexed her. Fear rattled her to the core. What was she afraid of? If she was pregnant, she'd have the family she wanted—at least partially. If she wasn't, she'd have to try again. But with whom? Now that she and Nathan were on the outs, he probably would want nothing else to do with her.

Why couldn't he understand? She wanted his loyalty. It wasn't always clear to her that she had it. That made her angry. So, she retaliated in telling him off. He was good at overlooking things and being the nice guy. He'd forgive her. She hoped.

Alex shook her head to clear her mind and keep from getting ahead of herself.

Kelly handed her the bag and her change. "Goodnight and good luck."

Alex glanced back at the man in the line behind her to see if he'd caught the meaning of Kelly's words. Unsure of what to say, Alex nodded and smiled at the cashier.

The time between walking from the store to her car and opening her garage door seemed to take forever. She scowled at every red light and gave the evil eye to every slow driver she passed. When she finally walked through her kitchen and placed her purse in a chair, she reached into the bag for the box. She read the directions carefully while taking quick steps up her stairs. One line meant her life would continue without any changes. Two lines meant she should start looking at daycare and preschools. Alex inhaled and exhaled. *Here goes nothing.*

She took the test in her master bathroom. Afterward, she migrated to her bedroom to wait three minutes. Three long minutes. Alex picked up her remote control and sat at the foot of her bed. She pulled her legs up to her chin as the sound of the TV filled the dark room. Searching for something funny to distract her, she clicked on the guide. She found an old episode of *Girlfriends*, where Joan thought she'd met her soul mate. Alex honed in on Joan's attempt to hide her exchanges with the man of her dreams from her boyfriend. She became so engrossed in the scene that before she knew it several commercials had passed and her three minutes were up.

She eased up from her bed and headed back to the bathroom. Alex walked in only to turn her back to the pregnancy test. *C'mon, Alex. You can do this. You have to do this.* She closed her eyes and slowly turned toward the test again. After inching closer to it, she opened her eyes and leaned over the bathroom counter. Her mouth dropped. *Two lines.*

"Oh my gosh!"

Still stunned, Alex migrated toward her room, fell on the bed and pulled the covers around her. She no longer paid attention to the television show. She closed her eyes and allowed a number of thoughts to run through her head, starting with the first.

How do I tell Nathan?

CHAPTER 39

Alex's steps are slow and languid down the shiny beige and brown marble floor. She glances down at her flats. They look ridiculous but, at 8 ½ months into pregnancy, she needs all the comfort she can get. She returns her attention to the stores on her right, specifically Baby Land. The store's cutesy clothes and colorful toys call to her. She walks in and strolls down the heavenly lit aisles. Alex fingers the impeccably stitched fabric until a sales associate comes up to her. The associate's dress glows like she should be donning a halo.

"Well, my goodness. When are we due?" she asks.

Alex bows her head and smiles. "Next month."

"I'll bet you can't wait."

"I can't. It'll be great to see my feet again."

The associate laughs and Alex joins in. Alex stops short when she happens to glance out the store window. She sees Nathan walking on the other side of the mall corridor with his son's mother. Alex's heart sinks as she watches him walk around carrying a drink and talking to her. Their son walks in front of them. Nathan is oblivious to her stare or that she is even in the vicinity. He has the same relatively carefree attitude he always has. It gives her the visual of what his life is like without her. Just fine.

"Alex! There you are." An older man approaches her out of the shaded area of the mall. His hair is gray and receding. He has slight stubble on his face. He moves quickly to meet her. "I've been looking all over for you."

"I'm looking at the baby stuff," Alex says, leaning closer to the sales associate.

"It's time for us to go." He reaches for Alex's arm.

"Are you sure there isn't anything I can show you? What do you and the father already have?" the associate asks as the older man leads her out of Baby Land.

"Nothing. We have nothing," Alex says.

The alarm sounded off. Alex jerked out of her sleep and slapped it silent. She peeped at the time like she didn't already know it. She fell back into her bed and closed her eyes. It took her forever to fall asleep last night and then she had to have that silly dream.

Her mind continued to ponder the future with her unborn child. As before, she wasn't worried about the financial outlook. She made more than enough to take care of a child but she wasn't sure what to do about Nathan.

Her mind flashed back to Roxie Miller's advice for aspiring mothers:

"No matter how scared you are, if you really want this, you can make it happen. I did it and I'm very happy with my decision."

Happy didn't quite describe Alex's feelings. Though she remained confident in her fiscal outlook, fear and sadness gripped her throughout the night and it hadn't let up that morning. Her easy plan didn't feel so easy anymore. While she'd gotten the result that she wanted, she didn't have the thing she really wanted: a full family complete with a husband for her and a father for her child.

Is this the best I can do? A tear rolled off the corner of her left eye to her ear. She'd made her decision. In nine months, she would have a baby. Now, Alex had to convince herself that it wasn't too late for her to have the husband she wanted. The decision to have a baby on her own did not make her happy. On the contrary, she felt ashamed that she had sold out—given up on her dreams.

Alex wiped the tear from her face and pushed her body out of bed. In the bathroom, she walked up to the sink and spotted the pregnancy test. She thought about the baby about to start growing in her belly and smiled. For a brief moment, she felt some of the happiness that she probably should feel. Alex looked in the mirror and saw her reddish, puffy face. She had to pull it together. Her staff had to see her usual calm and confident demeanor. This was no time to fall apart, especially after getting a promotion. She had to keep a positive attitude, regardless of how she felt.

Once she drove to work and the main door opened to the building, employees begin congratulating her on the promotion.

"Congratulations," Betty said when Alex approached the front desk.

"Thank you. I see word travels fast."

"When it's good news. Are you feeling all right?" Betty asked, staring at her.

"Yes. Why?" Alex stood straighter, fearing that her fragile emotions were too close to the surface.

"I heard about you fainting."

"Oh." Alex breathed a sigh of relief. "Well, I'm better now."

Betty searched her eyes. "Good."

Alex smiled and walked toward the elevator. After she reached her office, she closed the door, sat in her chair and pulled out her daily planner. Her morning meeting with Dan caught her eye right away. She glanced at the clock. He would be there in about twelve minutes.

They needed to start planning how they were going to execute this new area of the company. They'd already shown they could make events successful but they had to set more long-term goals.

On one hand, Alex welcomed the distraction from her issues but, on the other hand, it might be difficult to concentrate. She didn't want to waste time—his or hers. It wasn't a good idea to cancel the meeting. They had too much to do. She turned on her computer and pulled out her notepad and pen. No need to overreact. For the first meeting, they were only brainstorming.

As she logged into the Matrix computer software, she heard a knock at the door.

"Come in."

Dan opened the door and Alex looked up at him. She did a double take. Dan, who usually dressed professional enough for the office, seemed to have upped his game in that department. He wore a dark blue suit with a pale blue shirt and a purple tie. He topped it off with wing-tipped shoes. His current getup was a far cry from the beige slacks and cheaper shoes she'd gotten used to seeing.

"What is this about?" Alex asked, laughing for the first time in awhile.

He smiled wide and stretched out his arms. "I thought an updated position called for an updated wardrobe. You likey?"

"Nice choice."

He closed her office door behind him and walked over to the chair in front of her desk. He unbuttoned his jacket and sat down. "Are you much better?"

"Yes, I am better now."

"That was weird, huh? Do you know what caused you to faint like that?" Dan leaned forward.

"I had a little headache," Alex said. "Plus, I was probably tired. You know, after all the activity."

Dan nodded. "Yeah, we did work hard on the fair. Have you gotten a chance to go celebrate your promotion?"

Alex turned to her computer. "Not really."

"We should go for a celebratory drink. What about lunch today?"

"I can't."

"Why?" Dan asked.

His happiness made it hard for Alex to hold herself together. She should have been happy. A new position and now a new baby on the way. Yet, she felt like her life had turned upside down. How was she supposed to concentrate on a meeting with Dan while on the verge of falling apart? She couldn't.

He stared at her. "Alex? Are you okay?"

She inhaled. "I, um, think I need to postpone our meeting."

"Why? Are you sick or something?"

She shook her head and covered her mouth.

"Wait. I got an idea. Instead of staying in this stiff office, why don't we go across the street to The Skyline Café?"

Dan stood up. Alex watched him walk toward her door.

"C'mon." He motioned.

Alex took a deep breath and grabbed her keys. She and Dan walked through the lobby, passing Betty.

"We're going to a meeting across the street, Betty. We'll be back soon," Dan said over his shoulder.

The Skyline Café had a chic feel to it. Not only did it attract professionals but many singles frequented the café during its night hours. Alex tried getting Izzy to go to some of their events but her friend didn't like the atmosphere. Too stuffy, she'd said. On this particular day, the chairs on its roof were wrapped in a tan covering, which matched the tablecloths. Unlit candles in their glass holders sat on the tables. At night, the café lit them, creating an awe inspiring view against the lights of the city.

Dan and Alex walked to the rail at the edge of the rooftop. After a few minutes of watching the hustle and bustle of the drivers on their morning commutes, Dan broke the silence.

"What's going on?"

Alex inhaled and exhaled as a cool breeze blew through the air.

"You don't have to talk about it if you don't want to but I figured it might help, since you're obviously upset about something," Dan said.

She faced Dan. "Have you ever wanted something so bad but you couldn't quite get it?"

Dan cocked his head to the side. "What do you mean?"

"I've spent the past several years waiting for something to the point that I didn't believe that I would ever get it. Then, when it arrived, things went wrong." Alex shrugged. "And I still don't understand where or how."

"Well, I doubt things just went wrong. Something had to happen."

"No, it went wrong."

Dan shook his head. "It's like this, Alex. Physics teaches us that in order for something to move we have to apply force to it. The same is true for our problems." He faced her. "Nothing simply happens. Nothing goes amiss on its own. An action took place, whether it was someone else's action or our own action, somehow we put the situation in motion."

Alex focused on the traffic light below them. "I don't understand. What are you saying? That I made this happen?"

He turned his back against the traffic. "I'm saying that sometimes we do things, unknowingly. And those actions have an effect on the outcomes. Once we realize what we did, we can change things. We can replace the old action with a new action. One that will give us the outcome that we want."

"But I don't understand what I did to cause this. All I wanted was a husband and a kid."

Dan raised his eyebrows. "Will any husband do?" He laughed.

Alex smiled lazily. "No."

"So you have someone in mind? The man in the parking lot?"

"Yes, but it doesn't matter. He's gone." She frowned.

"What did he do? Leave the country?"

"No. He's back with his ex, I think."

Dan shook his head. "You think? But you don't really know?"

"His 'friend' suggested they might still be seeing each other. When he was helping me with my car the other day, she called him and he had to step away to talk to her."

"Did you ask him about it?"

"Yes, and he said he's not with her."

Dan shrugged. "Why don't you believe him?"

"Because it's hard to." Alex faced Dan. Tears started to well in her eyes. "And now I'm pregnant."

Dan leaned back. "Whoa! When were you going to tell me this?"

"I did." Alex scowled. "And you better not tell anyone else either." She pointed at him.

He widened his eyes. "Of course not. Congratulations! A baby." He leaned on the rail and looked at her. "So, you haven't told him yet?"

She shook her head.

"When are you gonna tell him?"

"What do you mean?"

"The dude? When are you going to let him know?"

"I told you he has someone else!"

Dan looked up at the sky. "Oh my gosh! I know you're not going to leave this man in the dark. This is crazy." He laughed and shook his head. "You know what I noticed about you?"

Alex crossed her arms. She had no patience for jokes. She was baring her soul to him, a coworker, which is something she never did. He could at least sympathize with her because, at this point, he knew more about her feelings for Nathan than anybody, including Izzy.

"What?" Alex asked, squinting at him.

"You are one of the most successful women I know. You just earned a promotion. You drive an expensive car. You probably even own a nice house—"

Alex stood up straight. "—I should. I worked hard for those things." She dug her pointer finger on the railing for emphasis.

"There you go!" Dan pointed at her.

She jerked her head back. "What?"

"You worked hard for those things. You don't make excuses. Like Nike, you just do it!" He paused. "Yet, when it comes to the area of your life that means the most to you, you're coming up with all these reasons why you can't do something about it. Why can't you make this happen like you made the car, the house and the job happen?"

Alex started to breath hard. She faced the traffic, hoping that the open air would help restore her normal breathing. "It's not the same thing."

"It's not? You've always known how to make things happen. This is what you *really* want but you'd rather play the victim than do what 'Alex' would usually do," Dan said.

"Now, wait a minute. I'm nobody's victim. I can do anything. I…" As she trailed off, tears ran down her face.

Dan stepped closer to her and softened his tone.

Alex covered her mouth and looked away. Tears poured down her face. She had one big problem; she did love Nathan and she really did want to be with him again but she feared that he didn't want her, after the way she acted. She feared it was too late.

Dan hugged her tight. "I know you're not a victim." He pulled her away from him so he could face her. "And you deserve all the love and happiness you can hold." He glanced down at her stomach. "It's time to give yourself what you want, Alex. To do anything less would be…insanity."

Alex cocked her head to the side. She had always heard about the "light bulb moment." However, she'd never experienced it, until then. All of a sudden, everything made sense. She knew what she had to do.

Dan smiled and nudged her back the way they came. "C'mon. Let's get you out of this air, Mama."

CHAPTER 40

Alex pulled into Nathan's driveway behind his Acura. She sat there, like she had done about a week ago. Except this time, the stakes were much higher. The last time she drove to his house asking for a mere fraction of what she really wanted. Now, she wanted to go back and renegotiate, which could be risky in business and relationships. She didn't have any bargaining chips. She'd aggravated him, yelled at him. They had a long history of not working things out and he had someone else he could more than likely go back to at a moment's notice. As Alex thought about all the odds against her, she felt herself wavering, feeling like this trip may not be worth it. Then, she remembered Dan's strong, yet compassionate words to her. She had to let Nathan know how she felt about him no matter what the outcome would be.

She fidgeted, as she mentally rehearsed what to say to Nathan when she saw him. She opened her car door and climbed out to take the familiar walk to his front door. Alex knocked on the door and waited. Silence. She knocked on it again. The anticipation of him answering nearly killed her. After a few more seconds of silence, her anxiety got the best of her and she turned to go back to her car. As soon as she walked down a couple of steps, Nathan's door opened.

"Alex?" Nathan said.

She heard him and stopped. Alex turned back around to face Nathan. He wore sweat pants and a T-shirt.

"Hi, Nathan."

"Hey. I didn't expect to see you here." He looked her up and down. "What's up?"

She took a deep breath. *I have to do this now.* "I stopped by because I needed to talk to you about something."

He paused. "Okay. Come in." Nathan pointed toward his door.

Alex settled the butterflies in her stomach. She followed him into his house. He closed the door behind him and headed toward the kitchen.

"Can I get you something to drink?" he asked.

"Water."

While he grabbed glasses out of the cabinet, Alex worked on her nerve to tell him the truth. Though she had rehearsed her words in the car, those same words had deserted her. Her mind could only grasp short phrases of the things she wanted to say. She took a deep breath and exhaled as he returned to her with a glass of water. She reached for it and took a gulp. The cool water soothed her parched throat. She felt momentary relief from her anxiety.

"Why don't you have a seat?" Nathan asked.

Alex sat down in a chair, holding the glass with both hands.

"Um. What did you want to talk about?" he asked, sitting down on the couch next to her chair.

Alex studied his face. She'd grown accustomed to the warm and supportive energy that seemed to radiate from his very core. He always made her feel welcomed, no matter what the situation. As she stared into Nathan's eyes, she got a slight chill. His eyes had become a bit cold, devoid of their usual positive emotion. Alex could tell she had a big mountain to climb and decided it was time to get started.

"I want to start by apologizing for my behavior a few days ago.

I was out of line and I really do appreciate you helping me with my car lock," she said quietly.

Nathan nodded. "Okay. Why did you go off on me?"

She glanced up at the ceiling. "Because I was afraid you were back with your ex. I feared that was where you really wanted to be anyway and that you had been playing me. So, I lost it."

He leaned forward and put his elbows on his knees. "Help me understand. What have I done to make you think I was 'playing you?'"

Alex sighed. "For starters, you stood me up."

"And I bought you flowers. What else?"

"Then, your friend called me Clarissa." Alex rolled her eyes at having to say his ex's name.

"And I told you he was mistaken."

"Then, he showed me the picture."

Nathan frowned. "What, what picture?"

"The one with you, her and your son."

"I haven't taken any picture with them," Nathan said.

"Yes, you did. You were wearing a blue and white striped shirt and your son was wearing a red shirt and some little jean shorts." *I'm trying to apologize to you, Nathan. Please don't lie to me now.*

He stood up and walked over to his book shelf. After shuffling through the books and photo albums on the bottom shelf, Nathan pulled out a black photo album. He flipped through a couple of pages and stopped.

"Is this the picture you're talking about?" Nathan had removed the photo from the album and handed it to her.

Alex stared at the printed replica of the photo she saw on A.J.'s phone. "Yes. I thought you said you didn't take any pictures with them."

He sucked his teeth. "Turn it over."

She did. In the left hand corner, Nathan had written the date 7/8/11. "This doesn't make any sense. Why did A.J. have this printed picture in his phone? Why did he have any picture of you all in his phone?" Alex asked.

"Last year, Clarissa and I took Keandre to a birthday party. Afterward, some of my friends were getting together to shoot some pool. A.J. came by to pick me up. I wanted to take a picture of us with my phone and have it printed later but my phone's battery was acting up. When A.J. arrived to pick me up, I asked him to take the picture and email it to me." Nathan shrugged. "I didn't know that fool still had it on his phone. Why would he need that?"

I am so stupid for believing anything A.J. said. Alex handed the photo back to Nathan. He took it and sat back down on the couch.

"She and I actually broke up a couple of weeks after the picture was taken." He stared at it. "Why didn't you tell me about this?"

Alex shook her head. "I don't know. I guess I thought where there's smoke, there must be fire." She put her glass of water down. "Nathan, these last few months haven't been the easiest. I broke up with a jerk and, on top of that, I had to defend my job. But, in the mist of all this, I felt like I was missing something. And then, you showed up and I didn't really know what to make of seeing you. I didn't want to believe that there was more to you and be disappointed all over again."

"Listen. I know I messed up years ago but I said I was sorry. You said you forgave me," Nathan said.

"I do and now I have to forgive myself for getting in my own way. You were trying to offer me everything and I was only accepting a piece of it." Alex glanced down at her stomach. She'd made a mistake but she hoped she wouldn't be punished for it. She didn't want to take care of her child alone. Yet, she didn't want Nathan to try and stick around out of duty. She wanted to know that he still desired a relationship with her, that he still loved her, even though she'd been hard to love. In order to find out, she had to step out on faith. She had to be honest.

Alex swallowed the lump in her throat and looked Nathan square in the eye. "I love you, Nathan and I want to try again. I want to make an honest effort to make our relationship work without the outside interference or my own previous doubts. I don't know if you're ready to move on or not but I want more than a baby with you. I want everything." Never in her life, did she remember being so vulnerable, so bare. It was a hard place to be. A cold place to be. After her little speech, she covered her face, afraid to look at the man she loved—scared that there was a big chance that he didn't feel the same way anymore.

A few seconds of silence passed, which frightened her even more. She slowly parted her fingers and found Nathan on one knee beside her chair. He reached out for her hand and she gave it to him, confused.

"You are the love of my life, Alex. No matter how it seemed or what I did or what you think I did, I've never cared for anyone the way that I've cared for you." He touched her face. "You're my best friend."

Nathan reached into the pocket of his sweatpants and pulled out a small box. He stopped and stared at it. "I've been struggling with this for a few days. I was hoping to get some kind of sign of what to do next."

He opened the box and revealed a two-carat, princess-cut diamond nestled in a platinum setting. Alex gasped and covered her mouth.

"Alexis Carter? Will you marry me?"

Alex opened her mouth but nothing would come out. When she realized she hadn't uttered any sounds, she nodded.

Nathan smiled at her. The warmth she'd grown to expect had returned to his eyes. "Is that a yes?"

"Yes," Alex managed to squeak.

Nathan slid the ring on her finger and stood up to hug her. Alex's heart nearly beat a hole in her chest. She couldn't believe her dreams were coming true. Suddenly, all of her worries disappeared. A tremendous sense of relief fell over her. For the first time in her life, she was completely happy. So happy, she almost forgot to make another announcement.

"Uh. Nathan?"

"Yes."

"There's something else I needed to tell you."

He pulled away long enough to give her his undivided attention. "What?"

"I'm pregnant."

He laughed and squeezed her tighter. "Great. Now, you'll never get rid of me."

ABOUT THE AUTHOR

Jaye Cheríe is editor and publisher of Entertainment Wire, an online entertainment medium devoted to news, reviews, and interviews. She has photographed, interviewed, and written articles on entertainers and personalities, such as *CSI: New York* actor Hill Harper, TLC member and reality show star Chilli, singer Eric Benét, and comedian J. Anthony Brown. She is the author of *The Golddigger's Club* and *The Cost of Love and Sanity*.

If you enjoyed "The Cost of Love and Sanity,"
be sure to check out

THE
GOLD
DIGGER'S
CLUB

by Jaye Cheríe
Available from Strebor Books

CHAPTER 1

Monica

"Hut, hut, hut." The quarterback seized the snap and stretched his arm backward, winding up for a throw. He fired the ball right into the arms of Tampa Bay Buccaneers wide receiver, Tony T. Hatcher. Tony cradled the ball and mustered all the speed and power in his six-foot-five, muscular physique to sprint across the goal line. When Tony stopped running, the head coach blew his whistle. All the players broke their positions, allowing waves of sweat to run down their sculpted chests and defined biceps.

The coach hurled his roll of papers to the ground.

"What are y'all doing? If we practice like this, we'll play like this during the season. Now, pick it up!" the coach shouted. The players trudged back to their line of scrimmage to practice the drive again.

Unlike the spectators perched on the bleachers, Monica Hatcher stood on the sidelines trying to play the supportive wife, but the sweat threatening to escape from her pores made it difficult to concentrate. As she watched her husband practice, she kept lapsing into daydreams of relaxing near the pool with a glass of iced tea at her side. That's where she preferred to spend the day.

Instead, she stood tall, hastily pulling her long, black ponytail behind her shoulders. Tony loved her manufactured mane but she yearned for her cropped haircut. She vowed to return to her signature tresses, at least while the heat index topped out at 102 degrees. In the meantime, she obliged her husband with her hair and her presence at the field. Monica figured this would stop him from complaining. Lately, he had harsh words for her absence at his practices. Tony claimed she was acting like a fair-weather fan because his team had a rough season last year.

While she would admit she wasn't attending like she did when he had first entered the NFL, it had nothing to do with the team's record. It was that practice, home games, and away games got old after eight years. She'd grown tired of feigning fulfillment in the NFL life. She was also tired of moving, tired of politicking and tired of smiling big for the cameras. She wanted to focus on activities more important to her, like planning the dinner for The Hatcher Scholarship Foundation.

The coach blew his whistle for the last time. The players broke their positions as if they'd been carrying a ton of bricks they were waiting to drop. Tony jogged over to Monica, wiping the sweat off his tanned forehead. "Hey. Where the kids at?" Tony asked, out of breath.

"They're with Marianna. I would never bring them out here. Too much open space for them to run or disappear, and I'm not running them down in this heat. Do you want your son running beside you on the field?" Monica asked.

Tony jerked his head back and frowned. "No."

Between the look on Tony's face and the looks from nearby players, Monica guessed she was a little too forceful in her response.

One player walked by, appearing to scowl at her. Self-conscious, Monica glanced around, while smoothing out the wrinkles in her sleeveless dress. She thought about how another passerby might view her as a bourgeois witch, but she really wasn't that way. She didn't consider herself a shallow, irresponsible woman—the type who let her "help" raise her children because she was too busy shopping and partying. She did, however, believe in using nannies and cooks to help her out.

But even with the extra help, her family was still priority number one for her; the children knew they could count on mommy.

A tiny bit embarrassed at her own behavior, Monica dropped her head and sighed. "I'm sorry. It's so hot out here. I think my brain is sweating."

"Well, it is spring and we are in Florida," Tony said sarcastically. "If you got a problem with the heat, why did you come here?"

"I came out here to support you."

"And you're doing that by standing on the sidelines mean mugging?"

"I wasn't aware I was supposed to be cheesing from ear to ear. You say I never come out. So, I'm out here." Monica placed her hands on her hips.

Tony threw his head back and pushed his thumbs inside of his sleeveless shirt. "All I'm saying is don't do me any favors."

Monica squinted at him. She'd sacrificed not only her comfort, but her time to make him happy. He could have at least acted like he appreciated it. If she'd known he'd react this way, she would have stretched out at her pool, or better yet, she could have used the day to check out a couple of venues for the scholarship dinner in August.

Now that Monica thought about it, she didn't know why she thought giving him what he wanted would make any difference. Nothing seemed to please him these days, especially since the season started. She knew the reasons behind his sour behavior—his smaller contract and unfocused teammates—but it was most disturbing that his attitude was rubbing off on her. Before she could address their growing discord, Tony turned toward the stadium exit.

"Where are you going?" Monica asked.

"I'm gonna shower, pick up the kids and take them to the park," Tony said.

"Fine. I'm going to meet Dee and Stephanie for an early dinner," Monica said.

Tony rolled his eyes.

"Don't start, okay?" Monica asked. Tony didn't care for Monica's friends. They didn't like him much either. She wasn't sure how it started but she was getting real sick of playing referee.

Tony placed his hand on his chest, faking innocence. "I didn't say anything. I'll see you when you get home."

Tony jogged off the field toward the locker room. When he passed two women sitting in the stands, he winked at them. They batted their eyes back and burst into giggles. The shorter one whispered to her friend, who howled in amusement.

The acid in Monica's stomach bubbled over like a boiling pot of water. She didn't attend Tony's practice to see him flirt with other women. Before the end of the day, she planned to read him about his behavior. Annoyed, Monica walked toward the exit, eyeing the two ogling women.

During the drive to meet her friends, Monica was still pretty hot with Tony. So much so she had to imagine the layout of the scholarship dinner to calm down. She envisioned an ice sculpture at the front entrance of the venue. Elegant crystal chandeliers in the dining area. Twenty-five tables with champagne tablecloths and floral centerpieces placed at the center. She'd present a plaque along with a $25,000 check for college to two eager high school students.

Thinking about the dinner instantly put Monica at ease. By the time she reached Henrietta's Bistro, she caught herself smiling. When she entered the quaint restaurant, her friends, Deidre Wright and Stephanie Robinson, were already sitting at a booth. With the Tony incident twenty miles away, she decided to avoid bringing it up to her friends because she didn't want to ruin the positive vibe. Besides, if given the chance, they'd only use the incident as ammunition against Tony's character, which she did not feel like defending.

"Hello, ladies," Monica said.

"Hey. What's up?" Dee said, glancing up from her pocket mirror.

"Same ole, same ole. What's up with you guys? Have you ordered yet?" Monica asked.

"Yeah, but here's a menu," Stephanie said, handing it to Monica.

Monica took the menu and glanced down at the choices, which included a special with collard greens, ham hocks and sweet potatoes. She shuddered to think she considered asking Henrietta to cater her dinner. Henrietta's food was savory in a soul food sort of way but she couldn't imagine serving collard greens and ham hocks to the bigwigs in August. She was going to ask these CEOs and politicians for hundreds of thousands of dollars. They had to take her seriously, and to do that, she needed to produce a high class event all the way—from the venue to the food. *Oh, well. Maybe I'll keep Henrietta in mind for future events, like a small birthday party.* Once the waiter returned to their table, Monica ordered the four-vegetable special and a tea. The waiter took her menu and she shifted her attention back to her friends.

"So, which one of you broads is gonna help me plan my dinner?" Monica asked the two women sitting across from her.

Dee looked up from her mirror with her trademark "no, you didn't" expression. She turned around to glance at people sitting at the tables behind her. "You must be talking to someone else because I know you ain't talking to me like that."

Deidre, or Dee to her friends, shifted her eyes back to her pocket mirror, while fixing her wavy weave with French-manicured fingers. As a fashion stylist, Dee was so appearance obsessed that she wore pricey hair, refused to leave the house without MAC makeup and shopped every week. She even liked donning hazel contact lenses and fake eye-lashes. They complemented her face, she said. Today, she was minus the lashes but she maintained her diva mode with the contacts.

"Since you're so style-conscious, I thought you might be able to help me with the decoration," Monica said with a wide smile.

"I do fashion. I don't do confetti."

"You're still styling a room. When you think about it, there really isn't any difference."

"There is a difference and you know it. Now, I'm not gonna sit here and debate back and forward with you about decorations and fashions 'cuz I know nothing about the former. So, I sure hope you have some-thing else to talk about."

Sometimes she is so impossible, Monica thought. She turned to her other friend. "What about you?"

"I would, but I'm not really fashion conscious. I don't even like those kinds of events. I mean, everybody gets all dressed up and acts like they're better than you. It gets on my nerves," Stephanie said, scrunching her round, baby face. The last rays of the setting sun shimmered over her cinnamon brown skin and long, curly hair, hinting to her Afro-Cuban lineage.

"You don't have to be fashion conscious. You can just help me make some calls. Besides, this is a dinner for a nonprofit organization. Nobody's supposed to be acting like they're better than anybody."

"You know those people aren't gonna act right," Dee said, peeking up from her mirror.

Monica shot Dee the evil eye for interrupting her volunteer campaign.

"I don't know," Stephanie said.

"You might meet some nice, rich men."

"When do you need help?" Stephanie asked.

"Well, I could use some help tomorrow afternoon."

"Oh, no. I have to get ready for the show. Natalie's gonna get me back stage at the Jam Fest. I already told her I would go. I need to network for more video gigs. I'm gonna spend the whole day getting ready. Sorry." Stephanie shrugged.

The waiter returned to the table with Dee's pepper steak and Stephanie's chicken fettuccine alfredo. Monica watched Stephanie divvy up the chicken chunks and sprinkle extra cheese over the pasta. It was amazing how much effort Stephanie put into the food on her plate, considering she didn't like putting effort into anything else. Whenever Monica or Dee asked her to do something—if there was any real work involved—they could forget about her. It was like she was allergic to any type of exertion. She knew Stephanie wasn't that sorry for ditching her on the dinner preparation but decided not to press the issue right then. *These chicks are going to help me whether they know it or not.*

"Sure. I'll let you know when I need help with something else." Monica tried her best to look dejected.

"How is the dinner going? Are you gonna use a deejay or an actual recording artist?" Dee asked, biting into a tender piece of steak.

"Well, since you don't intend to help, you're gonna have to wait and see like everybody else," Monica said, smirking.